LULU SMITH

KILLED IT

Killed It by Lulu Smith

© 2018 Lulu Smith

Published by **BoudiCat Books**

Huntington, West Virginia

Book design by Inkstain Design Studio

Paperback ISBN: 978-0-578-40457-8

Library of Congress Control Number: 2018961643

For Mardi
For twenty years of purring and snoring behind me as I wrote.
You were the sweetest of cats. You will be missed.

CHAPTER 1

ALL I WANTED WAS A cinnamon scone, a cup of coffee and to get through another day of dream and soul killing drudgery at the office. Instead, what I got was an unrelenting onslaught of First World problems and an anger that slowly percolated into a blinding rage which would not be contained until it reached its full head of steam. By the end of the day, I finally blew my gasket. I snapped. And that's how I found myself leaning over a railing in Central Park talking to the body of the man I had just killed. It's hard to believe that it was just three weeks ago and that my life managed to get even more complicated and that my pent up rage took me to even darker, although well-intentioned places.

That fateful morning began like any other Thursday morning. I was attempting to quietly sneak out of bed when my second foot hit the floor and landed smack in the middle of a recently coughed up and wet hairball. Naturally, I yelled, "damn it," and woke Drew up, which was exactly what I had been trying to avoid.

"Good morning babe." He grabbed me around the waist and pulled me back into the bed beside him.

There was no use fighting it. I knew I was going to be forced to cuddle and most likely have to lie to him.

"Hey honey, sorry about waking you." I let myself be pulled all the way back into nestling as the little spoon up against him.

"I'm glad you woke me up so we get to spend a few minutes together." He gently kissed the back of my neck. Any other day of the week I would have responded. God, how I would have responded. OK, I'm not going to lie, my body did respond. I let myself relax for a few seconds and enjoyed the nonstop flutter of kisses and the warmth of his hand as it made its way up my stomach to my left boob and its already hard nipple. Betrayed by my own nipples, damn it.

"So, how was your set last night?"

And there it was. Exactly what I was trying to avoid. Why do men always have to ruin sex by talking?

When he asks me about my comedy sets I have to lie, and I really hate lying to this man. I had now lied to him almost every Thursday morning for the past six months. It has been that long since I've actually done a set. He still thinks I do one every Wednesday night. The first lie wasn't planned. It just accidentally slipped out instead of a confession that I had frozen when I got ready to go up on the stage because I suddenly had nothing funny to say. I didn't have the guts to tell him, so I simply said, "It was OK. Not great." Ever the supportive boyfriend, he proceeded to give me a pep talk and show concern and ask if I wanted to run my new material by him, which made me feel even worse.

Now, every Wednesday, I go to the comedy club and sit and drink until it is late enough for him to have fallen asleep. I creep in silently and try not to wake him up before he asks me that dreaded question, "How was your set?"

How do I tell the man who asked me out after seeing one of my shows because he thought I was hilarious and feisty and who loved that I was foul-mouthed and brave that I had lost my voice and maybe my drive? Even worse, how do I tell him that I thought it was because I had it too easy now? My life was too cushy and kind of dull and there was nothing to find humor in and I just kind of muddled through my days. After all, he got me the legal assistant job at his dad's law firm making $75,000 a year doing bullshit paperwork that I could do in my sleep so I wouldn't have to continue schlepping food and relying on cheap tourists to leave me tips. He is the one with the amazing condominium where I live rent-free even though I have tried to give him money.

When I first moved from West Virginia to New York, I lived in a squeaker of an apartment in Brooklyn with three other struggling artists. It was the kind of place where you could hear every conversation and atrocity being committed by your neighbors on all sides because of the paper-thin walls.

3

But those cheap tourists and the shitty-ass neighbors gave me something to work with as material. Law firms and their employees? Mostly dicks, way too serious and not very funny. How selfish would it be for me to complain that I can afford to splurge on things for myself and live a good life but now I'm not funny anymore because I don't have to struggle and I've gotten too complacent? I can't do that. So, I lie and I hope like hell every Wednesday night that he doesn't decide to stop studying and surprise me at the club or that just maybe something absurd happens that brings back a spark in my creativity.

"How was it baby?" He repeated as he continued to kiss my neck while his finger gently circled around my Judas of a left nipple. "I bet you killed it."

I decided not to lie this morning. I wasn't going to tell the truth but I wasn't going to lie. I rolled over and pushed him on his back and straddled him.

"It wasn't as good as this is going to be." It was a delay tactic but it would at least get me through the morning and buy me more time to think of another vague response to throw out during our dinner with his parents tonight. Did I mention we always have dinner with his parents at The Manhattan Fifth's Club, an exclusive club for wealthy people, on Thursday? Yeah, it's great (rolls eyes). Well the food is great. It just means I have to lie to not only him, but also his parents. Every Thursday! And I hate lying. Yes, I'm aware that I've already admitted to killing a man, but I still don't like lying, damn it.

His parents can be as earnest and supportive as he is and it is slightly infuriating. I like to imagine that they are aliens because it is the only explanation as to why they are so nice and supportive to me. By most accounts, I'm from the wrong side of the tracks (what the entire country seems to think of West Virginia based on representations in the media) and I'm living with the son they have put through prep schools and have been grooming to become a lawyer and ultimately a politician. At least one of them should have taken me aside by now and offered me a large cash settlement to get the hell away from him. That would at least give me some material to work with for my sets.

After having some mind-blowing sex, Drew promptly rolled over and fell back to sleep. At least men are very dependable in that regard. I was able to get my shower and get out of the house without any further inquisition. I stopped on my way out the door and looked at both cats, who were curled up innocently on the couch. I sternly advised them that I would find out who left the hairball on my side of the bed and whoever it was would be grounded from snacks. They both yawned at me and laid their heads back down onto one another as if to remind me that the snacks were the fancy hairball reducing snacks so I could do so at my own peril.

I WENT TO THE STARBUCKS down the street before getting on the subway because clearly I hate myself. I had recently thrown out our "personal pod coffee system" after declaring it an environmental disaster of a machine. In a loud, profane-laced speech, I announced that we would be returning to a good, old-fashioned, normal-person coffee pot in order to save the world. I felt very triumphant in that moment. Drew simply shrugged his shoulders and said, "Sure, whatever you want honey."

It had been five weeks since my tantrum and I had not yet bought said coffee pot despite the Post-It note stuck to my computer screen reminding me to "get on Amazon and order coffee pot!!!"

I resolved that this was the day I would actually log on Amazon, which is the same resolution I made every single time I got in line. Since every time I was behind at least four nitwits who acted like they had never been to a Starbucks and stared dumbfounded at the menu trying to decide what they would order, as if there were serious consequences should they make the wrong choice. There should be a separate line for these dumb asses and it should actually say "dumb asses" above it so that they know to get in it. Of course, that is assuming dumb asses are self-aware enough to know that they are in fact dumb asses, and we all know that is clearly not the case.

I took some deep yoga breaths in and out and calmly talked myself down from using my purse strap to choke out the man who was standing so close behind me that I could feel and smell his disgusting hot breath on the back of my neck. Only two more people were in front of me. I could do this. I would get my coffee and I would log on to Amazon as soon as I got to the office.

The woman at the front of the line dithered back and forth between whether she wanted an iced coffee or a hot coffee. I clinched the strap of my purse and imagined whipping it around her neck and tightening it, watching her gasp her last few breaths. I was pretty sure everyone else in the line was having the exact same thought, so I was hoping someone would beat me to the punch. In case you were hanging on the edge of your seat, she finally decided to go with an iced coffee. I let her live, but I did silently curse her with a lifetime of never being able to get the plastic fruit and vegetable bags open at the store.

I got to the front of the line and the yak-breathed man behind me moved even closer as if I had been the hold up all along. I looked at Greg, the barista who I had become quite familiar with since my righteous coffee maker strike and smiled. I ordered my triple venti mocha and cinnamon scone, handed him cash, told him to keep the change and was out of line in 30 seconds.

It is not hard people. It is really not hard! Know where the hell you are and what the hell you are getting before you get in line.

As I stepped over to the waiting area to get my breakfast of a shit-ton of sugar and caffeine, I couldn't resist the temptation to say something. Rather than keeping my mouth shut, as we are trained to do in polite society, or so I'm told, I turned to face the close-standing man. He was in his thirties, hair slicked back, wore a suit and tie and would have been passably attractive aside from his complete lack of social graces and knowledge of personal space.

I jabbed my finger into the personal space that some might refer to as his face and hissed, "The next time you stand that close to a woman's back, you had better have bought her a very nice dinner and are helping her put on her coat. And even then you need to back it up a few inches. Personal space is not just a catch phrase."

I saw Greg laugh and then quickly cover his mouth to hide it. I felt a little something stir inside of me. It was only a comment. It wasn't even funny but I definitely felt a small spark after making someone that I didn't know laugh. Mr. Close-Stander attempted to save face by rolling his eyes at Greg like I was a crazy bitch, but Greg and I knew. I'm pretty sure I got some extra whipped cream on my mocha that morning. Score.

Amazingly, the train ride was relatively irritation free. I put my headphones on to avoid anyone who might make the ill-advised attempt to talk to me. I rarely actually listened to music because I liked to eavesdrop on everyone else's conversations for possible bits of material. Everyone around me was quiet that morning so I decided to turn on some Miley Cyrus and bopped along to "We Can't Stop" and "Party in the U.S.A." Don't even think about judging me over my music selection. Need I remind you about the dead man? Yeah, I didn't think so.

I have a three-block walk from the subway stop to my office. During this brief walk, I was run into by no less than six people who were not looking at where they were going because they were too busy texting on their phones. Look, I have friends. I text friends. You know what I don't do? Text my friends while I am walking. You know why? Because I am not an asshole.

Let's just pretend for a moment that my best friend Sarah sent me an urgent text that said *OMG, should I wear the black kitten heels or the slingback pumps with my outfit for work this morning?* Which is what I imagine to be the sort of critical content of these morning texts. Here is what I would do. First, I step aside from where other people are walking and lean up against a building out of everyone's way. Then, I immediately text Sarah back that we are no longer friends because that is a stupid ass question to be texting me this early in the morning. It is 8:45 a.m.! Nothing that important is happening in the morning that people have to be texting while they are walking to work. Nothing! I defy you to tell me any differently. I have very strong feelings on this subject. And my apologies to Sarah, I know you would never text me anything that stupid. And yes, I did text Sarah earlier this morning *Fuck this close-standing motherfucker behind me in line* and she responded, *lol*, but I was standing still in a line and as far as I know, Sarah was in bed after a late night at the theater.

I digress. The law firm where my boyfriend's father, Richard Andrew Stephens, Jr., is a partner and where I work is located on Fifth Avenue, so in other words, it is "fancy as fuck." And yes, my boyfriend is Richard Andrew Stephens, III. I'm living with a person who has a Roman numeral in his name. I would be embarrassed for myself if it weren't for the fact that I adore him and that he at least goes by the nickname Drew.

The firm website displays a quote declaring that it is a firm of "casual prestige" and "litigating masterminds." I have no idea where the "casual" part comes in because there is nothing about this office that even whispers "casual." I have a badge that I flash at Spencer at the front desk every morning before I get on the elevator and head up to the twenty-third floor where my open cubicle is located. The exterior walls are actually floor-to-ceiling windows so there is plenty of light, which is probably to keep all of us typing drones from killing each other. Everything is shiny and sparkly and the break station has an array of deep, fluffy couches and chairs that look out over the city. Granted, the view is mostly of just the building across the street, but it definitely beats the view of the misery on my face reflected back at me on the computer screen.

In my prior life, I would never have imagined myself working in an office, much less in a building on Fifth Avenue. I remember once in college, a girl at the dorms said she didn't care what her job was, she just wanted to wear expensive suits, carry a briefcase and work in an office. At the time, I scoffed at her since my ideal was a lot of drug-fueled, road trips to seedy nightclubs and trying to make people laugh.

Yet, here I was, dressed in what I would like to consider a stylish ensemble of a bright teal-colored sheath dress with a jacket and a somewhat loud pink and teal paisley scarf draped loosely around my neck and walking into a posh office, i.e. cubicle space. And yes, my boyfriend's mother, Carol, helps me pick out all of my clothes because my choice in clothing consists of the hard call between putting on pajama pants or yoga pants.

I sometimes wonder if the girl from college is living her dream or if by some freak accident she is the one having drug-fueled road trips. I barely made it off the elevator when Susan grabbed my arm and steered me to the break room.

"Have you heard?" Before I could even open my mouth to respond, she continued, "Oh, of course you didn't, you were out doing a show. Elise quit last night."

"What?! Why?" I screeched at a volume that was way too many decibels above the socially acceptable levels for an office setting. I'll admit I sounded a bit like a whiney school child. I immediately wanted to throw myself to the ground and roll around in a tantrum of protest.

Elise was the attorney who I directly worked with on all of my projects. I liked Elise. She said "fuck" just as much as I did and she was pretty easy to work for compared to some of the other attorneys in the firm. We worked well together.

"No one knows." Susan shrugged her shoulders and then turned to pour a cup of coffee.

"Apparently, she just took her personal shit out of her office and left without saying a word. An attorney on her floor walked by and noticed everything was gone. I've heard that she hasn't responded to any attempts to contact her. It's the most exciting thing to happen here in ages."

"Well, yeah. But damn it! I wish she would have given me a heads up. I wonder who is going to get her cases now."

I tried not to think of all the terrible potential replacements. My mostly benign but slightly challenging job could take a nosedive into "fuck this noise" territory pretty quick based on who took over her work. I had not consumed enough coffee or sugar for this news. I considered texting Elise *WTF?* but she might have been walking somewhere and I refused to be responsible for someone texting while walking even if they did just throw my work life into a tailspin.

After Susan broke the news of Elise's dramatic exit from the firm, I made my way to my cubicle and booted up the computer. I dreaded seeing the news of my fate waiting in my inbox. My cases could get assigned to any of the 60-plus attorneys in the firm. There had to be some non-raging assholes amongst them. Elise couldn't have been the only reasonably sane one.

I clicked the email open from Janet, the office manager, and the first two words I read immediately made me wish I had a bottle of vodka secreted away in my desk. I made a mental note to buy an emergency bottle of vodka for my office. I would now be needing one probably on a daily, if not hourly, basis.

To: Allison Brown; Tristan-Malcom Reynolds
From: Janet Goodman
Subject: Elise Newman's Work Reassignment

Tristan-Malcolm Reynolds will be assuming responsibility of Elise Newman's cases. Allison, you are scheduled to meet with Mr. Reynolds at 9:15 a.m. in his office to discuss the transition. Don't be late.

Fuck – my – life. I had just won the worst lottery in the world and I didn't even know I had bought a ticket. Tristan-Malcolm was legendary for running off employees. Since I have worked here, the longest he had a paralegal was four months. And don't even get me started on his name. He's so goddamn up his own ass that he makes people call him by two fucking "first" names. You get one damn first name people. One! It's called a "first" name for a reason. You can have ten other names if you want but I should only have to call you by one.

I would have walked out on the spot if it weren't for Drew and his dad and my recently discovered fondness for designer shoes and handbags and not smelling and feeling like salad dressing after coming home from work. I looked at the clock and it was 9:08. I thought about faking a ruptured appendix to get out of the office and buy myself some time to adjust to the news.

CHAPTER 2

I GATHERED A NOTEBOOK, A pen and a printed out list of my assigned cases and I started the walk toward the elevator and my doom. Prisoners on death row have been in a better mood on their long walk to death. I mouthed "Tristan-Malcolm" to Susan as I passed by her cubicle. Her eyes widened and her hands shot up to cover her suddenly gapping open mouth. She managed a slight, sad wave as if to say goodbye forever and that it had been nice knowing me.

As soon as I got on the elevator, I knew the other paralegals had started jockeying for ownership of my chair and office supplies. I should know, I had called dibs on my sweet-ass ergonomic office chair the moment Lisa had gotten assigned to him just three months ago. She only lasted two weeks.

I RODE THE ELEVATOR UP five flights and walked down the hall to where Tristan-Malcolm's corner office was located. I stood a few feet outside and again contemplated the ruptured appendix exit.

I had only spoken with him once and had seen him another handful of times at firm functions where I had Drew by my side. I'm usually not terrified of people but this man was the exception, mostly because I don't think he has ever smiled or laughed in his entire forty-five years of existence. I know this because upon being introduced to him and hearing "Malcolm Reynolds," I squealed, "OMG! Can I call you "Mal" like on *Firefly*? Fuck Fox for cancelling that show, am I right?" He scowled at me and immediately turned and walked away. He has stared at me with contempt ever since.

He looked out of place in his modern glass walled office where everything was sleek and linear. He had wavy, salt and pepper hair that hit his shoulders and a very severe eyebrow situation which always seemed arched and disapproving. He also had a salt and pepper beard and a mustache that he would sometimes twirl while looking you up and down as if he was trying to decide what you would taste like, and not in the good, fun going-down-on-you way, but in the stewed-with-a-nice-chianti way. Susan once confessed at happy hour that she thought he was ruggedly sexy, at which point I told the bartender to cut her off.

He stood with his back to me while looking out over the city. "Are you just going to stand out there quaking or are you going to come in here?"

Fuck. He obviously also had eyes in the back of his head. I put a fake smile on my face and headed in. I wasn't sure whether to sit down in one of the chairs across from his desk or stand.

"Sit." It was more of a command than an invitation and I thought maybe my appendix might actually burst out of fear before I got through the meeting, so there was hope. I obediently sat with my pen propped on my notebook ready to take notes.

He turned around, stepped over to his chair and stared at me without speaking for at least a minute. It was so uncomfortable that I was pretty sure I felt a small rupture actually beginning to formulate in my appendix.

"I don't like you." He announced as he sat down.

I hadn't thought that it could have gotten any more uncomfortable, but I had clearly been mistaken. I was used to dealing with hecklers and telling them to fuck off, but even I knew that would not be the appropriate response given the situation. I would be back trying to talk tourists into ordering dessert in a heartbeat if I dared open my mouth. Or dared to breathe. I was pretty sure that he didn't want me to even breathe. I comforted myself by thinking that maybe he only ate people that he liked and I was safe on that front. He continued to stare at me while stroking his mustache with his left hand and I hoped he was not trying to come up with a seasoning that might make me more appealing.

"I don't want to work with you any more than you want to work with me." He leaned forward and continued to glare at me. Instinctively, in an act of self-preservation, I leaned back further in my chair.

He continued. "I'm aware of the little office pools as to how long someone will last under my command. I don't find it amusing. I don't find you amusing. I understand that you think that you have some talent amusing people and I want you to understand that I have no interest in being amused. This is work."

Note to self, this dude does not want to be amused. As if this was a complete stop-the-presses newsflash. I adjusted my face from my forced pleasant smile to my somber oh-this-is-supposed-to-be-a-serious-moment face, which I have practiced for funerals. As with my Judas nipples earlier in the day, my appendix betrayed me by failing to spontaneously rupture.

"I've been told by Richard that I have no choice in the matter and that I have to take on Elise's cases, which means working with you."

He leaned back in his chair.

"I realize you are in some sort of a dalliance with his son, but I want you to know I will be making no special accommodations for you. I don't care who you are carrying on with. I expect you to be here when I need you to be here and I expect you to get your work done."

I sat there confounded thinking of all the various ways he could have appropriately used the word "fuck" or some variation in that soliloquy. This man was definitely not my people. My fear was momentarily forgotten as I thought about telling Drew that I wanted to dally and carry on with him after dinner with his parents. It took all of my effort to maintain the serious face.

"I spent half an hour going through Elise's office this morning and it is a disaster. She has hundreds of legal pads with handwritten notes stacked haphazardly all over her office. She knows we are a fully digital office and everything should be on the server so that it can be easily found. As you know, she and Richard were in the middle of overseeing a huge merger for one of our biggest clients."

I didn't dare let on that I didn't know anything about the merger at all. I just did what I was told to do and paid very little attention to the details of the cases that I was working on at any given moment.

"Of course." My first words spoken to my new scary and probably cannibalistic boss were a lie. This was not going to end well for me.

"I need to get up to speed on the case. I can't read a word of her abominable handwriting. So, I need you to collect all the notebooks out of Elise's office and I need you to type them up for me immediately."

"Yes, sir." I scribbled on my notepad to type up Elise's notes thinking that it made me look serious and concerned about my work. I kept my pen on the paper waiting further instruction.

"I said immediately. Why are you still in my office wasting my time?" His voice was a low and terrifying growl.

I scurried out of my seat and scrambled out the door desperate to go somewhere to quietly pee myself.

"And one more thing."

I turned around and was met with his cold, hard, blue eyes boring straight through me.

"If you ever try to use your relationship with Richard's son as leverage while working with me or in any way undermine me with Richard, I will fucking kill you."

And eat me. I just knew he was thinking it. I was going to be reduced to a nice Bolognese sauce, which he would then promptly spit out in disgust.

I am not going to lie. I did pee myself just a little at that moment. I walked quickly to the bathroom, removed the slightly damp underwear, and tossed them in the trash.

HE WAS RIGHT ABOUT ELISE'S office. It was a disaster. She was a notorious pack rat of paper who stood out in the digital office. All the other attorneys' offices were pristine and ready at a moment's notice to be photographed for *Fancy-As-Fuck-Attorneys'-Office-Weekly,* which I am pretty positive was the name of the magazine Richard once bragged about being featured in last year. It was hard to imagine that any work actually got done when you walked by and saw their clean desks which featured not one, not two, but three computer screens because they were obviously very important.

Elise's office had notebooks stacked on every flat surface. She had stacks and stacks of printed out pages which were highlighted and tabbed and scribbled on. Shit was scattered everywhere. There was a half empty cup of coffee beside one of the random stacks in the middle of her desk.

Honestly, it looked like she had left in the middle of going through a stack merely to take a break before returning to continue to sort and highlight and tab things for reasons only she knew. The only evidence that she was gone and not returning was the absence of her diplomas on the wall and her personal photos. I pictured her being halfway through a stack of papers and standing up and saying, "fuck this" and leaving. That was pretty badass. She would be my hero except for the fact that she left me behind to most likely be both figuratively and literally eaten by my new boss.

I called down to the mail room and asked for a cart to be brought up so I could load up the stacks of paper and notebooks and wheel them down to my cubicle space. I noticed that one of the large wooden file cabinet drawers was open. I tried to kick it shut to vent some of my frustration. It didn't budge.

I bent down to see what was jamming it and found two boxes of old audio tapes of various sizes and formats. I had no idea what case they were from and I was afraid I would look stupid if I asked, so I just piled them on the cart with everything else. I would stash them in the corner of my cubicle until I could somehow figure out if they had anything to do with this merger case. I sure as hell was not going to get stuck having to not only transcribe every notebook but also every tape if it was not necessary.

It took two carts and over an hour to load everything up. Tristan-Malcolm walked by the office at least twice and loudly huffed his disapproval that I had not even completed this "simple task" in a timely manner. I was in desperate need of that emergency bottle of vodka or a ruptured appendix. I really was not asking for much.

When I finally got back to my desk, I saw that I had three missed texts from Drew, two of which were simply emoji hearts and one which said, *I can't wait to hear about your set at dinner.* His supportiveness was enough to make me sick at times. For a few hours I had completely forgotten about having to come up with another lie.

I'm not going to bore you with the rest of the details of my work day. There is simply no way to make sitting at a computer and trying to decipher random words into something that might make sense to the crazy man upstairs sound even slightly entertaining. Let's just say there was a lot of squinting and fast and furious typing and yet, I still only managed to get half a notebook done by the end of eight hours.

I sent two *WTF Elise?* texts which were ignored. I briefly considered staying and burning the midnight oil to get at least one notebook finished but I found that my fear of the bearded asshole receded slightly by not actually being in his physical presence. I also reminded myself that whether he liked it or not, I was dallying with his boss's son so I was pretty sure I wouldn't get fired unless I seriously fucked up in a major way. I vowed to throw an extra pair of underwear in my purse for back up on days when I actually had to see him.

Dinner with Drew and his parents was at the fashionably late time of eight o'clock. I defiantly clocked out at six o'clock and walked down to the gym, which I was a member of courtesy of Mr. Stephens and the law firm. I needed to get a run in so I could survive dinner and any other shit shows this godforsaken day had to throw at me.

CHAPTER 3

IF YOU HAD TOLD ME when I was in college that I would be addicted to running, I would have taken the joint out of my mouth and laughed in your face. I was not exactly a health nut. I'm still not, because yes, I still inhale occasionally and I eat and drink like it is my part-time job, but I run.

I lived with Sarah when I first moved to the city and she signed us up for a running class, because I guess being a chorus line dancer in a Broadway show just wasn't enough physical activity for her. She said I needed to get off my ass and start moving because all I did was sleep, eat and get drunk and high. She wasn't wrong. I hated running. Absolutely hated it. Until one day about three weeks into the class. We were doing sprints. My lungs felt like they were about to explode. I thought I was going to throw up. I was mentally calling Sarah an asshole and a bitch. But my lungs didn't explode and I didn't throw up. The class was over and I thought about what I had just done and suddenly I felt like a badass. I had done it. Now, don't think for a minute that I stopped whining at Sarah and telling her how much I hated her whenever we would head off to class because I did, but somehow over those nine weeks I turned into a runner.

I changed into my running gear and headed out to run in Central Park. I will never tell my parents that I run in the park. My mother would be on the first plane here to drag me back home to safety. She watches way too many *Law & Order* reruns so she thinks the only way out of Central Park is in a body bag. To this day, she believes I have never set foot into the "Park of Death and Rape." The fact that I live in the city and take the subway is enough to make her curl up in bed with her rosary beads, praying for my safety.

After I graduated college and before I moved here, my mom made me take self-defense courses from my dad's blind Vietnam veteran friend, Bob. He terrified me. I have no idea how Bob knew I was doing things wrong but he yelled at me constantly and made me repeat and repeat my drills. I have not yet had to take anyone down with a rolled up magazine, but by god, I could do it thanks to Bob's tutelage. Every now and then when we are drunk, Drew, who is six-foot-four, or Max, his best friend since boarding school, who is six-foot-two, try to challenge me with a fake attack. And every time, both of them land on their asses, puzzled that a tiny slip of a girl who is five-foot-four, on a good hair day, has taken them down. It's all about the element of surprise and leverage. Well, and being absolutely petrified that Bob would suddenly appear and yell at me that I did it wrong.

It was late October and there was a chill in the air so I had on my bright pink windbreaker with reflective silver stripes and my running gloves. I wear the gloves even though it's fall because my hands are always cold. The women at the office laugh at me because I have a pair of gloves at my desk with the tips of the fingers cut out that I wear when my hands get cold at work but I still need to type.

My plan was to get at least an hour run in down by reservoir, take in the view of water, which always calms me, and just let my brain concentrate on keeping my legs moving and my lungs breathing. Every time my foot hit the gravel I was one step further away from failing to do a set the night before, lying to Drew, stupid iced coffee woman, Mr. Close-Stander, Tristan-Fucking-Malcolm and my new work hell. I breathed in and breathed out and listened to the sound of my breath and nothing else.

The stress was on the verge of dissipating, I was hitting that bit of a runner's high and then - - then I hit the ground like a rock.

I was dazed as I got up and looked for the source of my fall. I expected to find someone leaning over me and offering their hand and profusely apologizing for knocking me down. But no one was there.

The asshole just kept on going and he was about forty-yards away. He didn't even bother to look back because he was too busy texting. Texting and running! By now, I think you know me well enough to know the rage that boiled up and overtook my entire being. If not, I am going to need you to go back and start from the beginning.

I looked around to see if there was anyone in the area that I could say, "What the fuck? Did you see that rude-ass-motherfucker?" to, but there was no one. There had not been many runners or other people out since it was getting darker and a slight drizzle of rain had been coming down intermittently.

I could hear the blood rushing and pounding into my brain as I sprinted to catch up with the douchebag who was still texting. What is the point of running if you are going to text? What could possibly be so important that after you plow someone down that you would just keep going? This was not how society was supposed to function.

My blood pressure and anger were at a furious boil by the time I got a few feet away from him. I bent my head down and hurled my shoulder into his back and knocked him on his goddamn ass. He landed next to the railing and his phone went flying out of his hand. It landed several feet away from him. I hoped his screen was cracked. It was the least he deserved.

"What the hell? You crazy bitch." He looked up at me from the ground.

"Excuse me? Are you seriously saying that to me? Do you even realize you knocked me down back there? I want an apology douchebag." I stood glaring over him filled with the white hot rage that had been percolating all day. He tried to get up and I kicked him back down with my foot.

"You look just fine to me, you crazy bitch." He again tried to get up and I again kicked him back down. This time, I kept my foot on his shoulder close to his neck and I leaned all of my weight and rage into that one leg and kept him pinned down.

"So, I'm a bitch? I was running and minding my own business and you knocked my ass down because you were texting and not looking where you were going and didn't have the decency to stop and apologize, but I'm the bitch?"

He clearly had no idea just how bad my day had been and that he had been the last fucking straw and that I was going to get an apology from him if it was the last thing I did that day. My rage had made me six-foot-tall and bullet proof and he was not going to move off the damn ground until he said he was sorry.

He pushed his body up to get out from under my foot. He was able to get up just enough to crab-crawl around in an attempt to get himself away from being pinned between me and the railing. I kicked him down again.

"I need you to apologize to me." My back was to the railing and I was glaring down at him with what I could only imagine was the look of a deranged crazy person at this point.

"Screw you!" He lunged up off the ground and his arm came swinging forward as if he was going to strike me.

I honestly can't remember the details of what happened next but I could have sworn I heard Bob's voice in my head as I grabbed the man's arm, lowered my head into his body and flipped him over me. I heard a large-sounding thud.

Suddenly, I realized that I had let my rage place in me in a great deal of danger. I looked around for help. There was no one coming or going in either direction. I was alone. I was alone and I was going to get carried out of Central Park in a body bag as soon as this man got done with me. I could hear my mom saying she knew that would be my fate after moving to the city and daring to go the "Park of Death and Rape." I pushed the thought of either of those outcomes from my head and started running and realized that I was running in the opposite direction of the gym and possible safety.

I kept running and tried to figure out what to do next and where was I headed. I waited to hear him yell that I was a crazy bitch again and come after me. I got about sixty-yards away before I realized that there was no yelling and no pursuit. I looked back to see if he had grabbed his phone to call the cops. For the first time, it occurred to me that I might live but that I would likely get assault charges filed against me since I was the aggressor. I thought of how embarrassed Drew would be and how I would definitely lose my job and, most likely, Drew.

I didn't see anyone standing where I had left him. I didn't see anything at all. Maybe he ran in the other direction to get away from me. I ran a few yards back and saw the phone glowing on the ground where it had landed. Surely, the man who couldn't even get through his run without texting would have picked up his phone and not left it behind. I panicked. He was probably hiding somewhere waiting to come at me. I started running back in the direction of the gym. Even though it meant going past the scene of my break from reality, I needed a safe place to run toward.

As I ran, my head swiveled in all directions and my body was on high alert for an attack from any angle. "What would Bob tell me to do?" was playing in a rapid loop through my brain. That's when I saw it.

Out of the corner of my eye, I saw the glimmer of reflective light bouncing off the stripe on his jacket. The shimmer was low on the ground and coming from on the other side of the railing.

I froze expecting him to pounce on me from his position. The "What would Bob tell me to do?" chorus was getting louder and louder in my head. "Run as fast as you can," was the only answer I could conjure up.

But the jacket didn't move as I ran past. Some instinct, definitely not survival, made me stop. I could practically hear Bob swearing at me and saying this would definitely not be what he would tell me to do.

I walked toward the railing and peeked over it at. I was standing exactly where shit had gone down and he was laying on the ground not moving.

Somehow, in my rage, I had managed to flip him not only over me, but over the railing. His body was laying at an awkward angle and blood was oozing out of the side of his head onto the rock it had struck. I pissed myself for the second time of the day. I looked around and still saw no one in the vicinity. Where the fuck was everybody? It is no wonder people got raped and murdered in this park. I leaned over the railing. "Hey, are you OK?"

No response.

"I didn't mean to actually hurt you."

Still no response. I had no idea why I was talking to him and not calling for help.

"It's just . . . you really shouldn't be texting and running."

No response. No moaning. Just oozing blood and silence.

"All I wanted was an apology." This was more of a whisper to myself than an attempt to communicate with him, since I realized the conversation was one-sided.

I backed away from the railing and tried to decide what to do. I had left my phone in the gym locker because my run is my quiet time and I don't want to be bothered. Not to mention, I obviously don't text and run.

I walked over to his phone. I still wasn't sure if I was going to call for help or not. Bob's voice in my head kept warning me that I needed to leave. I thought about running and finding help and pretending I had just happened to find his body. But what if he wasn't dead? What if he was just in a coma? What if he woke up and was able to identify me? I'd seen that *Law & Order* before, where the first person on the scene not so shockingly turns out to be the murderer. No. I needed to leave this behind me and forget it happened. It was not my fault.

I considered sending a text to whoever he had been texting and asking them to send help before I left. I picked up his phone in my gloved, trembling hands. I saw the message that had been so important for him to type that he didn't see me, knocked me down, and didn't stop to offer help or to apologize: *I want u to suck my cock and drink my cum, u dirty slut.*

The rage came roaring back into my body and any fear or guilt was at least temporarily pushed out to make way for it. That bastard was sexting! And he couldn't even be bothered to spell out the word "you." I chucked the phone into the reservoir. I leaned over the railing and took one last look at him.

"Fuck you, asshole."

AS I RAN BACK TO the gym, the adrenaline and realization as to what just happened hit me with full force. I started to cry. Not tears of sorrow for him, but tears of rage and fear as I thought about how everything could have been avoided if he had just watched where he was going. If he had just shown an ounce of humanity. He had pushed me to my limit. This was his fault. This was his fault. I would keep repeating those words until I fully believed them.

I was just trying to get my run in so I could shake off my miserable shit filled day. Why couldn't he have waited until after his run to tell this unknown person he wanted his cock sucked?

And let me clarify, I have no problem with sexting. I sext with Drew all the time from work. Anyone who claims to have not sent a sext from work when they are bored shitless from the mundaneness of it all is either a liar or a prude. Just don't sext and walk or sext and run. Cocks and tits can wait. Damn it.

I had an hour to pull my shit together before dinner. I had an hour to sit in the sauna at that gym and replay the events in my mind. I replayed every detail while drawing upon knowledge from every detective show I had ever watched.

There had been no witnesses.

I had my gloves on therefore no finger prints. My finger prints are not in any databank because they had never been taken.

My hair was tied up. If any hair transferred onto him my DNA is not in any databank.

My running shoes are a popular brand and could be purchased at any number of places. I wear a size 6.5, which is one of the most common shoe sizes.

I do not live near or walk through any special soil or foliage whereby any traces possibly left on his jacket could be magically traced back to me. That detail always seemed to lead TV detectives straight to the killer.

My brain stumbled over the word killer. That is not what I am. That's not me. It's not my fault.

For all the police would know he could have bent over to get his phone and he fell over the railing himself. It could have happened that way. The police don't know about the crazy bitch that kicked him while demanding an apology for all the atrocities of her day.

And he was trying to strike me. At least I thought he was at the time. It was self-defense. I latched onto that phrase and kept repeating it in my head until the syllables lost their shape and any meaning as words. In a weird way, I felt like Bob would be very proud of me.

CHAPTER 4

I WAS STILL SHAKING AND flushed when the cab dropped me off in front of The Manhattan Fifth's Club, which is casually referred to as "The Club" by its members, as if to imply there is simply no other club that one would aspire to be a member of, provided you were deemed worthy of mingling with the upper echelon of wealth and society. In other words, I should never be allowed to pass through its doors, except maybe to scrub the toilets.

I was late even with taking a cab instead of walking. I had tried to reassemble myself at the gym and make myself presentable as opposed to the I-just-killed-someone look, which I'm surprised has not yet been the subject of a New York fashion show. Then again, it was entirely possible that it had been done since the closest I've gotten to following fashion is watching *Project Runway*. I smoothed the wrinkles out of my dress as I walked up to the door, which was being held open by Fred, the ever-present doorman.

"You are looking lovely as always, Ms. Brown." Whew! At least Fred couldn't tell that I was now a killer. I had half expected him to say, "Good evening, Ms. Brown. The cops are on their way."

"Thank you, Fred. You are looking quite dapper yourself."

Good lord, I just used the word dapper. What have I become? Who am I? I'm now apparently the crazy bitch that murders people for texting and running and also uses the word dapper. I tried not to think of the blood oozing from the man's head, because if I did, I would have either thrown up or peed myself, because, apparently, I have also become "the girl who pees herself." My mother would be so proud.

I walked into the lobby and to the bar, which was covered floor-to-wall-to-ceiling with dark, rich wood. The stodgy room was filled with groupings of high, wing-backed, leather chairs where very important men smoked cigars and drank scotch, because that was what they did and this was where the real money was made. It literally was the backroom where deals were made that kept this nation great. Or, so I've been told. I tend to believe the deals being made were less about keeping the nation great and more about redistributing the wealth upwards to keep the individuals in this room's lives great. But what did I know, I was just a simple girl from West Virginia.

I spotted Drew's tall, lean frame leaning up against the bar talking to the bartender and I instantly felt calmer. He turned around and saw me and smiled. I had to stop myself from running and throwing myself into his arms and crying and confessing everything. Instead, I walked briskly over to him and kissed him.

"How was your day, honey?" I asked hoping that my voice sounded normal and that my face was not wearing an expression of wild panic.

"Nothing too exciting. I worked on my brief for my Criminal Procedure class."

I make a mental note that I might need to read his text book for this class while he was sleeping.

He kept talking. "I heard about Elise and Tristan-Malcolm. How awful? Do you want me to talk to Dad about getting you transferred to someone else and put on some different cases?"

He looked across the room where his dad and mom were sitting with their pre-dinner cocktails and holding court with other very important people. People who I had been introduced to on numerous occasions but had forgotten their names despite their very important stature. My motto while at The Club or any of his parents' fundraisers or parties was always, "I'm just here for the food."

"No, honey. Please don't. I can do this on my own. I can handle Mr. Two-Named Prick Face all by myself."

He laughed.

"It will be a bitch but I can do it. I appreciate the offer to help me though." I kissed his cheek and smiled.

"Allison, how lovely to see you darling." Carol approached and made a hand gesture to Louis, the maître d', that we were ready to be seated. "I knew that teal color would look fabulous on you with your auburn hair."

"Thank you for picking it out. You always know what will work. I would be naked most of the time if it weren't for your good taste."

She responded with a light chuckle which was about as much as I have ever really elicited from her. Although to be fair, I had never seen her have a rip, roaring, throw her head back laugh. I've decided maybe her genteel breeding has taught her that a mere chuckle was how a proper lady laughed. I could never be accused of knowing how a proper lady was meant to behave.

Although Richard obviously made a good living at the firm, Carol was the one with the money. She was a blue blood through and through. Very proper and graceful. She was stunning to look at but her beauty consisted of sharp angles. She was tall like her son. Naturally skinny and lithe. Her cheek bones were as sharp as her eyes and the cut of her perfectly bobbed, blonde hair.

She hosted charity galas and brunches and fundraisers. She always knew the right words to say but she lacked the natural charm and warmth that radiated from Drew and his father. I believed that she could cut the balls off of any of the men in the room and that they would most likely thank her for doing it. I didn't know why she liked me, but I was grateful that she did.

We had been seated for almost fifteen minutes before Richard finally joined us at the table. He bent over to kiss my cheek to greet me before taking his seat beside me. Looking at Richard, I could see the man that Drew would age into since they looked so much alike. Richard was a tall, broad-shouldered, silver fox, with an ever-present wide smile shining across his face that spread up to his twinkling eyes.

So far, Drew had not mentioned the subject of my set or my fledgling comedy career, which was a good thing. He and his mother had spent the entire time discussing his cousin's upcoming New Year's Eve wedding and how she had still not selected a band. Apparently, this was a very big deal and quite the conundrum according to Carol. I have never been one of those women who obsessed about weddings. Frankly, I think the whole idea of spending a shit-ton of money on what amounted to a party where you got toasters, silverware, useless crystal goblets and candlesticks seemed like a stupid waste of money on everyone's part. I'm not a fan.

I mentally checked out of the conversation and concentrated on ridding my mind of the look on that man's face as I kicked him down to the ground.

It's not my fault. It was self-defense. The chorus continued racing through my brain. It was starting to take on the jaunty rhythm of a pop song which would soon become an endless earworm.

After placing his order and handing the menu back to the waiter, Richard turned his attention to me. He clasped my hand.

"Ally, I'm so sorry about assigning Tristan-Malcolm to Elise's cases."

"Oh, I will be fine. I can handle him." Tristan-Malcolm's words of warning began ringing in my ear briefly replacing the "self-defense" earworm. The fear of him killing me and eating me was briefly reignited.

"I know he is a bit of a bear to work for but with the merger taking place in a few weeks, he is the only one quick enough and bright enough to step into Elise's shoes."

I nodded as if I completely agreed that it was the right decision. I tried to look at ease with the fact that the cushy job I had held for three years was now a thing of the past.

"Now, if he gives you any trouble – you come tell me about it and I will make him back off. I can't have him running off the best thing that has happened to Drew." He turned to Drew, who was seated on his other side, and slapped his shoulder in a congratulatory manner.

"Dad, you know she's not going to be working there forever. Her comedy career is taking off."

Well shit. There was just no end to his loving support.

"Really?" Carol piped in. "I hadn't heard that your shows were going so well. You have been rather quiet about it lately so I didn't want to ask."

Thank you Carol. That is all I want. If I'm quiet about something don't ask. I love your son but can you get him to stop it with all this supportive nonsense.

I smiled and nodded, "Yeah, it has been going really well."

Lie. Such a super big lie. Although, the omission of killing someone just prior to dinner might have been a little worse so I was all in at this point.

"Well that is just lovely, dear. We will have to come see you one night. Are you still performing at the same club?"

Carol smiled at me as the waiter placed her salad in front of her. Her inquiry didn't worry me because I knew she was just asking to be polite. She would never step foot in a comedy club. It was just not in her nature. So, I lied again.

"That would be great, Carol. I would love that. Yep. I'm still at the same one down at the Village Underground. Now tell me all about the political fundraiser that you are hosting next weekend." See, I can have social graces too. Don't act so surprised.

At dinner, I usually clap with delight when my favorite meal of a rare filet mignon, with sauce chasseur, Boursin stuffed potatoes and haricots verts is placed in front of me. Sometimes that meal, followed by the chef's whimsy bread pudding dessert, is the highlight of my entire week. This night, I had no appetite, but I went through the motions.

As soon as I cut into the steak and the red juices poured out, I saw the blood on the rock and I saw the face of the man. I was never going to get that vision out of my head. I wasn't sure how everyone at the table could not tell I was now a sociopathic, killing bitch.

I looked at Drew and his parents and wanted to cry, but I didn't. I ate and I listened to all of the talk of the fundraiser interspersed with Richard quizzing Drew on his classes. I nodded and smiled in all of the right places and I asked what I imagined were insightful follow-up questions. Two hours later, I was finally able to seek the comfort of being at home and alone with Drew.

"YOU WERE QUIET TONIGHT, HONEY. Are you sure you don't want me to say something more to Dad about moving you to other cases?"

Drew was laying in the bed, petting the cats, and watching me change back into the clothes of my people, a T-shirt and pajama pants.

"I'm fine, babe."

I crawled into the bed and spooned up as close to him as I could get since the cats refused to budge from their prime belly rub positions.

But I wasn't fine. I put my hand behind my back and petted Daisy, the fluffiest and fattest of the cats who was wedged between me and Drew, and in return, I received tiny, warm cat-licks. I was relieved that at least Daisy and ZuZu would never know the truth if it came out. They wouldn't leave me. Then I thought about the possibility of being locked away and how I was pretty sure cats weren't allowed to visit their owners in prison. Fresh warm tears welled up in my eyes. I buried my face into the pillow so that Drew wouldn't see and then ask more questions. I didn't want to lie anymore for the night.

I wanted a do-over for the day. I'm sure the dead man wanted a do-over too, because he wasn't going to get his cock sucked ever again. But neither of us were going to get a do-over. I was just going to have to figure out how to push the whole thing down and try to forget it and hope to hell the cops never showed up at the door and took me away.

It's not my fault. It was self-defense. The rhythmic patter of the chorus returned.

"I love you, Ally Brown." Drew kissed the back of my neck and settled in to sleep.

"I love you, Drew Stephens." It was our nightly version of "Goodnight, John Boy" and I missed it on those Wednesday nights when I snuck in well after he was asleep. I still whispered my half to him on those nights, but it wasn't the same.

CHAPTER 5

I SLEPT SURPRISINGLY WELL THAT night and woke up the next morning refreshed. I guess looking back, that should have caused me some alarm about the functioning of my moral compass, but I was mostly just relieved because living with crushing guilt is no way to go through life. It's not that I didn't think about it at all throughout the day, but when I did, I summoned the earworm "self-defense" chorus and reminded myself that it had been a really shitty day.

Have I mentioned that I have remarkable rationalization skills? Sure, most of the time those skills had been of the non-crucial variety such as "a third bottle of wine is a great idea" or "spending $250 to get front row seats to see *Hedwig and the Angry Inch* so that I could get a 'car-wash' lap dance from Taye Diggs is a lifetime investment." But the years of honing those skills had finally paid off to assist me in this more serious transgression. And the money I spent on the lap dance from Taye Diggs? Worth every penny. And let's be honest, the third bottle of wine is usually not only a great idea, but also absolutely necessary on most occasions.

I got through the morning without Drew mentioning my set or my comedy career. There were only two people standing between me and my scone and mocha and they both knew exactly what they wanted. Not a single person bumped into me while texting and walking. It was almost as if the universe was rewarding me for ridding it of that jackass.

Sadly, I was not greeted with the news of Tristan-Malcolm's sudden departure from the firm or Elise's return. So, the universe wasn't sending me a huge "Atta-girl" but it also wasn't condemning me either. After yesterday, that was good enough for me.

I turned on my computer and found an email sent by Tristan-Malcolm at 6:15 the night before:

To: Allison Brown
From: Tristan-Malcom Reynolds
Subject: Your work ethic

I see that you have decided to leave for the evening. Do you not understand the concept of immediately? Did you even hear words when I spoke?

TMR.

I responded to this criticism in the way most reasonable adults would. I stopped reading, flipped my middle finger at the screen, and muttered, "I've killed people for less." Seriously dude, there were over 100 legal pads of scribbling. That shit is not getting done anytime soon, let alone immediately. I leaned back in my chair and contemplated not doing anything but playing Candy Crush for the day, like I used to do before Elise had left. My eyes rested on the file cabinet drawer where I had dumped the contents of the stupid boxes of tapes that I hadn't told anyone about. I really had to figure out what to do about those damn tapes.

I texted Elise. *What the hell is up with the tapes? Are these important? TMR is going to eat me and not in the good way. Eww! Ick! I just grossed myself out thinking about that. Seriously, though, how important are these tapes?*

She hadn't responded to any of my texts from the day before but I hoped that maybe it was because she was too busy walking. She was quite familiar with all of my rules. I get that she quit, but hanging me out to dry seemed kind of extreme seeing as how we used to drink together at least once a week. It briefly occurred to me that maybe I should have listened a little bit more when she talked about work.

I searched my memory to see if at any time over our after-work martinis she might have ever said something vague like ". . . and then I had to tell the summer law clerk, John, to move those boxes of very important merger related tapes out of the way so he'd have more room to go down on me from under my desk." Nope. I couldn't remember a single conversation about those damn tapes. Minus the detail about moving the boxes, the bit about the John the summer law clerk was totally a legitimate conversation that happened with her.

AT NOON, I MET SARAH for our usual Friday afternoon lunch. Sarah is the only one who I had confided in about the death of my comedy career. Like the best of friends, she would not bring it up unless I did first. Today's lunch wasn't about me though. Today was about Sarah. Wednesday night was the opening night of yet another new starlet taking on the role of "Sugar" in the hit musical *Salty but Sweet*. It was a dramedy about the rise and fall of a teenage pop star. Sarah had been the understudy for the possibly career-making part for over two years. In all that time, she had not yet gotten the chance to step foot on the stage as Sugar, but had to settle for playing a minor role.

Being the good friend that I am, I have never mentioned to her that a minor role on Broadway was still a pretty good gig and a far cry from where she was just five years ago when we first became roommates and she was desperately carrying around head shots and going on cattle calls. She was certainly further along in reaching her career goals than I was at this point. But, I don't say anything close to that because despite what some people might think, I am not a bitch. I know from rehearsing lines with her that she would be a fierce Sugar even if it was just for one night. Not to mention that she'd make history as the first African-American to play the role.

I wanted her to be successful more than I wanted success for myself. I wanted her to be "The Big Fucking Deal" that I knew she could be if given the chance. Sarah was everything I was not. She was tall, glamorous, health conscious, and had an unrelenting drive to succeed in life with a sunny and positive disposition. Her smile lit up the room and all heads turned to stare at her whenever she entered the room. She carried herself with the earned confidence of a warrior princess.

"I saw the reviews online. Is it true that Rena is actually good? I find that hard to believe since she's such a white-hot mess in real life."

Good friends know that you always trash talk the opponent regardless of whether that person was your first girl-crush growing up or that their songs are still on your running mix, and you follow their personal melt downs on the internet like it is part of your job. It was unofficially acknowledged by everyone that "Sugar" was loosely based on the life of Rena Harris, so when it was announced that she was taking over the lead, well, the internet lost its collective shit. Ticket sales skyrocketed. Everyone wanted to be there when the train went off the rails because no one believed that Rena would have the chops or the ability to stay sober long enough to pull it off.

"She's no Liza, no matter how much she runs around trying to get the crew to call her that, but she's actually pretty good. When she's sober. Rehearsals can be ugly when she bothers to show up."

She took a bite of her salad. "I hate to tell you this because of the girl-crush and all, but she is a dreadful and evil person. You will see for yourself at Saturday's after-party. You are coming Saturday, right?"

"Are you kidding me? You know I come to every Saturday show after a new bitch starts playing your role. Drew and Max and I will all be there, front-row center, to support you. Hopefully, Rena actually breaks a leg and can't go on and you get to have your big night. And hello . . . you know that I've moved on and my new girl-crush is Helen Miren."

"Bitch, please. Every woman on Earth has a girl-crush on Helen Miren. That's just common sense."

I shrugged. "I never claimed to be original in my choices."

I shoved a French fry in my mouth. "I can't wait to see the train wreck in person. And Helen aside, I can't promise that I'm not going to stare at her boobs. We all know that will happen."

Sarah grinned as she continued to daintily eat her salad. "Everyone stares at her boobs. It is unfair how amazing her boobs are in real life and they aren't even fake."

I stopped myself from taking a bite out of my burger. "Hold up. How do you know they aren't fake?"

"Because she walks around naked all the goddamn time and makes everyone touch them to confirm they aren't fake. So how is your work going?"

I wiped the burger grease from my chin, "Are you shitting me? That is awesome! You have the best job ever. Mine, on the other hand, is horrible. This new dude is totally up my ass all the time and Elise still hasn't responded to any of my texts."

"That's weird. You guys were tight. Even if she didn't give you a heads up that she was leaving, she could have at least said goodbye or sorry." She stole a fry from my plate.

"Thank you! My thoughts exactly! The worst part is that she left a giant mess at the office and I've got Hannibal all over me demanding that I clean it up and make sense of it for him. Speaking of which, I need a favor."

I reached for my workout bag that was beside me on the booth, raised it up, and attempted to hand it over the table to her.

Sarah refused to take it. Instead, she gave me a shade of side eye that I had unfortunately been the recipient of on more than one occasion. "Hell no, bitch, I'm not doing your laundry."

"It's not my laundry, asshole. Take it, it's heavy." I pleaded to her with a slightly exaggerated whine and what I hoped was a convincing pout. The bag was weighing down my arm and was in danger of falling into my ketchup.

She snatched the bag from me and rolled her eyes. She effortlessly put it down beside her.

"It's not that heavy. I told you to start doing arm workouts. You have weak-ass arms. I'm sending you a link to a workout. Now what the hell is in here and what am I supposed to do with it?"

"I found this shit-ton of tapes in Elise's office and I have no idea what they are and whether they are important. I don't have time to listen to them because I have five-bazillion notebooks to transcribe. I just need you to listen to them while you are working out and tell me what is on them."

She stole another fry off my plate. Normally, I would have pitched a fit about the stolen fries but I decided to keep silent since I had just asked her for a huge favor.

Her face turned serious. "I am not a lawyer, but I played one in a commercial once and even I know that you are violating a slew of ethics rules about client confidentiality or something by taking these out of the office and giving them to me. You know that right?"

I briefly thought about telling her that I killed a man the night before so violating some ethics rules was the least of my problems, but that was not the kind of burdensome information you saddle your rising star of a best friend with, so I just nodded. "I know and I wouldn't ask if I didn't need the help."

"Aren't there other secretaries or paralegals who can help you? Why do I have to do it?"

"Look. My new boss has a hobby of getting people fired and those are people he doesn't even know very well. He knows me and he hates me. He already thinks that I'm incompetent, which I think both me and you know is pretty much true."

I nervously folded and unfolded the napkin on my lap. "I wouldn't have this job if it weren't for Drew. My comedy career is not even on life support it is so dead so, sadly, this is all I have right now. If I go into his office and tell him I have no idea what is on these tapes, I might not get fired because Richard probably wouldn't let that happen, but my daily life would be even more miserable. Now, on the other hand, if I go in there and I've been transcribing the hell out of the notebooks and can say, 'Oh by the way, there were these tapes but I've listened to them and here's what is on them,' then, all of a sudden I look like I know what I'm doing. And I buy myself a little more time to live and not be turned into a stew."

She stole yet another fry from my plate and gave me a look that dared me to say something in protest. "You know, you could just work overtime and do this yourself. Or I don't know, maybe multi-task and listen to them while you do your other work."

I frowned at her because of the stolen fries and the fact that those were both valid points. It had made so much sense to me when I came up with the idea at the office and covertly transferred the tapes into the bag and snuck them out of the office. I suppose I was just trying to irresponsibly pass the work onto Sarah. I was truly terrible at my job.

"Fine. Give the bag back to me." I dejectedly hung my head and gestured to her to hand the bag back over to me.

Ignoring me, she unzipped it and looked inside. She picked out a large cassette and looked at it quizzically. "No. I'm going to do it. Mostly because I am curious as to what the hell is on them. These look like they came from the Cold War era. I'm not sure where I would even find the equipment I need to listen to them. Do RadioShacks still exist? Are those still a thing?"

"Thank you. You are the best friend ever." I would have hugged her if we weren't sitting at a booth and if she hadn't stolen so many of my fries.

"Don't thank me yet." Her face turned very serious and her voice lowered, "Someday, I don't know when, but someday, I'll call you up for a bigass favor." She then busted into a fit of giggles.

"What the hell was that supposed to be?" I asked.

"Brando? *The Godfather*? Ever heard of it?"

I laughed and shook my head. "That is possibly the worst Brando impersonation I have ever heard and I'm pretty sure that is not even close to the actual quote. But, whatever you want, I will take care of it."

"Oh, I know you will, bitch." She smiled at me.

I smiled back. "Asshole."

AFTER LUNCH, I RETURNED TO the office feeling a little more confident since the tapes were at least temporarily out of my hands and no longer a pressing concern. Out of sight. Out of mind. As soon as I sat down, an email from Tristan-Malcolm popped up onto my screen:

To: Allison Brown
From: Tristan-Malcom Reynolds
Subject: Your work ethic

Seventy-eight minutes for lunch? Did you have a few cocktails too? Do you even want this job?
TMR.

His office was five floors up. How in the hell did this man know everything I did? I searched around my cubicle for a possible nanny-cam. If there was one, things could potentially get very embarrassing the next time I sexted with Drew. Casually and discreetly taking tit pics from my cubicle and sending them to Drew was sort of my specialty and I didn't need to get an email from Tristan-Malcolm telling me to put my tits away and get back to work on the notebooks. I reluctantly kept my tits covered for the rest of the day and went back to deciphering Elise's scribbling.

Her notes made no sense to me but I hoped that maybe he would be able to put them in some context. There seemed to be a lot of legal case names and summaries of what each case had concluded. I gathered that the cases were antitrust cases based on the sheer number of times I had to type the words antitrust. Other pages contained random numbers that could have been dates or possibly times, along with abbreviations and initials. It could have been code for prostitutes or drug deals for all I knew. Now, that would have been the kind of twist to make the notes a little more fun, but I was pretty sure I would have remembered if Elise mentioned prostitutes or drugs.

By seven o'clock, I managed to make it through the first notebook and then a second one, which, thankfully, was only half-filled. I emailed the typed notes to the two-named son of Satan before I left. I wanted to add a note that I worked until seven on a Friday no less but I held my fingers in check. I had never worked that late before, which had alarmed Drew, based on the three texts I got:

Are you alive?
When will you be home?
Why were there no Friday tits?

I startled myself by packing up a few of the notebooks and my laptop to take home with me. Fear was apparently quite the motivator.

CHAPTER 6

I CAME IN THE DOOR to the smell of heaven which meant Drew had been cooking. I shut the door and he came out of the kitchen in his "Will Cook for Sex" apron and immediately handed me a glass of red wine. "Hey baby, I know you had a rough week. Dinner is almost ready." He kissed me and the stress of the day completely dissolved away. I was home and safe for the time being. He didn't know how terrible I was or that I had killed a man. He just loved me.

"I smell Italian. What did you make?"

"Lasagna. And of course, your favorite, tiramisu." He kissed my forehead.

"You are too good to me baby. I love it."

"And there is something else." He covered my eyes with his hands.

He led me into the kitchen by walking behind me and guiding the way. Finally, he lifted his hands from off my face. On the counter was a fancy, old-fashioned coffee pot with a big red bow on it. "I promise, I researched it on Amazon and it is not a piece of crap. It has an average of 4.5 stars."

My eyes welled up with tears. I turned and fell against his chest and the sobs that I had been holding back for days finally came pouring out. My whole body was trembling. He enveloped me in his long arms and broad shoulders and hugged me tight.

"Honey, what's wrong?"

"You are just too good for me and I don't deserve it." The sobbing became heavier and I could barely get the words out. He put his hand under my chin and titled my head up so that he could look into my eyes.

"It's just a coffee pot, honey. I know it's been a hard week. Elise left you in a mess and without saying goodbye and that two-named asshole has always been a dick. You know he desperately wants to replace my dad as the big dog at the firm so I know he will make it even harder for you because of your relationship with me. The least you deserve is to have your morning coffee without standing in line with all the dumbasses."

"I love you." I kissed him and attempted to wipe the tears from my face and caught the "ugly-cry" snot that was beginning to form under my nose.

"I love you too. Now go get out of that dress my mom bought for you and put some of your own clothes on and let's have a quiet, romantic dinner with our cats."

I went into the bathroom and washed my face. I looked at myself in the mirror and knew that I should tell him the truth. Not about the guy in the park, although I felt like he would even forgive me and understand if I told him how it happened. He at least deserved to know about the failure of my comedy career and my fear that I would never get my voice back. I should tell this man who loves me just how scared I was and how disappointed I was in myself and that I was lost. He would say the right thing. He always said the right thing. He always supported me. He would still love me.

Despite the pep talk I gave myself, the face looking back at me from the mirror revealed a coward. A coward who avoided and deflected intimacy by making jokes. A coward who instead of putting on yoga pants and a T-shirt put on a low-cut, long flowing negligee that had been a questionably appropriate gift from his mother. The coward who put on make-up and perfume to further mask any authenticity of emotion.

"You look beautiful. You are beautiful." Drew smiled at me from across the table while we ate the meal he had spent hours cooking for me instead of studying.

"Thank you, honey. This lasagna is amazing." I was practically moaning as I put another bite in my mouth. "Don't you have a paper due on Monday? I feel bad that you were making fresh pasta instead of working on it."

"I will get to the paper later." There was a brief flicker of something familiar on his face. It echoed the look that had stared back at me from the mirror. It caught me off guard to see what I perceived to be him being evasive or unhappy. Had I missed something going on in his world? I had become so self-absorbed and worried about my life that I hadn't even considered that something might be amiss in his.

"Honey, are you ok?"

"Of course I am, babe. Everything's fine." He sounded less than convincing. There had to be something that I was missing. I looked across the room at corner of the counter where I noticed his law books and notebooks remained untouched. They still had the stack of junk mail I had laid on top of them on Wednesday evening before I left for my "set."

I suddenly felt compelled to ask a question that had never occurred to me before. "Are you happy at law school? Do you really want to be an attorney?"

"What? Where did that come from? It has always been the plan for me to be an attorney."

He got up and grabbed more garlic bread from the oven and brought it over to the table.

"Yeah, I know that was always the plan. But whose plan? Does it make you happy? Do you enjoy it?"

"Of course not." He laughed and shoved a piece of the hot bread in his mouth. "Why do you think I took three years off to travel after college and then spent another two years helping to rebuild Haiti?"

"So, why do it?" I took a drink of my wine.

"You've met my parents, right?" He poured more wine in both of our glasses. "I'm already way behind schedule. My five-year delay was only tolerated because my father helped convince my mother it would make a compelling back-story when I ran for public office. You know how she loves a politician with a compelling back-story."

"Well, yeah. But they are supportive of me following my dreams, so wouldn't they support you if you decided to do something else and said you really didn't like law or politics?"

I leaned back in my chair with my glass of wine. "What would you do if you had the option?"

"I don't know." He swirled the wine in his glass. "I don't really have that option, babe. It has always been a foregone conclusion that I go to law school and take my rightful place at the firm. Then after a few years, I run for State Senate and work my way up. You know that."

He took a long drink of his wine. "It won't be that bad. I don't think anyone ever really loves their work. I'm not talented and creative like you so I don't have a dream to follow."

Suddenly, we had veered a little too close to the topic of my failed career and I regretted asking the question. I also briefly wondered how having a failed, foul-mouthed comedian partner from West Virginia would fit into his compelling back-story, but that was a worry for another time. "Future Ally" could deal with that shit. "Current Ally" had enough on her plate.

"Well, that's not exactly true. You are a genius in the kitchen." I tried to seductively take a bite of lasagna with the intent to emphasize my point but ended up wrestling with a long string of cheese, which ultimately bested me and got stuck dangling from my chin.

He roared with laughter, which always made me smile.

"Could you imagine the look on my mom and dad's face if I told them I wanted to be a chef and own a restaurant? That would be priceless. Right up until the moment my mother ripped my balls off and handed them to me."

"You would be amazing at it though."

I got up and walked over to the counter and swiped my finger into the tiramisu and straddled his lap. I put my finger into his mouth and he slowly sucked the sweet dessert off it. "See how amazing you are? Can you taste it?"

I felt him stiffen beneath me as I kissed him. His hands cupped my ass and pulled me closer to him. His warm lips worked their way down my neck as he slowly pushed down the straps of my negligee revealing my breasts. I closed my eyes and arched my back as his tongue lavished my hardened nipples with attention. I began rhythmically rocking my hips against his thighs and the hardened outline of his cock. A soft guttural moan escaped him.

I grabbed his head and pulled him up to kiss me. It was a deep, desperate kiss conveying that I needed him inside me. He picked me up and carried me to the counter as I pulled at his shirt to get it over his head so I could get my hands on his chest, all the while trying to maintain the frantic connection of kissing. I couldn't get enough of his mouth or his body. I wanted to melt into him. Everything else in the world faded away. There was just his nakedness against mine. His hard rippled chest against the soft curve of my breasts. My fingers dug into his hair and I pulled him harder into the kiss while he grappled with his belt and finally got out of his pants. He thrusted his cock inside of me. This time it was me that let out a low moan of satisfaction.

His thrusting knocked my head back into the cabinet. The pain jolted a memory in my brain of blood on a rock. I felt myself freeze and tense up for only the briefest of moments. I tried to force the memory back into the nothingness and refocus on the cock inside me but the pause had been enough for him to notice.

"Oh shit! I'm sorry honey." He gently cradled my head to protect it from hitting the cabinet again and kissed me tenderly.

"It's OK, baby. Just fuck me." I smacked his ass and he obliged. Oh my god did he oblige.

CHAPTER 7

I WOKE UP EARLY SATURDAY. I usually sleep in until at least eleven o'clock and then spend a good half-hour cuddling with the cats while refusing to acknowledge that it was time to get my day started. Drew, the usual early riser, was snoring. I rolled over and watched him sleep with a stupid grin on my face, thinking about the hours of sex and cuddling and laughing from the night before. He was the best thing in my life. I would never truly understand why he loved me, of all people, but I knew I would do anything to keep him in my life.

Don't laugh. I'm allowed to get mushy and sentimental every now and then. I'm not always a caustic, harsh and bitchy killer. I wasn't even a killer until the other day.

When Drew finally woke up a few hours later, he walked into the kitchen and caught me doing something incredibly embarrassing. I was sitting at the table with a cup of coffee from the new pot and the remains of my second homemade Drew baked muffin. Coffee and a pastries without the need to interact with dumb as hell strangers. Life was good. No, that is obviously not the embarrassing part. The embarrassing part was that I had my laptop open and I was transcribing Elise's stupid notebooks. I got busted working at home, and on a weekend no less!

Drew made an overly dramatic display of coming to a dead stop and audibly gasping when he saw me.

"What the hell? What have you done with my gorgeous, funny, carefree girlfriend?"

He grabbed a wooden spoon from the near-by utensil jar and raised it. "I don't want any trouble. I just need whatever demon is in there to get out."

I scrunched my face up and responded. "Ha ha ha. And we both know from watching *Supernatural* that a wooden spoon is useless on a demon. You are going to need some holy water and some fancy Latin words to purge any demon from this meat suit."

"So, you are admitting that you are a demon? My mother will be very disappointed."

He smacked the wooden spoon on the palm of his hand and grinned. "I can think of a few ways this wooden spoon might not be totally useless."

"BDSM night is on Mondays dear. Please put the spoon down until then." My deadpan response made him chuckle loudly.

"Fine." He put the spoon down on the table and walked over to pour himself a cup of coffee. "Seriously though, why are you working on a Saturday?"

"I don't know. Maybe I am possessed. Or just scared shitless. There is just so much shit here. Look at it." I lifted up the three notebooks stacked in front of me for dramatic effect.

"I have no idea what any of it means. I keep seeing this one name over and over again, though and it sounds familiar, but I'm starting to think maybe it's because I keep typing it. Does the name Benjamin Mars mean anything to you?"

For some reason this question made him laugh harder than my BDSM joke. "Honey, seriously?"

"What? Should I know him?"

"That's Uncle Benji. My mom's brother. Honey, he is at the house for dinner and holidays all the time. You do know he owns Mars News and Media, which is one of the companies that is part of the merger, right?"

"Oh!" I instantly felt embarrassed by my ignorance. Revealing to your boyfriend that you are a dumbass and have no idea what you are doing at the job he got for you is an even greater embarrassment than being caught working on a Saturday morning. "How did I not know Uncle Benji's last name or that he owned a media company?"

He sat down across from me with his coffee and smiled. "Well, we have always just referred to him as Uncle Benji and you do kind of zone out when people start talking about work. Which I totally don't blame you for doing, so I can see how you might not put it together. It doesn't matter, because when you finally make it as a comedian, you won't even have to worry about this tedious crap anyway."

He was being nice and giving me an out for my stupidity and I loved him even more for it. For once, I didn't even mind the reference to the career I had no longer been actively pursuing.

"Hmm. Well, now maybe some of this shit will make some sense." I highly doubted it, but I wanted to not come across as a complete dumbass.

"So, what you said about Mondays being BDSM night. Can that be a real thing? Maybe?" He playfully swatted the spoon against my thigh.

I took the spoon from him. "Oh, honey, what makes you think you are going to be the one doling out the spanking?" I grinned and went back to my deciphering of Elise's scribbles.

I worked six hours on a Saturday. Which was complete bullshit but it also wasn't so bad since I was working across the table from Drew. Twice he flicked water on me while chanting Latin and waited for a dark cloud of demon smoke to escape from my mouth. Looking at him, I thought about how my life with him would definitely have been worth making a crossroads deal with the King of Hell. I just hoped I got several decades of happiness with him before being drug off by the hellhounds. If you don't get any of these references, then you don't watch *Supernatural,* which pretty much means we can't be friends.

After pretending to be serious, dedicated to work and school grown-ups, we had sex in the shower before getting dressed to meet Max at the lounge at his father's hotel, Boutique. It was a few blocks away from the theater were we would sit in the front row and silently hope Rena was too drunk to go on so that Sarah's star could finally shine.

WE ENTERED BOUTIQUE'S LOUNGE AND immediately spotted Max with his arm casually draped over a male patron's shoulder and staring into his eyes intently. He was exuding charm that could be felt all the way across the room. Max is tall, slim, toned and perfectly put together at all times. I have always admired how effortless it seemed for him to look so perfectly attired for any occasion even if it was just a casual Sunday brunch and he was hung over. My effortless look is completely different in that it actually alerts everyone who sees me as to the little amount of effort that went into my appearance.

Max's jet black hair and blue eyes were piercing and seductive and he knew exactly how to wield every gift God had given him. He had never met a stranger. He came from a family even wealthier than Drew's. He really didn't need to work for a living but he did, in a manner of speaking. He lived in the penthouse of the hotel and managed it, although he let his assistant handle the majority of the tedious details of the paperwork. Max was more like the hotel's very expensive and luxurious concierge. He loved interacting with the customers and treating them as if they were his personal guests. He always knew the "perfect" restaurant or could get his hands on exclusive show tickets, which is how we got front row seats to the show tonight. He hosted a happy hour for the hotel's patrons and always worked the room and made every guest feel as if they were his personal friend.

The small upscale hotel was just a hop, skip and a jump from Broadway. If an attractive male guest happened to be single, well, Max would become their personal guide through the city and he would fall in love with them for a few days. He lived large and he loved large. His one flaw was that he was forever falling in love with men who would always be merely a temporary lover by the very nature of the circumstances under which they met. More times than I could count, I would come home from work and find Max bemoaning to Drew that he really thought this one would be different.

Drew leaned down and whispered, "Based on the look on Max's face, I highly suspect that Monday BDSM night will be temporarily delayed by broken-hearted drinking."

"Probably. But maybe this guy will be the one. Max totally needs to catch a break."

Max finally tore his eyes away from the man by his side and saw that we had arrived.

"Drew! Ally!" Max waived us over enthusiastically. "I want you to meet Conner. He's in from Vermont for the week on business."

"Sounds like Monday is still on babe." Drew whispered in my ear.

I ignored him. There was something vaguely familiar about this new man but I couldn't put my finger on it. His hair was a brown mop of wavy curls that dropped over his left eye. He was beaming up at Max.

"It's so lovely to meet you." I said and extended my hand.

I thought I detected a slight facial twitch from him when he finally tore his gaze away from Max to shake my hand. He stumbled over the words "you too" and immediately returned his attention to Max. Maybe he could sense that I was dangerous and a killer or maybe I was just overreacting, but he seemed to instantly not like me.

"Conner's going to be joining us at the play tonight and the after-party." Max was glowing. "You know, Rena, the star, is staying here during her stint on the stage." This comment was directed to Connor, who was once again his main focus.

"Shut up!" I shrieked. My loudness seemed to disturb the wine-sipping crowd as several daggers of judgment thrown in my direction. Had I cared enough, I would have thrown some daggers back of my own. Tourist fuckers.

"Max, you know Rena is on Ally's freebie list and you didn't even bother to tell her." Drew laughed. "There's a chance I might lose her tonight at the after-party." He grabbed my ass and squeezed it.

"I forgot about that." Max leaned over to Conner and pretend whispered, "When it comes to a few starlets, Ally likes to pretend that she would temporarily switch teams." Conner laughed and the two of them smiled at each other, most likely thinking about the team building exercises that would take place later that evening.

"Oh shut up, both of you. You aren't going to get rid of me that easy, Drew. Your parents would be too devastated if I were to leave you. And we both know if Ryan Reynolds walked through those doors you would be following him around like a whipped puppy."

Drew shrugged, "True. And Hugh Jackman, too. I can admit that man is just ridiculously sexy, and he can sing and dance like a dream. What's not to love?"

Max and Conner nodded in agreement.

I laughed. "Well, Rena was totally hot years ago but it is sad that now she is such a walking disaster. It is also sad how bad I want to witness the impending disaster up-close. But she is definitely Sarah's best shot at finally getting to play Sugar."

"Not only is she a total train wreck, but she's also a raving bitch. She has made at least sixty percent of my staff cry on a nightly basis." Max leaned forward and in a conspiratorial whisper announced, "And her mini-bar is cleaned out almost nightly, so rehab obviously did not stick."

"Ugh, Max . . . that is not exactly breaking news." I expected much better gossip since she was staying at the hotel.

Max frowned at me. He offered up a new tidbit of information, although it was not nearly as scandalous. "For some reason she throws all of the mini-bar bottles and food wrappers out on the hallway floor. I had the staff put extra trash cans in her room thinking maybe that might help with her bizarre litterbug habit, but just last night she opened the door and chucked an empty half-split of Veuve Cliquot and knocked Dave, one of our valets, out cold. He had to get five stitches."

The four of us continued to chat and drink until it was close to show time and time to leave. Connor continued to behave as if there was no one in the room but Max. I couldn't decide whether to be insulted or not. I decided that the evening was too important for Sarah so I just let it go.

CHAPTER 8

THERE IS SOMETHING THRILLING AND exciting about going to the theater, especially when sitting in the front row. The theater feels alive with the buzz of people out for the evening on dates. The dozens of gaping tourists fumbling for their seats with their adult beverage contained in the equivalent of an adult sippy-cup in one hand, and bags of commemorative magnets, shot glasses, and T-shirts for a show they haven't even seen yet in the other.

Although, until recently, I had always sought out the stage. The stages I sought out were tiny and insignificant compared to the theater. Over the years, Sarah tried to get me to audition for bit parts and expand my comfort zone from the mere holding of a microphone and attempting to make people laugh with my stories. But as much as I loved everything about the theater, I never made the effort. It was mostly because of my deep-seeded fear of forgetting every line no matter how many times I rehearsed it. I've been told I can tell a funny story and improvise to deftly handle any heckler who tried to inject themselves into my routines. But going out onto the stage and possibly forgetting every line and every movement from rehearsal and disappointing the other cast members? Nope. I can tank my own career, which I am currently doing at a very fast pace, but I don't want to be responsible for the failure of others. I can barely keep myself together on a daily basis, so no one should have to rely on me for help, let alone their careers. I'd probably do them more harm than good. It's not that I don't want to help, but I feel crippled at the thought of letting people down, so it's really just best that they feel let down by me not helping them rather than me trying to help and making an even bigger mess of things.

The bells chimed and the lights dimmed and the show started and I forgot everything else for the duration. I squealed for the second time of the evening when Rena took the stage. It had been twelve years since her first album skyrocketed her to fame. Being so close to the stage, I could see how hard those twelve years had been on her, even though the stage-lighting and heavy makeup.

I silently cursed my mom for not allowing me to go see her in concert all those years ago when she had been less than an hour away. The concert had been on a school night. According to my mom, there was no fun to be had on a school night. My mom also believed every group of teenagers out at night in a car would be doomed to die in a fiery car crash and most likely on train tracks. I am convinced that she watched the movie *Footloose* one too many times and that maybe she missed the whole point of the movie.

I clapped probably a little too loudly and wildly for the theater crowd when Sarah made her entrance on the stage, since it wasn't necessarily an entrance that warranted applause in anyone else's mind. I didn't care. They could think I had one too many sippy-cup beverages and go about their lives. At least I didn't illegally have my phone out like one of the rat bastards who was seated a few seats down from me. Asshole. It thrilled me to my core when an usher came down the aisle and without saying or even mouthing a word, intimidated the man into putting his phone away. Obviously, if I was in charge, I might have taken a more direct and violent approach to the situation, but I admired the usher's evil stare game. It was definitely on point.

After the show, we wove our way through the mobs of tourists on Broadway and back to the small, private bar that Max's hotel used to host private events. It had seen hundreds of opening night and closing night parties for various shows up and down "The Great White Way." Max's charm, money, influence, and love of the theater along with the bar's privacy from gaping onlookers made it the perfect venue. Although, Rene had made her official debut on Wednesday, the big welcome party for the new star was always thrown after the Saturday night show.

It took some time to weave through the throngs of people who shuffled like zombies while staring up at the view of the lights and spectacle of Times Square. As much as I hate slow, meandering people, and texting and walking, I actually don't actively hate the tourists who are walking while staring up in amazement and trying to capture the moment on their phones. It is a pretty ridiculously awesome sight and experience if you had never been here before. Sure, everyone has seen it in the movies and on TV. But, in real life, the experience is surreal.

There's the smell of the various ethnic culinary delights offered by the street vendors mixed in with a smell that your nose doesn't want to recognize as possibly urine. There's the noise of the cars, the horns, the street performers trying to get your attention and maybe a dollar or two. The artists hawking their work, the tables of not-quite-designer purses and watches. There are so many tables of purses. Then, there's the sketch artists and cartoonists. People dressed as popular movie and TV characters or some unique character of their own imagination. The girls just wearing body paint as a shirt. All who support themselves on the tips the tourists leave in exchange for a picture. Add in the flicker of the ads playing on the giant TV screens hovering above and the colorful billboards advertising the current or upcoming Broadway shows. It's frenetic and overwhelming trying to take it all in and make sense of it all.

My favorite time at Times Square is right around 1 a.m. when it's almost but not quite suddenly eerily quiet. The only foot traffic seems to be late night/early morning partiers, who are staggering and trying to find their way back to their hotels, and the various character performers who are walking home with their oversized heads in one hand and a drink or a cigarette in the other.

And for Pete's sake, please don't tell my mother that I have been in

Times Square at 1 a.m. I am not in the mood for that lecture.

ON THE WALK TO BACK to Boutique, I noted that Connor must be a regular visitor to the city because he did not succumb to the view or try to slow us down so he could take it all in. Maybe he just didn't want to make any waves with the new friends who had just delivered him front row seats to one of the hottest tickets in town. I still thought he was a bit odd but since he would be gone by the end of the week, and if he made Max even temporarily happy, then who was I to judge?

We had already finished off two bottles of champagne by the time Sarah and the rest of the cast started to show up. I had a glass of champagne and a plate of hors d'oeuvres waiting for her since I knew she was always famished after a show and that she also got super cranky if she had to talk to too many people before she ate.

"You were fabulous as always!" I clinked my glass against hers.

"Thank you!" She blew an air kiss at me. "And don't even bother lying to me. I know that bitch killed it tonight."

I felt a huge relief knowing that I wouldn't have to lie, but I still totally downplayed it a little bit and did not let the sixteen-year-old me start gushing praise.

"She did a lot better than I expected." See, totally the truth because I did think she would come out and be a disaster.

Max chimed in, "Here's an idea. What if I had the staff double the stash of alcohol in the mini-bar or just casually leave a bag of cocaine behind in her room? I mean, think of it, you get to star in the play and the hotel gets publicity for being the place where she goes on her worst-ever bender. The celebrity gawkers would be lining up to stay in the room where it all happened."

I laughed along with everyone else but was also slightly intrigued by the idea and wondered if we could pull it off. My albeit morbid mental diversion was disrupted by the sound of sudden silence followed by a loud round of applause as the devil herself appeared in the doorway.

She was tall and commanding without saying a word. Her long legs were highlighted by the shortest of black skirts and her apparently very real boobs were barely contained by the very low cut black sequined tank top she paired with it. It was only when she started to walk that you could see the slight weave in her step. One might think the unsteadiness was caused by her four inch heels, but as she got closer the glassiness in her eyes revealed she was well on the way to her intended destination of drunk.

"The show's been over for less than an hour. How did she get that drunk that fast?" I whispered to Sarah.

"She starts drinking at intermission."

"Really? How does she remember all of her lines when she is drunk? I can barely remember my own phone number when I've been drinking. Or sober for that matter. Hey, what the hell is my phone number?"

"I guess it's another one of her gifts. Just like her voice."

"Well, you have an amazing voice too and you aren't a mess. That should be your role."

"One day maybe. I haven't earned it yet. Oh shit! She's coming over here." Sarah took a huge swig of her champagne.

Inside, my inner sixteen-year-old screamed and passed out on the floor as Rena weaved her way straight towards us, or at least as straight as she could manage. Her long blonde hair somehow seemed to bounce as if it was in a shampoo commercial. She approached Sarah and grabbed her by the shoulders.

"Stephanie! Congratulations! You actually weren't entirely horrible tonight like you were last night. Maybe it won't be such a huge embarrassment to be on the stage with you every night."

My inner sixteen-year-old immediately jumped up off the floor and gave her a "what the hell did you just say?" look and leapt to my friend's defense.

"Her name is Sarah."

I could see Sarah shoot me her renowned side eye, warning me to shut the fuck up. My long time girl-crush turned and looked at me. I could actually see her physically looking me up and down because she was so drunk that her head actually moved with her eyes. I stood as tall as I could and glared up at her. This was not how it all went down in my head when I was sixteen. We were supposed to meet and immediately become best friends with benefits and I was supposed to follow her around on tours and meet all the cute famous boys who graced my *Teen Beat* magazine. Now, here I was, getting ready to throw down with her for insulting my real best friend.

"You have a problem with me?"

I couldn't tell if she was sneering or smiling at me, but the former glassiness in her eyes had now turned into a laser-like focus on me.

"I think you should at least know the names of your cast mates. And frankly, backhanded compliments are juvenile."

I heard Sarah whisper, "Oh shit."

To my own horror, I continued, "I mean seriously, what is wrong with you? You were drunk through the second act so she is the one who should be embarrassed to be on stage with you." At this point, I would never admit that she was good.

"Honey, I could start drinking hours before the show and still not be as bad as Stephanie over here." She jammed her finger in Sarah's face and spat out the words.

I felt Drew's hand settle in on the curve of my back. He had walked over just in time to diffuse a situation that he was blissfully unaware needed diffusing.

"Do you have a name?" The finger that had been in front of Sarah's face was now being jammed into my chest.

Drew, still blissfully unaware and drunk himself, answered for me, "Oh my god, Ally, I was in the bathroom and almost missed you finally getting to meet your girl-crush."

He yelled across the bar, "Hey Max, get over here. It's finally going down."

I could have killed him. Like, not literally killed him, but at least shoved him in a cab, taken him home, and given him the cold shoulder for the rest of the night.

Rena cackled and looked at me and I saw a glimpse of evil in her eyes. "Excuse us. Ally and I are going to have a little chat."

She grabbed my arm and pulled me away from Drew and my friends. I could hear Max humming porn music. She led me to the furthest end of the bar at the back of the room. She backed me up against the wall in the corner and leaned down to whisper in my ear with her cleavage deliberately pushed up into my face to distract me. I felt my skin grow warm.

She purred. "You try to act all tough and stand up for your friend and insult me and yet it turns out I'm your girl-crush."

She leaned in closer to me and her entire body was pressed up against mine. "It's sad and pathetic because I can just hear that teenager in you squealing because I'm this close to you. You want to hate me and judge me because of what you read about me. I'm a drunk. I'm a mess. I'm a train wreck. You can judge me all you want and I will judge you because I know how much you are going to enjoy this despite all of your claims to the moral high ground." She leaned in and kissed me.

I heard Drew yell in the background, "That's my girlfriend. Getting her girl-crush on and it is super-hot."

I wanted to kill him again but I also couldn't concentrate on anything. Her lips savaged my mouth and she grabbed my hand and pulled it up to her breast and I could feel her hard nipple pushing through the thin fabric. I refused to let my hand wander and explore. She slid her free hand up my skirt and between my legs. I wanted all of it to stop. People were looking now and probably getting out their cell phones. It didn't stop and she was right, I was enjoying it, despite myself. She continued to own me with her mouth and with her probing hand right in front of everyone, including Drew, who was probably enjoying it more than I was at the moment. I was pissed at myself. I was pissed at her. I was even more pissed at myself when against all of my better instincts, I finally started to respond by kissing her back. That is when she abruptly stopped.

She purred into my ear. Punctuating each sentence by licking the curve of my ear, "See, I knew you would like it. You want me so bad. I bet you would let me finish you off and make you cum right here in front of all these people. You don't even care if we are being filmed on people's phones. In fact, I bet you would even let me go down on you right here, right now."

Her fingers momentarily started to stroke me again to emphasize my wetness and my physical response to her. I felt myself flinch actually wanting her to continue what she started. She pushed herself off of me and sneered.

"Not so defiant and judgmental now are you, Abigail? Or is that not your name? I totally forgot."

She walked off and left me trembling against the wall, hot tears wanting to streak down my face. And at that moment, I knew that I would somehow exact revenge for every insult she spat at Sarah and for what she had done to me.

Drew was immediately by my side and drunkenly oblivious that anything happened other than his hot fantasy coming true. He grabbed me and kissed me, "That was so hot, babe. You must be so excited right now. Was it amazing? I hope you don't mind that I recorded it on my phone. I thought you might like to have a souvenir."

I didn't want to talk about it. I didn't want to think about it. I grabbed him and kissed him hard.

"Just take me up to one of the hotel rooms and fuck me, honey. I want you to finish what she started."

"Yes, ma'am. I will go get a room key from Max. Best night ever!" He practically skipped over to Max.

I took a deep breath, found the use of my legs, and pulled my skirt down. I headed back to find Sarah at the other end of the bar.

"Sarah, I'm so sorry. I should have kept my mouth shut. I hope my mouth didn't just cost you your job. I'm so sorry. I don't know why I couldn't just keep my mouth shut."

"It's OK. She won't remember any of it in the morning. She never does. You were just standing up for me. How could I possibly be mad at you for that?"

She handed me a glass of champagne. I downed it in one long drink.

"I'm really sorry. I just couldn't let her talk to you like that."

"Honestly, that was actually the nicest she has been to me since she has been here. I told you she was terrible." She studied my face. "She said something horrible to you didn't she?"

I nodded and tried to keep the tears out of my eyes.

"Well, I don't know what she said to you and you don't have to tell me. Just shake it off. Treat her like a rude heckler and move on."

"I will be fine. And hey, at least my inner sixteen-year-old got to live out her fantasy." As usual, I resorted to a joke to deflect and distract. I glared over to where Rena was standing just a few feet away and pondered how I could go about scoring a large bag of cocaine without getting arrested.

LATER, DREW WAS COLLAPSED IN the bed, dead to the world from a long night of drinking and some aggressive sex. While he slept, I slipped back into my clothes and quietly left the room.

I rode the elevator to each floor, got off and wandered down each hallway. Finally, on the twentieth floor, I found what I had been looking for just outside of room 2008. The empty contents of at least half of a mini-bar. I leaned against the wall and stared at the door. I knew I would not do anything tonight because I wasn't sure what the hell I was going to actually do, but at least now I knew exactly where she was so I could come back once I figured out a plan.

I heard a loud clamor come from inside and realized she was getting ready to open the door. I panicked and turned around and pretended to be fumbling with my key to get in the room across the hall.

"Hey!" I heard her slur across the hall. "Hey, you have a smoking hot ass. Turn around so I can see if your face is just as hot." Out of the corner of my eye I saw a bottle hit the floor and roll to a stop near my foot.

Shit. I couldn't stand there with my back turned forever since my room key was not actually going to work on the door I was pretending to open. I tried to stand still and hoped she would just go back in her room. Suddenly, I felt her hand on my ass. Good god! This woman had no sense of boundaries.

She started caressing my butt and once again my body betrayed me by responding to her touch. I slowly turned around and waited for the recognition to cross her face followed by another string of hateful words.

There was no recognition, just a seductive smile. She was completely naked. How the hell does she have that banging of a body when all she did was drink and eat the contents of a mini-bar. This is bullshit.

"Ohh, your face is even hotter than your ass." Her hand reached up and she stroked my cheek.

Sarah was right. She had already completely forgotten meeting me earlier. I was momentarily hurt by the fact that I was so forgettable, but then I realized this would make my plan even easier. Dealing with a blackout drunk made everything easier. She mistook the smile for an invitation and she leaned in and kissed me. It wasn't an angry and spiteful kiss this time. I kissed her back. It was a slow kiss. Her lips were soft and velvety. Her tongue found its way in my mouth and I heard myself moan. I backed her up, across the hall, and against the wall near her door. She wrapped one long leg around my waist and pulled me in closer. My fingers traced down her perfect breasts. Her nipples responded to my touch. I pulled away.

"I'm so sorry. I realized that I'm on the wrong floor and my boyfriend is waiting for me. I have to go."

Her face was flushed and flustered, "Are you sure? You could come in for a quickie and then be on your way." Her smile was almost predatory.

"I'm sure. If I came inside, there would be nothing quick about it. How about a rain check?"

"You can come by anytime you want."

I pulled away again, "I will definitely be back. You can count on it." I turned and headed down the hall.

"Hey, what's your name?" She called out to me as I got to the elevator.

"It's Abigail." I smiled as the doors closed.

CHAPTER 9

THERE ARE FEW GREATER JOYS in life than room service breakfast. When you're hung over, room service is like a gift from God. A benevolent God who knows that you need at least four fluffy pancakes, a river of syrup and a mountain of bacon while languishing in your hotel-supplied robe and slippers. And a giant carafe of coffee to wash it all down with. Drew always laughs at the mess I make with every new cup of coffee that is poured as I scientifically try to find the correct ratio of coffee to sugar and creamer, which is always heavy on the sugar and creamer. The tray was littered with empty sugar packets.

Luckily, I had a mouthful of bacon when he said, "Last night was so hot, babe. I'm so glad you actually got to experience it."

I took longer to chew my bacon then necessary as I thought of how best to respond. "You know she isn't the first girl I've kissed, babe. I'm bisexual. It was no big deal."

"Yeah, whatever. You were just kissing the woman who has been your idol for years and whose songs are all on your iPod. You know, you can admit that it was a big deal to me. I'm secure with what we have."

His face was so sincere and he was being so sweet. "I know, babe. And I love that about you. So, yes, you are right. It was a big deal." He didn't need to know the real reason why it was a big deal or that I was going to somehow destroy her. "I'm glad you were there for it."

He sipped his coffee and flashed the crooked smile that always gave away his intentions of being ornery. "She's going to be in the show for two months . . . so maybe it can happen again. I don't necessarily have to be there. But, let's just say that the opportunity presents itself, we should do it. Or just you should do it. Then you can tell me all about it. Like all about it. Or not. You don't have to tell me if you don't want to tell me."

He had no way of knowing how that helped alleviate my guilt about what happened the night before in the hallway when he hadn't been there and what might happen in the future if I had to seduce her in order to get my revenge. I tossed some empty sugar packets across the table at his face. "You are such a pervert. I love you."

"I know you do. I love you, too. So, how much sleep do you think Max and Connor got last night?"

"Probably less than we did, which is hard to believe. You know that Max is going to be a mess when Connor leaves."

"I know. I will stock up on his favorite beer and have *Galaxy Quest* and *Hitchhiker's Guide to the Galaxy* queued up and ready to go."

"You are a good friend. Is it wrong that I wish his cheer-up movies involved a *Magic Mike* double feature so you could learn some moves?"

"Are you saying I don't have moves?" He pretended to look hurt.

"I haven't seen you rock a pair of tear-away pants and a G-string yet, so yeah, that is exactly what I'm saying."

"Oh really? Next time we are in a store with a water bottle display cooler, just you wait. I'm going to hump the hell out of that cooler."

"That will be fabulous. I will film it and we can use it in your future campaign ads. You know how much your mom loves good photo ops."

He stood up, picked me up, and threw me onto the bed. He awkwardly started humping my face and attempted to sing "Pony" while I cackled with laughter.

CHAPTER 10

I WAS PRETTY PLEASED WITH myself on Monday morning. I had gotten home on Sunday and finished transcribing all four of the notebooks I had brought home for the weekend. Knowing that Uncle Benji was one of the owners of the companies involved in the merger only helped to the extent that I finally figured out Elise was not randomly adding in dates for badminton games with a man named Mark, which I had thought was a bit particular. Instead, the dates obviously had something to do with Benjamin Mars. What can I say? Her handwriting was really atrocious. It was a small victory, but I was willing to take it.

I had never worked on a weekend before and it was weird. I didn't care for it. Neither did the cats, who aggressively expressed their displeasure by slowly and methodically knocking everything, including the notebooks, off the table. As much as I had hated it, I was totally going to enjoy taking my work up to the asshole and throwing the proof that I could be a somewhat dedicated worker in his face. Screw him and his bullshit critical emails.

I happily sat on the subway trying to come up with an amusing and totally off-the-cuff comment that I could make as I handed my work over to him. I was itching to blatantly disregard his "I don't want to be amused policy." I also considered how I could get my hands on some cocaine so I could set Max's plan in motion. It may not totally destroy Rena but at least I could lay down another piece of track for the inevitable train wreck and give Sarah the opportunity to be the star for a night.

At one of the subway stops, two douche-bros boarded and proceeded to sit down beside me.

I could immediately tell they were douche-bros before they even opened their mouths to confirm it. They had all of the douche-bro affectations and accessories down to the entitled sneers on their faces, Deepwater Horizon levels of product and pomade in their hair and beards, the immediate waft of an offensively obscene amount of cologne that assaulted my nasal follicles, and the way they openly ogled every pair of boobs they passed.

They elbowed each other as if to say, "Take a look at this pair," and stared down at my cleavage before sitting down beside me. Gross. I shifted and turned my back to them.

I mean for Pete's sake, I was dressed in a totally modest tan scoop neck A-line dress, houndstooth scarf and riding boots. I could easily be found lounging and staring vacantly on the cover of a Talbot's catalog, all courtesy of Carol's good taste. Of course, she would be offended that Talbot's is my go-to label for referring to clothes as classy. I grew up with those catalogs and I paid no attention to the current labels on my clothes because I just didn't care. Seriously, Carol literally picks out and usually buys all of my clothes, including accessories. I basically have the adult version of Garanimals. In the mornings, I put on exactly what she picked out and there is zero thought process to it on my end. She first took me shopping after I moved in with Drew and took the job at the firm. It was under the guise that she finally had a "daughter" to shop with, but I knew it was more of a "we can't be seen with her in public wearing clothes of her own choosing" kind of situation.

The douche-bro beside me used the jerk of the train starting up as an excuse to dramatically fall into me and attempt to put his hand on my upper thigh to brace himself. I am not a subway amateur so I had already shifted my computer bag over as a barrier which effectively blocked his lame-ass attempt and probably saved his life from me chocking him out. I was reaching for my phone to turn on the situation-appropriate Pink's "U and Ur Hand" when I heard one of the guys say, "Dude," because of course he did.

"Dude, I finally got that new batch of Kit-Kat from the guy I know down in Hell's Kitchen."

I held off turning on my "fuck you douche-bro" anthem so I could listen because I was pretty sure he wasn't talking about chocolate.

The shorter douche-bro sitting closest to me, who had just narrowly avoided death, responded, "Awesome. They might not know it but the bitches love taking a ride down the Black Hole and letting us run a train."

Tall douche-bro nodded. "These girls today like to run around screaming about feminism and how hard they have it in life but we both know that really all they need is to shut the hell up and let us give it to them hard."

My rage stroke response to their words was so intense and immediate that I had a sharp stabbing pain behind my eye. I had to actively keep my ass planted in the seat instead of getting up and beating the shit out of both of them. Without moving my head, I looked over at the elderly lady sitting across from me to see if she had overheard the snippet of conversation and was on the verge of a similar rage stroke. She looked pretty nonplussed so I assumed she either didn't hear it or maybe didn't understand the reference.

Shorter douche-bro piped back-up. "Bitches keep taking over everything and claiming it's for equality. They want everything to be about them. They don't even really know what they want . . . . except to take our jobs and make us apologize for every imaginary slight. Then they cry about how hard it is to work and raise a family after they've taken all of our jobs. It was bad enough Hollywood put some bullshit woman in the new *Mad Max* but then they pull that shit with *Star Wars* too. It's bullshit, man."

Original flavor, taller douchebag was getting riled up and was practically shouting. "That's why we have to take back the reins one filly at a time and break them in nice and good. There will be lots of prime meat to choose from at the ROE show this week. I have got to make up for missing out on the training session last week."

My rage stroke had rendered me speechless. I started to wonder if there were hidden cameras somewhere and I was unwittingly on an episode of *What Would You Do?* I highly doubted that they could use any footage of me killing these two jackasses for the show, but they probably could use it as evidence in my murder trial.

"I know man. I got pictures of that feminazi bitch. She was a handful at first but her body was smoking." He "accidentally" nudged my boob as he reached into his jacket pocket to grab his phone. I closed my eyes and started humming the du-du-du-du melody from Suzanne Vega's "Tom's Diner" song for the dual purpose of acting like I couldn't hear the conversation and for planting an ear-worm in his head that he would never be able to shake. Although, I'm not sure they actually would have altered their conversation in anyway if they thought anyone was listening because they seemed pretty proud of themselves and not in the least bit ashamed or secretive.

Short douche flicked through his photos until he found what he had been looking for and then held it out at arm's length for the other douche to look at.

Tall douche let out an appreciative grunt. "Damn, there isn't anything better than some pussy on some cat Valium."

At that point, I was not only horrified that they were openly discussing on the subway that they enjoyed drugging and raping women all in the name of men somehow taking back their stolen masculinity from the evil feminists of the world, but I was equally disgusted that they also used so many ridiculous names for whatever drug they were using. I glanced again at the old lady across from me but her expression still hadn't changed. She was either deaf, had perfected the "I have no fucks to give" look, or secretly enjoyed hearing stories about young girls unwittingly having trains run on them. At this point, for all I knew, maybe she invented the train run.

The douches continued yammering about the ROE show, whatever the hell that was, and the high grade of pussy they were going to be able to score. I was officially done with humanity by the time I got to my stop. I had considered every manner in which I could kill them and how painful I could make it. I was hoping they would get off when I did (as if they ever cared about women getting off) so I could push them off the ledge and into an oncoming train since they loved trains so goddamn much. Sadly, they didn't get off at my stop, so they got to live and rape another day.

I stared after the train as it rumbled past. I couldn't move. I thought of all the girls and the lives that were ruined by the garbage pieces of shit who had just sat next to me. I counted myself lucky that at least I only got ogled and side groped. I felt helpless. I should have said something. Why did I just sit there and not say anything? I should have told them how gross and disgusting they were that they could only get women who were rendered helpless by drugs. Why didn't I say anything? I should have said something. Done something.

A vision of the blood on the rock flashed through my memory and I realized that I could do something and that I wasn't done with these douchebags.

I WAS SO DISTRACTED AND disgusted on the walk to the office that I didn't even count how many people bumped into me, or openly scowl at them, or flip them off. I know it was more than two, but their offenses seemed trivial compared to what I had just overheard. I flashed my badge at Sam and got in the elevator. On the ride up, I googled ROE to see if I could find out the location of the next crime scene. Both theirs and mine. The results were mainly articles on how to get a good return on equity. I also learned that a roe was a mass of ripe eggs contained in the ovaries of a female fish or shellfish, i.e. caviar. Both unhelpful and gross.

I got off the elevator and headed straight to Susan's cubicle. Everyone knows that Susan Carlson can find anything on the internet. Need a picture of a naked man wearing only hard black shoes, a top hat and a monocle? Susan can find it in under ten minutes. Yes, there was a very serious reason that picture needed to be found. Don't judge me.

"How was your weekend?" I tried to engage in a bit of idle chit chat before asking for her services so as not to be rude.

"Not too bad. I finally binge-watched the first season of *Supernatural*. You are right, that's a good show."

"I told you. I'm glad it only took three years of me hounding you about it for you to finally get on board. How many times did I say, 'It's two hot guys hunting demons and monsters but actually a really clever show with a plot too?'"

"I'm pretty sure you said it at least once a week. And sweet Jesus those two are hot."

"Ridiculously hot."

Susan nodded in agreement and looked at me with an almost guilty look on her face. "I couldn't help but think that Drew kind of looks like Sam Winchester."

"Don't think that doesn't come up on role-playing nights."

"Eww. TMI about the boss' son." She laughed.

"Sorry. You know how I blurt. Now that I have introduced you to the hotness of the Winchester brothers, do you think you could do me a favor?"

"Sure. What do you need? Another naked guy in a monocle? A guy in a shower? Tattooed? Butts? Some full frontal?"

"While all of those sound like great options, what I really need is to figure out where and when a band that goes by ROE might be playing in the city this week."

"ROE? Never heard of them. I will have the answer to you by lunch though."

"Like it will take you until lunch. Don't act like you aren't tapped directly into the NSA's computers. And if you could throw in a naked guy in the shower with a tattoo, I wouldn't mind that either. I could use a treat after I come back from meeting with the asshole upstairs."

"And you're telling me that you still don't see his hotness factor?"

"He is not hot Susan. Stop it. You aren't even drunk this time."

"Whatever. His hotness is real. Can you find out if he's single?"

"Eww. No. Are you a masochist or something?"

"Do you want to know when and where ROE is playing or not? My services aren't free. The monocle guy was just to get you hooked."

"Fine. I will see what I can find out."

She smiled satisfactorily. "I will too."

I went to my desk and it took me a few minutes to figure out how to reconnect my laptop since I had never actually disconnected it before. I finally got it set up and launched my computer to see what delightfully cheery email awaited me. I was not disappointed.

To: Allison Brown

From: Tristan-Malcom Reynolds

Subject: Your work ethic

It is nice of you to finally join us this morning. I've been here since six. TMR.

"Well, aren't you special." I muttered to myself. I looked around my cubicle again for a possible nanny cam because it freaked me out that he seemed to know my exact whereabouts. I printed out the pages of notes I had typed up. I was not going to let myself be intimidated by him. I could have emailed them but I wanted to get some acknowledgement for my hard work and dedication this weekend even if that acknowledgement was just a slightly less menacing scowl on his face.

CHAPTER 11

I BRAVELY TOOK THE NOTES and strolled to the elevator, feeling moderately confident that I was not going on a suicide mission, but also comforted by the fact that I had a spare pair of underwear in my purse should things go awry.

I took a deep yoga breath as I stepped off the elevator and walked down the hallway towards Tristan-Malcolm's office. He was staring at his computer as I approached his door.

"What the hell are you doing up here? Did I ask you to come up here?" He didn't even bother looking away from the screen.

"I didn't know I needed an invitation to come bring the notes that I worked on all weekend for you." Yes, I can do this. You don't intimidate me. If I repeated this in my head enough it might become true. I held the papers out towards him.

He finally looked directly at me. His glare moved slowly up from the papers which were now visibly shaking in my hand and then up at my face.

"That meager amount of paper is the result of you working all weekend?" He leaned back in his chair, scowled, and made no effort to take the extended papers.

I mentally told myself that I was not going to fall to pieces in front of him and I wasn't going to pee myself. I had worked harder this weekend then I had in three years so I was going to own it.

"Yes, it is. As you said the other day, Elise's handwriting is abominable. I'm doing the best I can and working as fast as I can. Now, would you like the notes or not?" I tried to appear confident as I took a few steps closer to his desk and continued to hold the notes extended out towards him.

He crossed his arms in front of him. "No, I would not. If you recall, I also said that we are a paperless office so you can go back to your desk and email the notes to me like you should have done in the first place. Did I ask you for paper copies?"

He's no worse than a heckler. You can do this. "I suppose you didn't. I just thought I would save you the trouble of printing them off."

"I never print things off. That is the whole point of being paperless. Or do you not understand the concept of paperless? Do you see any paper in my office?"

My eye started to twitch because now he was just being a dick to be a dick. I had already had my fill of dicks for the day. Of course, people in the office used paper. I used paper all the time. I scanned his desk and his shelves and couldn't even find evidence of a Post-it note. Shit.

"It was a mistake for me to have come up. I apologize." I started to back out of his office.

"You know what I think?"

I really didn't want to know what he thought. I wanted to just quietly retreat and never come back again.

"I think that you came all the way up here to brag about working over the weekend. Working over the weekend is really something that should go without saying considering the time frame we are working under and the circumstances of Elise's abrupt departure."

The tone of his voice shifted to a patronizing one normally used with a child or a dog. "Did you come up here looking for a treat? A reward for being a good girl?"

He opened the drawer to his left but made no effort to look in it.

"Ahh! I'm sorry young lady. I'm all out of lollipops. I must have given the last one to Joe, the intern, for his extraordinary act of wearing pants to work today."

I imagined repeatedly jamming the drawer shut on his fingers until they broke.

"Got it. Won't happen again." There was really no other way to respond so I turned to leave.

"By the way, pathetic is not a good look for you."

I kept walking. I didn't turn back to face him. I didn't pee myself. I just left. It had been a stupid idea to come up to his office. He was right. I was seeking approval and acknowledgement. I was choking back hot tears of embarrassment by the time I got on the elevator. I looked down at the notes and the work that I had been so proud of and realized that it was probably not as impressive as I had originally believed. I wasn't good at this job. I was no longer good at comedy. I had no idea who I was anymore or whether I was good at anything. I wiped the tears off my face and tried to regroup. I couldn't have a breakdown at the office. Richard would find out and then Drew would know.

I got off the elevator and was grabbed by Susan as I walked past her cubicle.

"What's he wearing today? Did he look hot?"

Don't snap at her. She has no way of knowing. Don't snap at her. I took a deep breath.

"I didn't really notice what he was wearing because he was too busy being a brutal asshole."

Her face morphed from an excited fifth grader with a crush to one of genuine concern. "I'm sorry. You OK?"

"I'll be fine. Actually, I think it might have been a gray suit and red tie." I attempted to smile at her and started to head back to my work space.

"Remnants of Evil."

"What?"

"That's the name of the band. Remnants of Evil. They are doing a show on Wednesday night at 10 at Hitches in Alphabet City. I had no idea there was a genre of music called Post-Industrial Urban New Grass. Please tell me this is not something you like or I might have to withhold the showering tattooed guy."

It figures that the douche-bros had found a band that was on par with their own level of ick factor.

"Good God! No. Not me. There was a guy hitting on Sarah this weekend who kept talking about the band ROE and neither of us wanted to admit we had no idea who he was talking about. I think Sarah gave him her number so I was trying to help give her a heads-up. Pretty sure douche-canoe music is going to be a deal breaker for her. So thank you for saving her from what sounds like a horrible date."

"Thank God. I was trying to envision you liking that kind of music and was very confused. Always glad to help another woman avoid a bad date."

I started to walk away and then stopped. "Hey, one more favor. Do you think you would be able to find out Elise's address for me?"

If she wasn't going to respond to my calls, maybe I could ambush her at her apartment and beg her to help me understand which notes were important and tell me if the tapes were work-related or whether she had just inherited her parents' college mixed-tape collection.

"Sure. I can snoop through the accounting and payroll department files. Angela's passwords are easily cracked."

"Should I be worried that this is something you have done before?" I laughed.

"Should I be worried about why you need Elise's address?" She countered.

"Just need some help reading her handwriting. It might help smooth things over upstairs and then I can find out his current dating status." At this point, I was pretty sure it involved a deep well, a basket, and lotion, but that would be Susan's problem.

"I'm on it. It might take me a few days. I will have to chat up Angela and see what she's currently obsessed with in the way of either a TV show or movie."

"Alright then. I'm just going to head back to my computer and change my password to some random numbers and letters."

"Whatever. You'd never remember it and have to come get my help to log back in."

"You scare me." I backed away from her desk.

The rest of the day sucked. I kept my head down and typed as fast as I could read. Squint. Type. Save. Squint. Type. Save. That was pretty much how I spent the next eight and half hours of my life. I took a twenty-minute break to eat a bowl of cheddar Goldfish crackers for lunch and snuck in a quick tit selfie for Drew. Thankfully, I did not get an email from the dick upstairs about my sexting, so I ruled out the possibility that there was a nanny cam in my vicinity.

Nothing I typed made a damn bit of sense. Entire notebooks were just random letters which possibly could have been initials, and random numbers which were maybe dates or times and more abbreviations. Another notebook seemed to be summaries of case law pertaining to arbitration law.

Drew texted that he would be out late studying so I stayed at the office until 8:30. I finally realized I was starving. I texted Sarah to see if she wanted to meet at our favorite Cuban restaurant and eat an unhealthy amount of empanadas since it was her night off.

She responded: *Would love to but can't. Running lines with a friend to help her with an audition.*

I texted back. *Fine. I will get them to go and eat them with my cats. Not nearly as fun.*

A few minutes later my phone beeped: *Run after work tmrw? Been listening to tapes. That shit is bizarre.*

I still like to pretend I hate running with Sarah but I don't think she believes me anymore. I replied: *Sure. But I want drinks after.*

I got off the elevator on the ground floor and realized I had worked so late there was a new security guard at the desk. I had never actually seen the night shift guard. I hoped this wouldn't become a habit.

"Hey, how are you this evening?" I smiled and waved. He looked at me like I was crazy. I suppose it is a holdover from my southern upbringing but I simply can't make direct eye contact with someone without acknowledging them.

"I'm good. You new here?" He grabbed his clip board to look for the name that was on the badge that I flashed. I never understood why they needed to check us out when we left the building.

"No. Just new to working late." I looked at his badge. "Greg, no offense, but I hope I don't see you very often."

His laugh echoed through the empty lobby.

"Don't blame you one bit. Have a good night."

I ate my empanadas on the couch with a bottle of wine and binge watched my favorite episodes of *Veronica Mars*. I needed a dose of the spunky and adorable TV detective to get the taste of the morning douche-bros out of my mouth. What would Veronica have done if she overheard that bullshit this morning? Taser them, most likely. Maybe I should get a Taser. I could walk the city and just Taser the hell out of all the assholes I encountered every day.

I smiled as I imagined a trail of people curled up in the fetal position post-Taser and rendered unable to text and walk, or drug and rape. I picked my phone up and googled "black hole," "cat Valium," and "Kit Kat" and quickly learned they were street names for Ketamine, which can be in liquid or powder form. It is apparently very fast-acting and the user/ victim could be aware of what was happening but unable to move. Fuck those douchebags up the goddamn ass!

My rage stroke returned with a vengeance as I read all of the potential side effects their victims endured along with the torture of being on the receiving end of their dicks. Distorted perceptions of sight and sound; lost sense of time and identity; out of body experiences; problems breathing; convulsions; memory problems; numbness; high blood pressure; loss of coordination; and slurred speech. I had to stop reading because I was having problems breathing and the blood rushing through my head was making me want to get violent.

I put my phone down and skipped to the episode of Veronica and Logan's first kiss and re-watched the kiss several times. Veronica and Logan must have soothed my frayed nerves enough that I finally fell asleep on the couch. I startled awake when I felt myself being picked up and carried to bed.

"Hey, honey." Nothing soothed me like the sound of Drew's voice.

"Hey, babe." I nestled into his arms as he sat us both down on the edge of the bed.

"Must have been a bad day if it was a VMars night. Want to talk about it?"

"Not really. Just work stuff."

I crawled up into the bed where I was joined by the cats and then Drew after he undressed.

"Just hold me."

He curled up behind me and I pressed as far back into his chest as I could get. He was my safe spot. He helped keep the rage at bay. A rage he didn't even know about. I tried not to think about whether he would still love me if he knew.

"I love you, Drew Stephens."

He kissed the crown of my head. "I love you, Ally Brown."

CHAPTER
12

I DRUG MYSELF OUT OF bed at 6:00 a.m. on Tuesday and was at the office by 7:30. Sam at the security desk seemed as confused to see me there so early as I was myself. There had been no drugging, raping douche-bros on the subway, so that was a plus. I hardly moved from my desk all day except for the rare trip to the bathroom or to the employee lounge to restock on Goldfish crackers and Coke. I made no effort to go up to Tristan-Malcolm's office and I received no snarky email from him. Squint. Type. Save. As I typed I let my mind bounce back and forth between ways to stop the douche-bros and ways to destroy Rena. I had definitely been getting in touch with my violent side and I guess I should have been more unnerved by how easily and quickly my mind went straight to violence. I also should have been alarmed at how I was now starting to draw on the image of the blood on the rock as inspiration as opposed to curling up in the fetal position and being overwhelmed by guilt. The guilt was still there but I couldn't acknowledge it or I would break and I had too many things to get done to have a breakdown.

I texted Elise for what had to have been the hundredth time asking her to please call me and that I needed her help. Sarah texted that she would meet me down by the reservoir at our usual spot at 6:30. In the two hours before I met with her, I tried but failed to come up with a single reason to suggest we run on a different path. I could think of no excuses that wouldn't lead to her questioning me. I had always demanded that if she was going to force me to run that at least we should run somewhere with a view.

IT WAS CROWDED WHEN WE met. It was an unseasonably warm day and everyone seemed to be out enjoying the evening. Where were these assholes when I needed them? I stopped myself from following that train of thought. Then I thought about trains. Everywhere I turned there seemed to be a rage trigger.

"So, Stephanie, how is it going at the theater? At least you got out of there at a decent time today."

I was having to run at a pace faster than usual to keep up with her and her ridiculously long legs.

"You call me Stephanie again and you will be taken out of here in a body bag."

"My mother would probably secretly love to finally be proven right."

I was getting short of breath and dizzy. Sarah must have noticed because she slowed her pace down a bit.

"So, what's on the tapes? Do they say anything about a merger?"

"Not so far. They are crazy though. Some of them sound like they are being recorded by a person in the room and then some of them sound like they are made by a wiretap."

"What? A wiretap? Why do you think that?" I suddenly felt like there was a brick sitting on my chest making it almost impossible to breathe, but I was determined to run through it.

"Well, here's where it gets weird. I swear that I listened to a twenty-minute phone conversation between the actors Jeff Jax and Vinny Stevens discussing which restaurant in LA had the best burritos."

"What? Have you been drinking with Rena today?"

"I'm serious."

"Why do you think it was them and why the hell would Elise have a recording of it? That makes absolutely zero sense."

"Well, for one thing, the conversation started with 'Yo, Jax, what's up?' And, for another, I feel like I know their damn voices better than my own parents' because when we lived together you always watched their stupid tv show when you were stoned, which was all the damn time by the way."

"This is true. Well, at least it doesn't sound like there's anything important on the tapes. Maybe Elise was a secret star fucker or stalker. That could be why they were hidden. Maybe she hasn't responded to my texts about them because she is embarrassed."

I was still struggling to breathe and things were starting to get blurry. I should have eaten more protein before my run. My steady diet of boyfriend-baked muffins and Goldfish crackers was obviously not enough to fuel a run.

"I wouldn't say that there's nothing important on them. I was about to give up on listening to them after the burrito debate, which actually got a little heated. Then the next recording started. This was one of the recordings where it sounded like the conversation was happening in person. There is always the same gravelly voiced dude talking in these tapes and he was talking to some woman who I swear he kept calling "Burt." They were discussing licenses and antitrust rulings. It all sounded very cloak and dagger but no other names were mentioned. Burt said she was 'taking care of it' and not to worry."

There was a ringing in my ear and dark spots floated in and out of my vision. I suddenly couldn't breathe at all. I was frantically gasping for breath when I fell to the ground.

"Ally!"

Everything was pitch dark for a few seconds and I could hear her but couldn't respond.

"Ally! What's wrong?"

I felt Sarah crouch down on the ground beside me and then cold water was being sprinkled on my face.

"Ally. Talk to me." She was gently shaking my shoulders. "Just breath normal. OK. You sound like you are hyperventilating. Follow my lead.

Inhale for two. Exhale for two."

I followed her count and finally got my breath to slow down. I rolled my head to the side and opened my eyes. I immediately knew exactly where we were. I knew this spot. Five days ago this spot changed my life. I wondered if there was still blood on the rock just on the other side of the railing. How long had it taken someone to find him? Tears started to form in my eyes.

"It's going to be OK, Ally. You are going to be fine. Can you sit up?"

Sarah gently nudged me up from behind and helped me sit up. "Stay here. Don't move. Wait for me. I will be back in just a few minutes."

She ran off. She left me. Just like I had left him. I kept breathing. Two breaths in and two breaths out. I wanted to throw up. I wanted to stand up and run but my legs wouldn't let me move. I felt paralyzed but I couldn't stay here. I needed to get away. I was struggling to get to my feet when Sarah returned.

"What did I say about staying put? Sit your ass down."

I reluctantly obliged. She sat down beside me and handed me a soft pretzel and a Coke. "Eat this. I think your blood sugar dropped."

I was clearly not going to get away from the scene of my crime until I followed her commands. I ripped off a piece of pretzel and stuffed it in my mouth.

"What did you eat today?"

"A muffin, coffee, Goldfish crackers and a lot of Coke."

"Damn it, Ally. You need to eat healthier."

She must have noticed the tears welling up in my eyes.

"I'm sorry. You just scared the shit out of me. Not the time for a healthy living lecture. Is work that bad?"

I nodded and continued to stuff the pretzel in my mouth to keep myself from blurting out where we were and what I did.

"Screw that damn cannibal. I will not let him eat my friend." She gave me a side hug and held me tight.

I managed a faint smile. "Thanks."

"Do you think you can walk now?"

"Yes." I was so eager to get away from the spot that I practically screamed my answer.

"We are going to walk very slowly out of this park and we are going to go find a restaurant and you are going to eat a big-ass salad with some chicken on it to get some protein in your body."

"Ick! I was just on the brink of death and now you are trying to kill me with rabbit food. Shouldn't I get something that will make me happy and cheer me up? Like chicken wings? Ohh! Let's go inhale a shit-ton of chicken wings."

"Oh my God! You were not just on the brink of death. I swear you are a bigger drama queen than Rena."

I got to my feet, pretended to stagger a bit and gave her my best pout face.

"Fine. You can have some chicken wings. Let's get out of here. It's getting dark and creepy."

She had no idea how dark and creepy that place could get. I vowed never to go back.

CHAPTER 13

I WOKE UP EARLY WEDNESDAY. I was antsy but also a little bit excited to confront the douche-bros that night. I had no plan at all other than I knew they had to be confronted and they had to be stopped. I wouldn't be able to live with myself if I knew that they were still out there rendering women helpless and taking advantage of them and videotaping them when they were at their most vulnerable. I was also practical enough to know that not even with Bob's fierce and relentless tutelage would I be skilled enough to take down two men at a time. I was good, but I wasn't Sydney Bristow from *Alias* by any means. Although, I suspected guys who needed to drug women for sex were pretty soft and would run away from any direct confrontation or fight. I was also pretty convinced that I was not mentally cut out to kill them based on my physical and mental meltdown at my prior crime scene the night before. I would have to think on my feet and improvise once I got to the club and surveyed my surroundings.

While Drew slept, I stealthily combed through my closet and all the "ladies who lunch" dresses and outfits that Carol had bought for me over the years for something to wear when I went out hunting douche-bros. I had no idea how the people attending a Remnants of Evil concert dressed. I assumed they were hipsters or some variation thereof and I had no idea how to dress ironically.

It was 6:30 in the morning so I just randomly started throwing things in my gym bag that I thought might work. I definitely needed the tights covered in *Pride and Prejudice* quotes that Sarah gave me as a joke. I grabbed a flannel shirt, a knitted beanie, and my *Firefly* "I'm a Leaf on the Wind" T-shirt. I know, fellow *Firefly* lovers, it is still too soon. RIP Walsh. I decided I would need to go out at lunch to buy some fake glasses and some denim cut off shorts to complete the ensemble. I tossed several long necklaces and a scarf into the bag. I was going to look like a fool and I hoped to hell I didn't see anyone I knew.

It occurred to me that this was the first Wednesday night I wasn't actively dreading in a long time because I wasn't even thinking about pretending to do a set. I wouldn't be drinking at a bar by myself listening to other comics either succeeding in making the room laugh or spectacularly failing. I had a distraction from my own failures. I might not have a plan but I now had a hastily thrown together hipster outfit and an agenda of making those two men miserable in some fashion or another.

On the subway, having learned my lesson about listening to other people talking, I cranked up my girl-power playlist of Britney, Beyoncé, Pink and Miley. It was a good morning. I felt a confidence blossoming inside me. I was sure it was going to be cut short in no time once I got to the office, but I leaned back and closed my eyes and listened. Yes, Pink, you are right. We do need to "Get This Party Started."

At work, I had a hard time concentrating on transcribing the notebooks and the whole task started to seem like pointless busy-work. There wasn't a bit of logic to Elise's notes that I could discern and I couldn't imagine how Tristan-Malcolm was getting anything useful out of them either. As much as I hated getting up earlier in the morning, at least my early arrivals had stemmed the tide of snarky and hateful emails greeting me on my arrival. If I was lucky, I could get through this day without any interaction with him at all.

After finishing another notebook of antitrust case law summaries, I decided to take a break. I clicked on the Mars' file and opened the file that was labeled "merger documents." I was not sure why I wanted to read it because I knew that I wouldn't understand half of it because of all the legalese, but I was hoping, just maybe, I would understand enough to put the notes into context.

The first four pages made my eyes gloss over. Why in the hell does it take so many words to just identify the parties to the merger? Jesus, I get it. Mars News and Media, a New York-based corporation is buying and acquiring the assets of Rusk Communications, a North Carolina-based corporation for the sum of twenty million dollars. Holy shit! I should pay more attention to Uncle Benji because apparently he will just throw around the Benjamins. I admit - that was lame, but I'm trying to entertain myself, people. This work is soul-killing. Seriously though, that is a lot of money. I stopped reading the document because it basically read as "blah, blah, blah, party of the first part, blah, blah, blah, party of the second part, blah, blah, blah." This document was as useless to me as Elise's notes. I closed the file.

I looked at the notebook sitting on my desk. I knew I should be transcribing it, but I still couldn't bring myself to face it. I got on the internet and googled Mars News and Media to see exactly how big of a player Uncle Benji was and how much attention I should actually be paying when he was talking. Turned out – a lot. His corporation not only owned and operated MNM, a 24-hour news network, but it also ran GTrendz, the celebrity gossip site I read every damn morning, along with a multitude of other pop culture websites.

Damn it! Maybe I needed to start paying attention when other people are talking at these boring functions at Drew's parents' house. I'm sure his 24-hour news network was very important and prestigious and whatnot but I don't watch the news. I know that's a real shocker to you. The real tragedy was that I could have been pumping Uncle Benji for celebrity gossip over the past three years instead of just reading about it online. There were so many blind items and I bet he knew all of the answers. I'm not going to lie. This information is a game changer in terms of my life.

Maybe it was best that I didn't know. I could just imagine the look I would receive from Carol if she heard me ask Uncle Benji if he could "leak" the exact current whereabouts of Taye Diggs to me for very important, serious and not at all stalker-related reasons.

I went to the break room and got more Goldfish crackers and Coke and continued to ponder how to subtly use this new information to my benefit. I had so many burning questions I wanted to ask Uncle Benji but I wasn't sure where to start. I might actually enjoy the fundraiser this weekend.

My temporary high was cut short by the phone at my desk ringing. I've received less than ten calls on my work phone over the past three years, so it startled me enough that I actually jumped in my chair. As I reached to answer it, I saw "TM Reynolds" on the caller display. This couldn't be good.

"Hello?"

"What the hell were you doing in the merger documents?"

"What? How did you –"

"I can see on the document trail that you opened it. What the hell were you doing in it? If you changed something and messed it up, I swear to God I will get your ass fired."

"I didn't change anything. I . . . I was just . . . looking . . . at them," I stuttered my way through the words.

I felt like I was in school and being accused of cheating in front of the whole class. I had no idea I was not allowed to look at the documents in the case. Granted, I had never been compelled to look at documents in any case unless I was specifically asked to, and even then, I just typed and didn't really pay attention to the words or meaning of anything I typed.

"Let me be clear. You don't need to be looking at them. You don't need to be touching them. You need to type up the damn notes. I've asked you to do one thing. Do it."

I tried to find courage through flipping him off and making faces at the phone. God, I hoped there was no nanny cam.

"Absolutely. I will get back on it immediately."

He hung up on me. I immediately missed the days when the harassment was just transmitted via email. Now that I knew phone calls were on the table, I reminded myself I needed to get that emergency bottle of Vodka for my desk. Once more, I was grateful for the spare underwear in my purse.

I DEFIANTLY LEFT THE OFFICE for lunch and went in search of the additional items I needed to complete my hipster attire for the evening. I had to go to the fifth floor of Bloomingdales to find an over-priced pair of denim cut off shorts. I actually kind of loved them. They felt like home. They were the first clothes I have bought in years without Carol's approval. I looked at my ass in the mirror and was pretty sure Drew would approve.

It took longer to find a pair of glasses. All of the fashion glasses were reading strength or what we call "cheaters" back home. I knew I couldn't take hours to search through different stores for glasses with just clear plastic lenses because ass-face would know how long I was gone. I needed the glasses to Clark Kent myself so the douche-bros didn't recognize me even though I was pretty sure they only looked at boobs and never made it up to a woman's face.

I finally settled on a pair of purple cat's eye-shaped glasses with rhinestones in the corner. They were a +1.25 strength which was the lowest I could find and they made the floor look wavy and I stumbled a bit when trying to walk. I figured this feature might come in handy at some point and hoped that I didn't give myself a massive migraine before I accomplished my as yet undefined mission.

I grabbed a hot dog and a pretzel from a vendor and practically ran back to the office so I could try to make it back in under an hour. I failed.

To: Allison Brown
From: Tristan-Malcom Reynolds
Subject: Your work ethic

An hour and fifteen-minute lunch? You have work to do.
TMR

Damn it. This was some major bullshit. I sat back at my desk and resumed my dreary routine. Squint. Type. Save. According to Susan, Remnants of Evil was not set to start playing until 10. I decided to work until 9 since I had no place else to be and I didn't want to get there too early and prolong my suffering. I had discovered over the past six months, being a single woman at a bar can be exhausting. You have to be on constant alert to avoid unwanted conversations and if one happens to occur you have to be prepared to shut it down quickly and walk away. I have pretty much perfected a resting bitch face which wards off those with at least some survival instincts. Unfortunately, not everyone has honed survival instincts.

Everyone on my floor had already left for the day so I went to the women's room to change into my hipster persona, who I had given the name "Payden." Susan had stopped by on her way out and asked if there was anything she could do to help me. I requested a naked picture of a guy with a man-bun. I could say that I asked just so I could make her feel helpful in some small way, but I suspect you now know me well enough by now to pick up on that lie. Don't judge my kinks and I won't judge yours. We all have them.

I was mortified by the results of the multi-layered horror show of an outfit staring back at me from the mirror. I instantly regretted not buying a trench coat to cover the sartorial disaster that adorned my body. With any luck, the only person I would see who knew me would be Greg, the night shift security guy, and I could play it off as a joke. I would take a cab down to the bar to avoid any stares on the subway. It would help if I had some plan as to what I was going to actually do to intervene, but plans were a luxury that I didn't have time to come up with because I was too busy jumping through hoops for the ass face upstairs.

I looked into the mirror and tried to summon a coquettish look. I talked out loud to myself because I was now officially a crazy person.

"Hi! I'm Payden. It's like Hayden but with a 'P' or Peyton but with an 'a' and a 'de.'" Isn't this band ama-huzing. I saw them before they actually became Remnants of Evil. They used to go by the name Residuum of Garbage and they only played Steampunk Country-Western Jazz."

What are you doing? Seriously? Are you actually doing this?

It certainly wasn't me in the mirror. This strange creature Payden stared back at me. I reminded myself of the douche-bros and the unsuspecting hipster girl who didn't deserve to suffer at their disgusting hands.

"OK, Payden. We've got this."

As I waited for the elevator to arrive, my confidence was growing. I was beginning to get a feel for Payden and how she might speak and interact with the douche-bros before somehow kicking their asses. I was in deep thought wondering if it was too late to stop and get a Taser and where I could get one. The elevator doors opened and to my horror, Tristan-Malcolm was standing before me.

It is hard to say who had the most horrified look on their face between the two of us. I was tempted to turn and run down the hall screaming, but the damage was already done, so that wouldn't change anything. I summoned Payden and bravely stepped into the elevator and stood as far away from him as I could.

He stared at me with a look that was equally perplexed and disgusted. After a few moments, he finally broke the silence that had somehow managed to be even more awkward than any of our other encounters.

"Have you recently suffered a head injury?"

"Well, Drew did bang my head on the kitchen cabinet the other night when we were fucking on the counter top."

Oh my God! Where the hell did that come from? Payden – you are a stupid bitch.

His upper lip curled in disgust as he glared at me. We rode the rest of the way down in a silence that bespoke our mutual hatred of one another. I had never been so happy to hear the ding announcing our arrival on the ground floor.

I practically ran off the elevator and over to Greg. Thank God for Greg! He was bound by a security guard oath, which I'm sure exists, to protect me from an enraged cannibal.

"Hey Greg. How is everything going in your world?"

Greg was now my best friend in the world. I would never leave Greg's side. At least, not until Tristan-Malcolm was safely out of the building and far away from me.

"Doing good. Better than my Giants."

"They are a hot mess this year. Tomorrow's game against New England is going to be brutal."

Love his heart, Greg didn't even bat an eye at my appearance and was more than happy to talk with me for as long as I wanted. We chatted about football until I finally saw Tristan-Malcolm get into a town car. I was sure I had not heard the last of this encounter, but I would have to worry about that later. I had bigger douche-bros to fry.

CHAPTER 14

THE OUTSIDE OF HITCHES LITERALLY had half a dozen hitching posts where its patrons tethered their bikes. I hadn't even gotten inside yet and I hated everyone and wanted to burn the building to the ground. When I saw the interior, my eyes rolled so hard that I almost detached a retina. It could best be described as a tribute bar that desperately wanted to be a saloon in the days of the grand Old West.

There were Mason jar pendant lights hanging from the ceiling and the drinks were also served in Mason jars. Wooden signs on the walls advertised baths for five cents along with an array of Wanted Dead or Alive posters which I suspected used photographs of staff members. The bar stools were fucking saddles. The tables were poker tables and several patrons were playing poker. I didn't want to know if the bar provided the poker chips and cards or whether it was a bring your own chips and cards. I wished Drew were with me so we could mock the hell out of the place. I couldn't tell if it was earnest or ironic, so I guess I was the fool here.

This was going to be a long ass night and I still had no plan. It was not yet ten o'clock and the bar was only about half full. Some of the people had dogs with them, because of course they did. I scanned the room and there was no sign of the douche-bros.

I found a stupid ass saddle stool near the end of the bar as far away from where the band was setting up as possible. I had a clear view of the entrance. I would see my targets as soon as they arrived.

I watched the band getting organized. There was a washtub bass, jugs, a banjo, an accordion, and of course an Old West saloon piano. Way too many men had actual handle-bar mustaches and they were all pomaded to an inch of their life. I'm sure if I had asked, I would have heard long and death-inducing stories about how the pomades were all made with all natural ingredients that only came from the finest of residue shitted out of the rarest of yaks or some such nonsense. My resolve to not actually kill anyone was getting weaker and weaker.

The bartender approached me and was dressed in a white shirt with black arm bands on both arms, a red and white striped vest, a bow tie, and the obligatory handle-bar mustache. I wondered if he hated his life or if he thought that he was living the dream. I considered killing him just to put him out of his misery.

"Good evening Lassie, what can I get you? Our specialty drink is the

Apple Jack, which is a cider brandy that the owner distills himself."

Dude, blink twice if you want me to mercy kill you. I ordered a Wild Turkey and water and stared at the door. If these assholes didn't show up after I went to all this trouble, I swore that I would track them down and kill not only them, but everyone they loved. My head was starting to hurt. I wasn't sure if it was the reading glasses or the anticipation of the fresh hell that was sure to assault my eardrums when the music started.

I checked my phone for and saw I had a text from Drew.

I hope you kill it tonight. Love you, babe.

In all of the preparations for tonight I had forgotten to worry about what lie I was going to tell about my set. I had such bigger lies that I was telling or willful omissions that I was keeping from him. I was going to have to find a way to make it up to him. Maybe I could bring him and Max here one night for an evening of mockery.

I sipped my drink and watched the door. The band was getting ready to start and still no douche-bros. Maybe Susan had been wrong when she found this band. I briefly worried that there was another band with the initials ROE playing somewhere in the city tonight.

The lead singer stepped up to the microphone and thanked everyone for coming out and informed the audience that they had some new songs they were anxious to debut. I noticed there was now a female with a flute in the band. The crowd cheered and clapped, but not too loudly, because that would make them look eager. The tables playing poker continued to play and couldn't be bothered to look up and acknowledge the band. I suspected they were just playing it cool and keeping it real, as hipsters do, and that they were probably the band's biggest fans and were squeeing inside like twelve-year-old One Direction fans at the thought of hearing brand new songs.

I would love to say that once the band started playing I was blown away with their talent and the uniqueness of their sound, but we all know that didn't happen. It was a total mish mash clusterfuck of noise that had no rhythm or melody. I highly suspected there were not any actual written songs. It sounded as if the approach was more of an "everyone do your own thing and it is going to sound awesome." At one point in the middle of a song, the singer suddenly morphed from a bad Mumford & Sons impression to a Vanilla Ice-style rap. One of the dogs started barking.

This was a real thing that was happening in my life and I had no one to share it with me. I was so mesmerized with it all and trying not to laugh out loud that I almost missed the douche-bros show up. I watched them take a spot standing around a tall table with no stools in a corner to my right. The bar started to get crowded and there was an influx of young women coming into the bar as the "band," and I use that word very loosely, continued to assault everyone's eardrums. I guess hipsters like to be fashionably late or maybe even they recognized that this "band" was preposterous.

I kept the douche-bros in my sight and followed their gaze. I saw her at about the same time as the taller douche-bro and knew she would be his prey. She seemed to be alone, like me, but as opposed to giving off a violent, I will kill you if you look at me attitude, she was gazing lovingly at the lead singer, clearly infatuated. She looked vulnerable and innocent. Maybe it was the floral baby doll dress, ankle boots and flower in her hair. From a distance, she was beautiful in a serene way and the baby doll dress did not hide that she clearly had what the douches would consider a banging body, including very ample boobs.

The taller douche-bro slinked across the bar and approached the girl. I hopped off the saddle and made my way towards the two of them. I stumbled and almost fell down because I forgot I had the damn glasses on my face and the floor looked wonky and distorted. I was frantically searching my brain for what to do as I got closer.

I went with throwing myself at her to hug her and knocking her drink onto her dress. "Oh my God, Christy! I haven't seen you in ages!"

"I'm sorry, my name is not Christy. You must be confused." She politely pulled out of my half hug and looked down at the stain on her dress.

Douche-bro used the opportunity to take a napkin from the bar to "help" her clean the spill off her cleavage. I grabbed the napkin from him and slapped his hand away which earned me a glare from him. I pretended not to notice.

"I'm so sorry. You look just like my old roommate from college."

"It's no problem. It happens all the time. I'm Ariel."

She was being so nice about being doused with a drink by a "drunk" stranger that I resolved not to mentally mock her name.

Tall douche decided to make his move. "Ariel, I'm Steve. I was just coming over to offer to buy you a drink since it seems you don't have any friends with you. It's a real shame that you had to come out all alone. What can I get you? I hope you aren't drinking cranberry and vodka. That is such a ridiculous drink for a grown woman . . . but I guess with that dress and flower in your hair . . ." He put his hand in his left pocket as he was reaching for cash and I caught a glimpse of a plastic bag.

Really. That's your play asshole. Negging? No wonder no one screws you without being drugged. Not on my watch douche-bag. Not tonight.

"I'm Payden." I reached out my hand to shake hers and boxed Steve out of the picture momentarily. "Can I help you clean up that stain? I'm so sorry because your dress is adorable and I think the flower is an awesome touch. Is that cranberry juice? OMG! I love cranberry juice and vodka. We should probably go to the bathroom and clean that up."

"You are probably right. It is starting to get sticky." She started tugging on the baby doll dress near her cleavage. The douche was taking advantage of the situation with his height to look down her dress.

"You don't want to get sticky so early in the evening. Save some of that for later." Another killer pick-up line from Steve. I will end him. Ariel and I both side-eyed him with a slight sneer of our upper lips, the universal female look for "he's super gross."

I GRABBED ARIEL'S ARM AND lead her to the bathroom. Steve was left standing there basically holding his dick in his hand and smoldering with hatred and misogyny. I had saved her, but only momentarily. I was sure he would try again and if not her, then someone else. I wasn't sure how many times I could get away with the "OMG Christy" move throughout the night. I had to do something to at least get Ariel off my list of worries. Even though I was pretty sure his sticky remark had sealed his fate, he could still drug her drink.

I closed the door of the bathroom and checked the stalls. No one else was present. I turned to her with what I hoped was an authoritative and serious look on my face.

"Ariel, my name is not Payden. It's Marianne and I'm an undercover cop."

"What? Am I in trouble? I swear I'm not stalking Sloan. OMG! Did he say I was stalking him?" She spiraled into a free fall of panic right before my eyes. "I know we are supposed to be on a break but I just had to see him. Oh God! I've ruined everything by coming here tonight. Please don't arrest me."

Well, this was a turn I had not expected. I quickly guessed that Sloan was the lead singer of that atrocious band.

"No. It's OK. This has nothing to do with you and Sloan." I placed my hand on her shoulder to try to stem the tide of panic I saw on her face. "I am investigating a string of rapes. Young women like you are getting drugged. That man out there that approached you is one of my main suspects. I just wanted to get you away from him and warn you."

"Oh my God! Really?" Her face grew even more panicked.

"Unfortunately, yes. Now based on what you just told me, I think the best thing is for you to leave and go home for the night. That way you are safe from harm and you can also give Sloan a little space. Make him wonder why you left. I bet that will make him come looking for you. OK?"

She was visibly shaking and I felt bad for scaring her but I needed her to be scared and to leave and get away.

"Yeah. You are probably right. It was a mistake coming here."

She hugged me. "Thank you for saving me."

It felt good to help her but unfortunately, I wasn't done for the evening. I would still somehow mete out some justice for the girls that didn't get so lucky.

I walked her out of the bathroom and scanned the room for the douche-bros. They were both back at the tall table and no girls were near-by. Steve watched us as we headed to the door. I endured several more hugs from Ariel before I finally got her in a cab. I went back inside to my saddle and ordered another Wild Turkey and water and planned my next move.

THE SCREECHING NOISES COMING FROM the stage had reached a pitch that caused one of the dogs to hunker down with its paws over its head. I thought about calling its owners out for animal abuse. Not long after, the band mercifully took a short break to "wet their whistles." I would not have been surprised if when they took the stage again that they would actually have whistles to add to the mayhem of the next song. I didn't want to be around for the next set so I had to take action. I needed to "grab the bull by the horns" as one of the signs above the bar announced.

I called the waiter over and nodded in the douche-bros direction and asked what they were drinking. I should have known it would be Pabst Blue Ribbon Pounders. I ordered three. I opened all three and removed the pull tab from only one of the cans. I drank some of the swill from the can with no tab.

I dismounted the saddle stool and headed straight towards Steve and short douche. I stumbled again because of the glasses and was about to rip them off my face and yell "fuck it" when I decided to use the stumbling to my advantage. I swayed and stumbled my way over to the tall table carrying the three beers in a triangle with the one with the removed tab closest to me.

"Oh my God. Steve. I'm sooooo sorry about accidentally cock blocking you with Ariel. I bought you a beer to make up for it. Is there anything else I can possibly do to make it up to you?"

I slurred my words a little and leaned forward to flash some cleavage as I strategically placed myself between two of the most disgusting men in the world. I hated myself but it had to be done. I slid the two beers that still had their pull tabs over in each of their directions.

A self-satisfied smile spread over Steve's face as he accepted the offering. "I'm sure we can put our heads, or some other body parts, together and come up with some way you can atone."

I nearly threw up in my mouth. Steve was the worst. Or at least I thought he was before short douche spoke up.

"I'm Damon. You might not have cock blocked me but you sure did something to my cock just now. Anyone tell you that you have amazing tits? Although it looks like one might be smaller than the other. Ever had that looked at?"

It was the worst attempt at a "Neg" ever, but it still managed to trigger a rage stroke. Keep it together. Stay focused. I saw tall douche-bro's left hand reaching for his pocket. Yes, I realize that I know their names now but they don't deserve names.

I turned to face the shorter man but kept the corner of my eye on my drink. Hating myself, I flashed a smile at him and tugged my T-shirt down a bit to give him a better look.

"I've always worried that was noticeable. Is it that bad? Maybe that's why I have so much trouble finding a man." I simpered as I tried not to gag at the thought of him getting hard just from looking at my cleavage. Based on the face he made I was pretty sure he did. Thank God I wasn't standing close enough to feel it. Sure enough, while I was engaged in the gross encounter with him, out of the corner of my eye, I could see tall douche's hand hover over the can that was in front of me and then quickly retreat to his pocket. I wanted to punch him in the balls and then beat his face in but that would come later.

I turned to include tall douche in the conversation and grabbed the can. "How about you? What do you think of my tits? Is the size difference that noticeable?"

"I didn't want to say anything, but a little. Maybe it's just the way you dress that emphasizes it. I'd have to get a closer look at them naked before I could decide if it would be a deal breaker."

That certainly won't be happening, fucker. I put the can up to my lips and pretended to drink out of it. I was careful that not even a drop of the liquid touched my lips. The two guys practically high-fived each other with their eyes.

"You know what would make this night more fun? Shots! Damon, would you mind terribly to go get a round of Fireball?"

"On it. This night might end up being fun for you after all."

"So much fun." At least fun for me. For you two, not so much.

After he was gone, I turned all of my attention to the tall one. I pressed up against him. His back was against the table. I put my knee between his legs and put my beer can down beside his. I leaned in and his gaze immediately zeroed in on my boobs again. Men like him were so predictable.

"I was worried you were going to be an uptight bitch earlier. You don't seem so bad though."

Oh, I'm a bitch. You are going to find out just how bad of a bitch I am, very soon.

"Who me? Never. I was just getting rid of the competition. So, while your friend is gone, why don't you whisper in my ear just how much fun you want to get into this evening?"

He leaned down close to my ear with his eyes laser focused on my boobs. "I'm going to pound you so hard. You are going to finally learn what it is like to have a real man in charge, which is how things were meant to be."

I restrained myself from kneeing him in the groin. Instead, I put my hands on both sides of him and leaned in closer. "I love it when a real man takes control. It is just so hard to be a woman today and have to pretend like we want it all when all we really want is a man to tell us what we really need." I tried not to gag as I giggled and pulled my shirt down a little lower and revealed more cleavage.

He was sufficiently distracted by my boobs, desperate for a possible nip slip, and impressed with my apparent agreement with his life philosophy that he didn't even notice when I used one of my hands to switch the beer cans so that the drug-laced beer can was now in front of him. I grabbed the unlaced beer that was now in front of me and pulled away from him.

"I think we should drink to that." I suggested.

He grabbed the laced beer and took a long swig out of it. Drink up asshole. I once again pretended to drink out of the can I held. I wasn't about to let any of his disgusting backwash into my mouth. One down. One to go.

Short douche reappeared with the round of requested shots. I wasn't about to trust that he didn't have his own special pocket of drugs. I stepped forward to grab one and stumbled and fell into him knocking the glasses so that most of the liquid spilled out onto him.

"Oh my gosh, I'm so sorry." I grabbed a napkin and patted his scrawny as chest. "I'm suddenly getting a super good buzz. The floor is getting all wavy on me." I shook my head for exaggerated effect.

I turned to the tall one. "You know what great right would be now, is body shots. Could you go get a round? I promise I won't spill this one. But you can spill the shots on me and lick them off."

He and the shorter one exchanged excited looks and he headed off to the bar. I then preceded to use the exact same lean-in, whisper in my ear shenanigans with short douche and switched beer cans to get the laced one in front of him. It was almost too easy the second time.

Again, I pretended to drink out of the non-laced drink while he guzzled down a portion of the laced one.

Tall douche returned with the shots. I needed to get them out of the bar soon before the drugs kicked in and they realized what I had done.

I broke out the fake stumble again and fell back onto the shorter douche. Ick. He was definitely hard.

"Yikes. So sorry. I'm all of a sudden getting really hammered. Are you all hammered? I'm seriously hammered." I slurred my words and pretended to be unstable on my feet. "You boys want to take me home?"

"Your home or ours?" The tall one leered.

God, I hoped they had enough of the laced drink. My research indicated Ketamine was fast-acting so I needed to get them somewhere private fast.

"Yours."

The two guys toasted each other with the shots and slammed them back. The shorter guy followed it up by finishing off the laced beer, so I knew at least he would have enough drugs in his system. I could take down the taller douche even if he wasn't knocked out, if I had to do it. I was suddenly very grateful for all of the drunken sneak attacks by Drew and Max.

CHAPTER 15

IT WAS WELL AFTER MIDNIGHT and they were both alert enough to give the cab driver their address. Just before the taxi arrived I took the beanie off my head and let my long hair fall forward over my face. In the cab, I made several comments about how everything was so distorted and I felt like I was having an out of body experience. Then I closed my eyes and let my head roll loosely forward and sway back and forth. I kept my head down and hair in my face the entire ride so the cab driver would not be able to accurately describe me. If questioned, he would testify that the girl they were with was clearly out of it. I had to subtly fight off short douche's attempts to grope my boobs and tall douche's fumbling attempt to slide his hand up my shorts.

When we got to their apartment building, both of them were visibly unsteady on their feet and the drug had obviously kicked in. Tall douche dropped the keys to the apartment three times while trying to get the door open. Short douche leaned against the wall waiting and started to slide down to the ground.

"Damn it. Get the door opened man. Maybe those shots weren't such a good idea. I'm starting to feel hammered."

His words were slow and slurred and his eyes were drooping closed as he tried to feel his way back up the wall to a standing position.

"Dude, I'm trying. I'm seeing at least three key holes and I can't find the real one."

I didn't bother to conceal the self-satisfied smile on my face. I wasn't going to get all prematurely mission accomplished and break out the flight suit just yet. We all know how that worked out.

I grabbed his hand and steadied it so that he finally got the key in the lock and got the door open. He stumbled forward and fell on his face and crawled back up to a standing position. I helped the shorter one into the apartment and directed him over to the couch.

"Where's your bathroom? I need to go get ready."

The taller one slowly raised his arm and pointed down the hall.

"I expect you boys to be naked by the time I get back."

I saw them fumbling with their shirts as I walked down the hall. I quickly shut the door and locked it behind me. My adrenaline was pumping and my hands were shaking. I looked at myself in the mirror and saw the crazy persona of Payden reflected back at me.

"Are you seriously doing this?" I whispered to my reflection.

"I mean you kind of have to at this point. Right? They are rapists. They need stopped. Will this even stop them?"

The truth was, I didn't know if my hastily cobbled together Scooby-Doo plan would work and actually stop them from raping again, but I had to try.

It was quiet out in the apartment. I expected them to yell in and tell me to "hurry up, bitch" but it was silent. I stayed in the bathroom another ten minutes giving myself a pep talk. It was still silent on the other side of the door. Hopefully that meant the impaired motor function and loss of coordination had reached its peak.

I took off the stupid fake glasses and shoved them in my small purse and pulled out my running gloves and slipped them on. I grabbed a towel and wiped down anything I might have touched upon entering the bathroom. I took out my pepper spray and had it cocked and ready just in case shit went sideways. I rubbed down the outside bathroom door handle. I was alert and ready to fend off attacks from any direction as I walked down the hallway.

I found both of them sprawled out on the couch not moving. I heard what sounded like incoherent mumbling. Tall one was completely naked. Shorter one, who drank the largest dose, had his shirt off but appeared to have only gotten his pants half-way down before either giving up or losing his coordination. Neither seemed to register my fully-clothed entrance into the room. I braced myself for what I was about to do. I thought of all the girls who had been brought here before me under much grimmer and helpless circumstances. Thinking about the other girls rendered into the state of the two men before me and stripped of their freewill and choice and being subjected to these two disgusting excuses of human beings was enough to trigger the rage that I needed to carry through with the plan.

I would like to say that I didn't enjoy it, but once the anger kicked in, I felt a rush of power.

"Hey boys. I don't know if you can hear me or will remember this once the drugs wear off but you two are the most pathetic examples of the male species I have ever encountered."

The tall one managed to slightly open his eyes and lift his head, "sssay . . . whhhhatss . . . happenin . . ." and then his head fell back and his eyes closed again.

"What's happening, Steve, is called payback for all the girls you and your douche-bro over there have ever drugged and raped."

I pulled the belt from short douche's pants. His body didn't even respond to the movement. I hoped he wasn't dead but if he was, then it was not my fault. It was his own drugs that killed him. Rather him than some innocent girl.

"Let me tell you something, Steve." I jerked his head up by his over-gelled hair and looped the belt around his neck.

"You are a pathetic piece of human garbage." I tightened the belt and gave it a tug that was enough to make him open his eyes wide in panic. He lacked the coordination of his limbs to do anything in response to try to stop me. I relaxed the tautness of the belt.

"You and your friend are gross and disgusting." I yanked the belt tight across his neck again.

His eyes remained open and I could sense real fear starting to set in.

I released it again.

"There is a reason that girls won't voluntarily sleep with you. And it is not because of feminism or because they are uptight bitches. It's because you are vile and putrid."

I yanked the belt tight again. "Men's rights are not a fucking real cause, Steve. You know why? Because men have had ownership of all the rights since the beginning of time. Women wanting to be treated equally doesn't take a damn thing away from men. Women who don't want to date you aren't violating your rights. The only men who think that are pathetic losers."

His face was starting to turn red so I released the tension of the belt for a moment. I gave him a few seconds to breathe.

"How does it feel to be so vulnerable, Steve? Is it scary? I bet it's scary."

I pulled the belt tighter. The fear in his eyes only emboldened me.

"Do you feel vulnerable and afraid?"

I managed to pull the belt just a little tighter and held it. I imagined if he had any coordination he would have fought me and struggled for air.

He gasped for breath and I released the pressure for just a moment before reapplying it again.

"Do you think any girl you drugged and raped ever felt any actual enjoyment? They didn't. They were scared and vulnerable just like you are now. You and your friend have failed as men. Do you understand that now?"

Again I released the belt for just a few breaths before pulling it tight once more. He continued to look at me with sheer panic on his face.

"I want you to blink your eyes if you understand what I'm saying to you."

He blinked. I released the pressure for just a millisecond and then yanked it back.

"I want you to blink again and let me know that you now see how you and your friend have failed as men and promise that you won't ever drug another woman and take advantage of her."

I held the pressure tight until he began blinking rapidly. I released the pressure of the belt.

"Steve, I know where you live now. I'm going to look in your wallets and get your full names and driver's license numbers. So, I want you to remember that I can come back for you at any time. And the next time, I won't hesitate to kill you and your friend over there. I'm feeling generous tonight so I'm going to give you a chance to make better choices and to find a way to atone for what you have done."

I tightened the belt one last time.

"Blink if you appreciate the opportunity that I'm providing you."

Again he blinked rapidly. I let go of the belt and let it drop down on his chest. I inspected his neck and was satisfied that he'd been inflicted with a long lingering bruise to serve as a reminder of our conversation.

I turned to the shorter douche who had not stirred or made any noise during my assault on his friend. I leaned down closer to his face and was able to hear breathing sounds. I was almost disappointed he wasn't dead. I grabbed his head and pulled him over closer to his dude-bro. I forced open his mouth and shoved it onto his friend's dick. I agree that might have been a little overkill, but I was in the moment and totally feeling a *Heathers* type of vibe.

An iPhone was laying on the end table closest to the taller douche. I grabbed it and used his fingerprint to unlock the screen. I then proceeded to take several photographs of my handiwork to serve as further warning once they recovered from their unexpected trip down the "black hole" of pussy Valium. In the notes section of his phone I typed, "Looks like it can happen to you too, assholes. The more you know."

I found their wallets and took pictures on my phone of their driver's licenses. I picked up Steve's pants off the floor and pulled the plastic bag of powder from out of his left pocket and shoved it in my purse.

I scoured the area for close to half an hour, wiping off anything that I might have touched when I first got in and inspecting their clothes and bodies to make sure that I left no hair behind, even though I had put it up into a tight bun in the bathroom and put the beanie back on. I doubted they would go to the police given the circumstances, but I was going to do my best not to leave any trace evidence behind. I was calm and methodical as opposed to the crazed person who had just been choking the shit out of a man. I didn't have time to stop and think about how I was farther down the road to becoming a sociopath.

"It looks like your train got derailed this evening douche-bros. Sorry. Not Sorry." I announced as I closed the door.

I pulled the beanie down over my face as far as it would go and kept my head down as I left the building just in case there were security cameras. I walked four blocks with my pepper-spray cocked and ready before hailing a cab to take me home to Drew. I tried not to let my mind think about what Drew would do if he found out what I had done and who I was becoming.

CHAPTER 16

IT WAS CLOSE TO TWO in the morning when I got home, so thankfully Drew was in bed and snoring as I stripped off the nightmare of an outfit I had been wearing and shoved the clothes and glasses into an old gym bag in the back of the closet. I crawled in beside him and watched him sleep, grateful that I had found him and I wasn't out in the dating world being subjected to the likes of the douche-bros. I hoped after tonight no other women would be subjected to those specific douche-bros.

The next morning, I woke up in a panic. I couldn't breathe and I felt a crushing weight on my chest. In the first few moments of panic, I thought maybe I was back in the douches' apartment and I had been drugged and that one of them was on top of me. Maybe my vigilante outburst had just been my imagination during a drugged up state as a way of disassociation.

I opened my eyes to find Daisy, my fifteen-pound cat standing on my chest staring at me. Upon seeing the whites of my eyes she chirped and meowed and stomped her front feet on me. This was her ritual when it was past time for wet food. I rolled over and looked at the clock on my night stand. Shit!! It was 8:30. Drew was still snoring. He was usually an early riser and was my backup alarm. I jumped out of bed and ran to the bathroom. I didn't even have time for a whore's bath, as my grandmother used to call it. I frantically brushed my teeth, put on deodorant and enough make-up so as to not frighten any children. I don't exactly have a super complicated beauty routine on a regular day, but today it was even more rudimentary.

I was in the closet fighting to keep my balance while attempting to put tights on while standing up and picking out a Carol-approved outfit for the day when I heard the low growling sound that Drew always made when waking up and stretching in bed. I was so worried about having my ass reamed out by Tristan-Malcolm that I hadn't even thought about the fact that it was Thursday morning until I heard Drew call out from the bed.

"Good morning, babe. You had a really late night. How did it go?"

Shit. I grabbed a jade green dress from the hanger.

"It went much better than I expected." That is not a lie. I told myself as I squirmed into the dress.

"Did you kill it?"

"Not exactly, but I got really close." Still not a lie. I was hopping around on one foot pulling on one of my riding boots and trying not to fall on my face.

I looked at the clock. 8:36. Not bad timing but I still should have been at the office by now. I ran over to the bed and kissed Drew.

"We can talk about it later. I'm running super late. Can you give the cats their wet food?"

"Sure. By the way, I'm going to go by a church today and get some holy water because I'm still not convinced you haven't been possessed by a demon. The girl that I moved in with never cared about punctuality before."

"You can stage an exorcism for later tonight." I grinned at him playfully, but truthfully I was starting to wonder if maybe I wasn't possessed. That would explain a lot and it would be a great excuse. "Love you."

"Love you. See you tonight at dinner."

Yay! Something else that I had completely forgotten about. I grabbed a muffin from the kitchen and raced out the door.

I kept my headphones on for the entire subway ride, having now thoroughly learned my lesson about the dangers of eavesdropping. I was on high alert when passengers boarded at the stop where the douches had boarded on Monday. Once I assured myself they weren't in my car, I was able to relax a little as Aretha Franklin sang to me about "Respect" and Whitney sang about being the "Queen of the Night."

It was 9:30 by the time I got to the office. I went straight to the break room and made myself a large cup of coffee, heavy on the sugar and cream. I sat down at my desk and booted up my computer and held my breath, waiting for the insult to appear, and there it was.

To: Allison Brown

From: Tristan-Malcom Reynolds

Subject: Your work ethic

I'm concerned about your mental health. Fashion choices aside, I simply cannot understand how you don't seem to comprehend the concept of work hours.

TMR.

My boyfriend thinks I'm possessed by a demon, my boss thinks I'm mentally disturbed, and I was tempted to agree with both of them. This day was off to an auspicious start. I picked up a notebook and started typing. I was starting to give up on Elise ever returning my texts. She was either on a really long walkabout and didn't want to break my no texting while walking rule or she was ignoring me. I couldn't understand what I had possibly done to warrant such a response. Maybe she was the mentally disturbed one? That would explain the nonsense in these notebooks.

I resumed my tedious daily routine. Squint. Type. Save. Three bowls of Goldfish crackers, five Cokes, and eight and a half hours later, I had three notebooks typed up and it was only six o'clock. Dinner was not until eight o'clock. I had two hours. A week ago I would have used that time to go run. After my last two runs, I was not so gung-ho to hit the pavement. Sarah had a show. Elise was no longer around for happy hour drinks. Susan had plans. I wasn't sure what to do with myself. The thought of starting another notebook was enough to make me want to voluntarily take a trip down the black hole.

I got online and searched Rusk Communications to see if there was any information that could help me decode the notes and also to sate my curiosity as to exactly what Uncle Benji thought was worth twenty million dollars. I found no website. I found no news articles. I found no Facebook page or Twitter account. Maybe I read the name wrong. I didn't dare open the document back up to check the spelling lest I incur the wrath of the asshole upstairs. I was trying to keep a low profile on that front. One insult a day delivered via email was already more than my fair share.

I got frustrated by the lack of information so I gave up and went to GTrendz, my favorite gossip site, which I now knew Uncle Benji owned. I was going to catch up on all the very important news I had been missing while slaving away on those damn notebooks. Back in the glory days of Elise, I used to spend hours at work reading the site and unofficially held myself out as an expert on the comings and goings of all celebrities. I used to wear Drew out at night telling him the latest ridiculous thing that a celebrity had done or said. Max and I had long discussions about the rumored closet cases and their contractually obligated beards.

I was reading about a country singer who got busted in Texas with pot on his tour bus when I remembered I still had the illegally obtained Ketamine in my purse. I was an idiot to be walking around with it. It wasn't like I was planning to use it. I was getting ready to grab my purse and take it to the bathroom to discretely flush it when I had a Eureka moment.

Rena! It was so brilliant, I couldn't believe it had taken me all day to think of it. I could use the Ketamine to ruin Rena and help Sarah get her big break. My mind began to race with all of the possibilities. I got so lost in concocting a plan that time raced by and it was only when I got a text from Drew with a heart emoji and *See ya in twenty babe* that I remembered dinner with his parents.

Greg was working the front desk as I left. "Hey, I hope the Giants win big for you tonight."

"Me too. I've got a meatball sub riding on it with Sam. I've had to buy that bastard his dinner for the past four Friday nights. You need to stop working so late."

"You got that right."

I MADE IT TO THE Club with three minutes to spare. I did not want to be late two weeks in a row. I found Drew at the bar waiting for me. It occurred to me that I never saw him take a place in the glad handling and power talks his parents seemed to be engaged in all the time. I kissed him and ordered a glass of wine.

"How was your day, honey? Did you get a lot of studying done?"

"Unfortunately. I hate my criminal procedure class. It's not like I'm every going to use it in real life."

I wanted to warn him that he shouldn't be too sure about that, but thought better of it.

"That's not true. Next time we visit my mother and are forced to watch *Law & Order* marathons you can tell us what is accurate and what is completely wrong."

"I'm sure your mother would just love that."

"Actually, she really would. Where are your parents?" I scanned the room and didn't see them holding court as usual.

"They were having a heated conversation when I got here so I think they stepped into one of the private rooms."

"What? I've never even heard your parents even raise their voices at each other. What are they fighting about?"

I hated being present when people were fighting. I had a tendency to get exceedingly awkward and over talk and over share in an attempt to fill any potential lulls in the conversation. I didn't want my favorite dinner of the week ruined for a second week in a row. I checked the clock behind the bar. It was 8:10. Carol always insisted on being seated on time.

I sipped my wine and my stomach growled. I had been mentally picturing my steak all day.

"Any word out of Max this week? How are things with Connor?"

"Tonight is Connor's last night in town." He took a sip of his drink.

"Uh-oh! So tomorrow night is cheer up Max night."

"Maybe not. He said Connor comes into town a lot for his job so they are talking about trying the long distance thing."

"Good for him." I wasn't crazy about Connor, but if Max was finally happy, then I would learn to live with him.

"I know. Here comes mom. I'm sure dad will be out once he's licked his wounds."

I wondered why Drew did not seem surprised or phased about his parents fighting, but didn't have time to ask because I was quickly caught up in Carol's embrace followed by socialite kisses on the cheek.

"Allison, how lovely to see you as always." Her demeanor was completely at odds with the fact that she had just been in a heated argument with her husband.

"You too."

She motioned to Louis and we were guided over to our usual table. Luckily, Drew picked up the conversation ball with her while we waited for Richard to arrive and they discussed the upcoming fundraiser for Senator Bridget Davis' re-election campaign and the latest hijinks of her competition, an upstart politician who was threatening to start slinging mud.

"Mr. Antonini will be swiftly advised that the opposition research done on him has produced more mud than he could ever hope to wade out from under."

I am sure you won't be surprised to learn that I don't closely follow politics so I mentally checked out of the conversation and went back to plotting the demise of a certain pop/Broadway star. Our entrees had already arrived by the time Richard joined the table. Carol had ordered for him.

"Sorry to keep everyone waiting. I had to make an important call on the merger."

He bent over and kissed my forehead as he took his place beside me. "How are you holding up? Are you keeping Tristan-Malcolm in line?"

Since adherence to my no lying policy flew out the window the week before, I heard myself responding, "It's all fine. Just typing up Elise's notes that seem to be mostly gibberish."

I could have sworn I saw Carol's lip stiffen more than usual at the mention of Elise's name.

Richard patted my hand. "I'm sure her notes aren't that important. I don't know why he has you doing such a project. I will talk to him tomorrow."

Shit! No! I was pretty sure Tristan-Malcolm would go through with his death threat if he thought I went over his head.

"Oh, please don't. I think he is finding them very helpful in getting up to speed." Boom. Another lie. "It's a lot of case law that I just don't seem to understand."

"OK. If it is helping him then keep at it."

"I do have a question that I didn't want to ask him because I thought it would sound stupid."

"There are no stupid questions. Ask away." He started cutting into the steak in front of him.

"Why does Uncle Benji's company want to buy Rusk Communications? It's so much money and I couldn't find out a thing about them on the internet."

Richard stopped mid-cut and put his knife down. I could have sworn I saw Carol's lip stiffen again. I immediately regretted my question. Maybe I wasn't supposed to talk about company work in front of Carol and Drew. Did I just breach attorney and client confidentiality? I knew I already breached it when I gave Sarah the tapes, but at least no one knew about that.

"Good question. It involves a lot of newly developed technology. Trust me. You'd get as bored as I did when listening to the details. I'm pretty sure I didn't even understand the half of it." He again patted me on the hand and then resumed cutting his meat.

I hung my head and quietly returned to my steak, embarrassed that I had tried to talk about a case I clearly knew nothing about and was obviously way over my head. I was savoring my medium rare filet when the dinner conversation took another swerve into Unpleasantville.

Carol piped up. "So Allison, how was your show, or set, or whatever you call, it last night?"

Et tu, Carol? I thought we had come to an understanding last week.

"Oh my God, honey. I totally forgot to ask when you came in tonight. I'm so sorry."

"It's OK, babe. You don't have to ask every time. I know you support me." I smiled across the table at him.

"No matter what you say, I bet you killed it. You are so awesome." He smiled at me with pride.

"I wouldn't say that, but I did strangle it and make it my bitch." Mostly accurate. Not entirely a lie.

"That's wonderful news, Allison." Carol made a signal to Louis and I hoped it wasn't for the check because I needed the chef's whimsy bread pudding like my life depended on it. The waiter had already told me it was pumpkin bread pudding with a spicy caramel apple sauce and vanilla bean crème anglaise.

Instead of the check, Louis brought Carol a rather large red square box with a bow on it. She handed it to me. I looked over at Drew confused. He shrugged and made a face that let me know he had no idea what was in it.

"I don't understand. It's not even close to my birthday."

"You've been working so hard for Richard and at the same time chasing your dream. I just wanted to get you a small token to celebrate and thank you for being part of our family."

I carefully opened the box, which, thank God, was one of the fancy boxes that just looked like it was wrapped and all you had to do was lift the cover. Laying inside was the most beautiful red handbag I had ever seen. I knew better than to call it a purse because Carol had corrected me on that before. Purse was a term "ordinary people" used on "ordinary bags," and this was no ordinary bag.

"It's beautiful!" I held it up to admire it and was careful not to get any sauce from the steak on it. I had a tendency to ruin good things and I didn't want to ruin it immediately upon receiving it. "You really didn't have to do this Carol."

"It's a Hermès. You deserve it dear."

A Hermès. I shouldn't even be allowed to look at a Hermès bag through a store window let alone touch one or own it.

"Mom. That is an awesome present, but now you've made me look bad for not getting it for her myself."

"Stop, both of you. I don't deserve this. It is the most beautiful thing I have ever seen but, I can't accept it."

"Well, you have to accept it. I won't hear any further argument about that. Drew, tell her."

"Honey, you have to accept it. My mom will fight you on this and no one ever wins a fight with my mother."

Richard was in the middle of taking a drink and made a slight choking sound. "Sorry. I think the bartender put a bit too much gin in this martini."

Carol scowled across the table from him. I got immediately uncomfortable.

"Well, I love it! Thank you. And I can't imagine ever wanting to get in a fight with you, Carol."

"That's good dear." She laughed her polite ladylike chuckle. "And Drew isn't wrong, you know. Not many people have ever come away from a fight with me that aren't at least badly bruised and severely shaken."

Her eyes never moved from my face and her voice was jovial, but I was quite certain she was firing a warning shot in Richard's direction. I was suddenly very glad I wasn't her target. I just wanted to get my pumpkin bread pudding before the dinner came to an awkward and uncomfortable conclusion. Drew finally navigated the conversation to safe water by talking about law school.

Once the bread pudding was placed in front of me I was able to zone out of all further conversations and concentrate on the orgasmic delight. A few low moans escaped my mouth as I savored every bite. I don't know why I always seemed to be the only one at the table who took pleasure out of eating the food every week. I guess maybe they had been eating such fare for so long that it just didn't even register to them how delicious it all tasted. I was sure I would never develop such ennui towards a good meal having grown up on a steady diet of macaroni and tomato soup and grilled cheese sandwiches, which I still love. I would never throw shade at comfort food.

When we got home, I pulled the Hermès bag out of the box to admire it. It really was the most beautiful thing I had ever owned. I wrapped it up carefully and was putting it up on a high shelf in the closet for protection when Drew walked up behind me.

"What are you doing?"

"I'm putting it up somewhere safe so I won't destroy it. You know I tend to get ketchup or salsa or grease on everything I own. Have you seen how much I have to pay the dry cleaners?"

He reached up and pulled the box off the shelf and handed it to me.

"She will be hurt if you don't use it."

"But I will ruin it. I ruin things. I don't know why she got me something so expensive and nice." I opened the handbag and looked inside. Even the inside was perfection and no one ever sees the inside. I was sure I would get food crumbs in it on the first day.

"She got it because she likes you. Look, my mom is not like yours. She isn't very good at showing or expressing affection, so she gives people things. If you think she's wound up tight you should have met my grandparents."

"I just don't feel like I deserve it." If she knew everything that I had done in the past week, she would have ripped the handbag out of my hand and possibly choked me with it. I thought back to the night before and choking the douche-bro and a smile crossed my face.

"There's that smile I love. Now put whatever it is that you women carry around in that purse and use it."

"Don't ever call it a purse in front of your mother. I've heard that lecture before." I admired the bag again. "It is just so fancy for carrying around duct tape, matches, tampons, gum, super glue . . . Oops! I've revealed too much secret women's' stuff."

He laughed. "I always knew you had a MacGyver starter kit in there. I'm super jealous."

"Well, maybe if you are a good boy your mother will give you a murse and you too can be prepared to disarm a nuclear weapon with a hair clip and breath mint."

"I have no interest in being a good boy tonight."

He took the bag out of my hand and tossed it onto the floor and kissed me. I was torn between checking on the bag to make sure it wasn't damaged and melting into the kiss. He picked me up and carried me to bed and for the next hour I completely forgot about the bag. There is nothing better than that feeling of falling on top of him naked and out of breath, completely satisfied and curling up beside him. We have had some of our closest talks in those moments before we both drift off to sleep.

That night as I lay there safe in his arms, I thought about how I could just confess everything to him in that moment and how maybe, just maybe, he would love me enough to stay. I tried to think of the right words to say and where to start but I knew I wouldn't do it. I was too much of a coward and too afraid of losing him.

CHAPTER 17

I WOKE UP THE NEXT morning and found ZuZu sleeping contently in the new Hermès. Carol would be horrified if she knew a cat was in such an expensive purse. She wasn't a cat person and I could tell she merely tolerated my cat stories. I took a picture of ZuZu with my phone to show Drew and shooed her out so I could transfer the contents of my old bag into it. I took both bags into the bathroom and shut the door so Drew wouldn't see the bag of drugs that I pulled out of my old purse. I secreted the drugs into an inside zippered pocket in the new handbag. The new bag had a long strap so I could drape it across my body. Based on the quality of the leather, I was pretty sure I could choke a bitch out with it, which is always a handy function, but one that is rarely advertised, particularly with a higher end bag. On the subway I clutched that bag to my chest and practically hissed at anyone who got close to me. I suspected that protecting this bag was going to exhaust the hell out of me.

I got to the office, turned on my computer and found my cheerful morning greeting from the dick from five floors up. As usual, I was not disappointed.

To: Allison Brown
From: Tristan-Malcolm Reynolds
Subject: Your lack of work ethic

I remained shocked at your lack of commitment to this project and the lack of both quantity and quality of your work product. How did you even get a job here? Oh, I remember. I suppose you must have some talents. They are just useless in an office setting.

TMR.

Weak sauce this morning Tristan-Malcolm. And I will have you know my "talents" have been used on Drew in this office building and they were far from useless. I resolved that in the very near future, Drew and I would further explore my "talents" in Tristan-Malcolm's office setting.

I looked at my precious red bag and twirled around in my seat looking for a safe place to store it so it wouldn't get Coke or coffee spilled on it or covered with crumbled Goldfish crackers or grease from the rare times I dared to make a run down to get lunch from a food truck. Not to mention, I didn't want any of the other employees to see it and create the impression that I got favorable treatment. Surely, getting assigned to work for Tristan-Malcolm should have dissuaded any of those beliefs, but I was always acutely aware of what they must think of me and how I got the job, as pointed out this morning by the ass face.

I cleared out the bottom filing cabinet drawer and stacked the contents in the corner of my cubicle. I had no idea what was even in the folders since I hadn't opened the filing cabinet in months. It is quite possible that I did have a work ethic deficiency. I went to the employee lounge and got a roll of paper towels and created a fluffy nest to cradle the bag. Yes, I realize I was treating the bag like a newborn kitten and I'm not in the least embarrassed about it. I shut the drawer and reluctantly returned to my dreary world. Squint. Type. Save.

It was 3:00 when I was finally briefly spared from monotony by Susan's sudden appearance at my cubicle.

"Timothy Olyphant." She said the name as if it would have some great meaning to me and then looked around to make sure no one was in the vicinity.

"He is very hot." I wasn't sure if that was the response she was looking for since I didn't know what the hell she was talking about.

Her eyes darted around furtively to again make sure no one was paying attention. She was acting completely over the top crazy but I appreciated the brief moment of excitement.

"He is Angela's current obsession." She leaned in conspiratorially and handed me a Post-it note with an address written on it.

"Oh my God! You did it!"

"Shhhh. Don't call attention to us."

I didn't dare make fun of her theatrics because she had just gotten me Elise's address and I might finally be able to get some information that would help me not get eaten alive.

I lowered my voice to a whisper. "You are the best. I don't know how to repay you."

"Oh, you know how. You just haven't done it yet."

She was clearly crazy, but I guess the heart wants what the heart wants. "I'm sure it will be easier for me to get what you want now that I have this information."

I wasn't going to make any promises I knew I couldn't keep, but I was willing to keep her hope alive for the moment. I was definitely going to stage an intervention for her after the stress of this merger was over and he was temporarily off my back.

It was Friday but I worked until 6:00. I texted Drew and told him I would be home by 8:00 for dinner and movie night with him and Max. I wanted to give Elise enough time to get home from her new job, assuming that she had one by now.

I GOT TO ELISE'S APARTMENT AND rang the doorbell. No response. I texted her that I was at her place and that I was going to wait for her to get home and that we needed to talk. I was leaning up against her door and as soon as I hit send, I could have sworn I heard the faint ding of a text notification come from inside. That bitch was inside and ignoring me. This shunning had gone way too far. I hadn't done anything to deserve this shitty ass treatment. My rage was once again triggered.

I started banging on the door with my fists and screaming. "Elise, you motherfucking bitch! Open this goddamn fucking door and talk to me right now!"

No response. I banged harder and continued screaming louder and more desperately. "Elise, this isn't fucking funny. I need your help. God damn it Elise!! Open the door or I swear I will kill you with my bare hands."

Suddenly, I heard the door across the hall open.

"Dear, I don't think she's inside."

I turned and saw an elderly lady peeping out at me. I felt like I had been caught looking at porn by my grandmother and neither of us knew how to respond. She was a tall woman whose height was betrayed by the hunch in her back. Her hair was white with a tint of pink in it that I wasn't sure was intentional or not. She wore a paisley muumuu and held a glass in her hand. I could smell the whiskey from across the hall.

"I'm sorry. I hope I didn't scare you. I just really needed to talk to my friend."

"I've lived in this city for forty years. A tiny slip of a girl like you yelling at a door certainly isn't going to scare me." She stood up as tall as she could and looked at me like I had just insulted her very core.

"You aren't the first person to be banging on that door yelling. Frankly, I'm just getting tired of hearing it. Of course, none of it's as bad as the yelling a few weeks ago when she was in a fight with her boyfriend."

"What? Elise didn't have a boyfriend." Elise "dated" i.e. screwed practically all of the young interns that came through the office, but she never had a serious boyfriend in the three years I had known her.

"She certainly did!" The old lady glared at me again for insulting her.

"You must not be very good friends with her if you didn't know about her boyfriend. Although, he wasn't much of a boy . . . more of an older man. Very handsome, tall, a kind of silver fox who most likely was born with a silver spoon in his mouth based on his clothes."

I was pretty sure this woman was off her rocker and getting Elise's love life mixed up with her soap operas because I couldn't possibly believe that Elise would date an older man, even if he was a sugar daddy.

"He was such a nice gentleman. He helped me carry my bags in one night." It looked like she was searching her memory for something. "Richard. That was his name. So very handsome and nice. I was really shocked when I heard them screaming at each other last week."

My mouth literally dropped open when I heard the name Richard and matched the elderly woman's description with Drew's father. Holy shit!

"Dear, you look all shook up. Do you need a drink? I've got whiskey."

I desperately needed a drink as my brain tried to comprehend the news. Unwillingly, an image of Elise and Richard having sex flashed through my head, which was quickly followed by the knowledge that I couldn't let Drew find out. Was Elise the reason his parents had been fighting? Did Elise quit because the affair ended? Had she disowned me as a friend because I was dating her ex-lover's son? I had so many questions. I needed to talk to her now more than ever.

"Thank you for the offer. But I think I should wait out here for her. I don't want to run the chance of missing her. I really need to talk to her."

"I hate to tell you this honey, but I don't think she's been home since the big fight last week. You might be sitting out there all night. Wait here."

She shut the door. I stood there not knowing what to do or what to think. I rang the doorbell. "Elise?" I didn't scream it this time. It was more of a desperate plea.

The old lady opened her door, walked across the hall, and handed me a large goblet full of ice and whiskey.

"If you are determined to wait for her. You might as well have a drink."

I took the glass and sipped from it. Momentarily forgetting the lesson from the night before about never drinking from a glass given to you by a stranger.

"Do you know what the fight was about?"

"I don't make it a habit to eavesdrop, young lady." Her tone made it clear I had insulted her again. "I think she must have left town not too long afterwards because I haven't seen her since. She always used to bring me her paper after she finished reading it so I could do the crossword and her paper has been out there all week not touched."

I looked across the hall and didn't see any evidence of the papers she was talking about. I started to think again that maybe this was all just a mistake and a combination of the lady drinking too much whiskey and watching too many soap operas. She picked up on my doubts.

"Well, of course they aren't out there now. I took them. I still like to do the crossword. It's not stealing if she would have given them to me eventually anyway. Right?" She looked a little bit embarrassed to have admitted to a crime as minor as it might have been.

"I agree. That's not stealing at all."

"Well, it's time for Wheel of Fortune. Just put my glass by my door when you are done with it." She closed her door. I stood there with the full goblet not sure what to do.

I sat on the floor, leaned against Elise's door, and drank the whiskey. I waited to see if maybe the old lady was wrong and Elise would show up and tell me that she was the building drunk. We would share a huge laugh over the thought of her sleeping with Richard and she would share with me all of the secrets of her crazy notes and the tapes. After half an hour I texted her again. Again, I heard the faint sound of the notification alert on the other side of the door. She obviously didn't take her phone with her wherever she went, so I had to finally accept that I was all kinds of fucked on the work front.

I placed the empty glass in front of the old lady's door and headed home. Home. Now, I had even more lies to keep from Drew. Fuck you, Elise.

I GOT A TEXT FROM Drew asking me to pick up wine for dinner so after I got off the subway, I headed straight to the corner bodega and made my way to the wine section. Not sure what Drew was cooking, I texted back, *Red or white?*

I stood in the aisle and waited for Drew to respond and watched a couple heading down the aisle, arm in arm, laughing and smiling. The woman looked like she was about six months pregnant and was beaming up at the man with a smile on her face that I knew well. She was ridiculously in love with him. I bet she wasn't burdened with keeping horrible secrets from the man she loved. The buzz of my phone alerted me that Drew had responded, and as I looked down to see his answer, I noticed the couple seemed to come to an abrupt stop and the man appeared to steer the woman back down the aisle away from me. Weird. I must really be giving off some "fuck my life" vibes that he didn't want to ruin their evening. I grabbed three bottles of red wine and headed to the front to pay.

As I walked past the next aisle over, I glanced down it and saw the couple again. He was standing close up behind her while she was reaching for something from the top shelf. Suddenly, it all came into focus. His hair was slicked back like it had been the first time I saw him at Starbucks, and not curly and hanging in his eyes gazing up at Max like it had been the second time I met him. Mr. Close-Stander was Connor and he had a pregnant girlfriend or wife. I almost dropped the bottles of wine on the ground as I realized why Connor had been so uncomfortable around me the night we met.

I wanted to run down the aisle and confront him but I stopped myself. I wasn't in the mood to make a scene. I'd been involved in way too many scenes lately. I was already reeling from the Elise/Richard revelation. I was on sensory overload. I was now going to have to lie to poor Max as well as Drew. Fuck everyone. I wasn't going to let Connor slide on this transgression, but his payback would have to wait.

I hurried to the counter and paid and then lurked outside around the corner and waited for the "happy couple" to come out. Five minutes later they appeared. Connor held the bag of groceries in one arm and she was snuggled up against his other arm as they walked away from me. I knew I should be getting home with the wine, but instead I decided to follow them.

Four blocks later they stopped in front of an apartment building. I grabbed my phone and took a picture of them walking past the door man holding hands. I wasn't planning on showing the picture to Max. I could never hurt him. I really wasn't sure what I was going to do, if anything, with this knowledge. As I walked home, five blocks back in the opposite direction from the bodega, I became hopeful that Max would find someone new soon and I could just let this knowledge slip into the forgotten abyss of shit I knew about. I had a lot of things I wanted to throw into that abyss.

I OPENED THE DOOR TO find Drew and Max in the kitchen dancing and jumping in the air like a couple of lunatics while listening to "Jump" by Kris Kross.

"Is this what you two do when I'm not here?"

They both smiled, nodded, and body slammed into each other while jumping. I saw a half empty bottle of Wild Turkey on the counter. Max motioned his hands upward, indicating that I needed to join in with the jumping. I put the bottles of wine on the counter and decided to play along. I quickly found it was quite cathartic to just jump up and down and listen to the music. The song ended and I was tempted to hit replay and just jump for the rest of the night.

"Hey, honey." Drew grabbed me and kissed me and I could smell the alcohol on his breath, but I could hardly judge since I had a large goblet of an old woman's whiskey while sitting on the floor of an apartment building.

Max grabbed a corkscrew from the utensil drawer and began opening one of the bottles of wine I had just put down.

"It doesn't look like you two even need wine." I nodded over to the Wild Turkey bottle.

Max responded, "Ally, honey, we are civilized people. We have wine with dinner. We just had a little pre-dinner shot or two to get me over being sad that I won't be seeing Connor again for a whole week."

I wasn't sure how long I would be able to hold my tongue so I grabbed a wine glass from the cabinet, held it out for Max to fill, and guzzled down a long drink to compose myself. Max continued talking.

"I'm not a fan of long distance, but at least he lives close enough so it is doable and he's not half-way across the world."

I should tell him that he's not even half-way across the damn city and that he's merely blocks away. I should tell him about the pregnant girl he is obviously living with and who does not appear to be his sister based on the kissing I had witnessed. I had so many secrets I should just unburden myself from keeping. Instead, I just drank and pushed them even further down into the abyss.

"So what does he do that allows him to come into the city so often?" I would just play along and continue to hope that Max would meet someone else and move on.

"He's in computer technology and development or something like that. I saw his badge and it looked like it was from a federal government agency, so I told him I would just assume he was a spy. I'm not exactly sure of the details, but it means he comes to the city a couple of times a month, so that is good enough for me."

Max was smiling and happy and I felt horrible. I drank more wine.

"So what has the sexy chef made for us tonight?" I had to change the subject before I cracked and showed Max the picture.

"I kept it simple tonight. Just a Caesar salad and lobster and seafood risotto. And of course, chocolate mousse parfait for my sweetheart."

"Aww. Thank you, sweetie." Max leaned over and kissed him on the cheek.

"Max, you know damn well I didn't mean you." Drew playfully pushed Max off of him.

I laughed. "Well, I don't care which of your sweethearts you made it for. It sounds amazing and the complete opposite of simple, so I can't wait to eat it."

I walked over to the cabinet to get the plates to set the table. I noticed that the junk mail was still stacked and unmoved from the top of Drew's legal books which included his criminal procedure book. I rationalized that maybe he just didn't need to look at the books and everything was on his computer, but again I couldn't help but think I wasn't the only one keeping secrets in this relationship. I resolved to just drink myself into a stupor. It seemed to be the theme of the evening for everyone. We devoured Drew's meal and quickly finished off the three bottles of wine by the end of *Galaxy Quest*. A unanimous decision to switch back to

Wild Turkey was made during the viewing of *The Hitchhikers Guide to the Galaxy*. It seemed no one wanted to remain the slightest bit sober for the evening. For a few hours I was able to forget all about work, the man in the park, the douche-bros, Elise and Richard, and Connor.

CHAPTER 18

WHEN I FINALLY WOKE UP, every muscle in my body ached and my head was pounding. Drew was not in the bed so he must have woken up feeling much better than me. I tried to sit up and my stomach protested and threatened to hurl. I laid back down and regretted all of the drinking from the night before and how I mixed wine and whiskey, which was never a good combination. I managed to roll over without vomiting to check the time on the clock. 11:30. I had six hours to rally and be presentable at the fundraiser. The thought of drinking again made my stomach pitch forward as if my body threatening a full revolt for even thinking about touching alcohol again ever in my life. I needed grease and soda if I was going to recover, but the thought of getting out of bed and standing up straight was not getting any traction with the rest of my body. I heard the apartment door opened and closed.

"Babe? You out there?" I called out and the words stung my raw throat.

Max stuck his head in the bedroom door. "First Drew calls me sweetie and now you call me babe. I feel so loved in this house."

I had forgotten that Max was so drunk he crashed on the couch.

"I went out and got you something that will help. Wait here."

My body was definitely up to the task of waiting. That was about the only thing it was willing to do. Max returned with a bed tray that held a small vase with a rose, a plate with hash browns, a sausage biscuit and a large fountain soda. I was both grateful and puzzled.

"I don't remember us owning a bed tray."

"Oh, you didn't. I had to go buy it and the vase, and the rose, when I went to get breakfast. Drew told me to make sure you had some grease so you could rally."

"So, you had to buy a breakfast tray?" I sat up against my stomach's various protests and took a bite of the biscuit.

"You know if I'm going to do something, I'm going to go full out and do it the right way. And now, there's no excuse for Drew to not bring you breakfast in bed."

Max settled in on the bed next to me.

"That's true. And I really do appreciate it. Where is Drew?"

Max rolled his eyes. "He had to go meet his mother and help with last minute things for the fundraiser. I can't believe that after all these years he still basically asks how high whenever that woman asks him to jump and do something."

I had never heard Max talk about Drew's relationship with his mother in such a negative tone before.

"Well, she is his mother."

"I guess. As much as a barracuda can be a mother."

I laughed but immediately felt guilty as I looked into the walk-in closet filled with clothes she had picked out and bought for me and the beautiful red bag that was down the hall in the kitchen.

"Well, she's very nice to me. Did you see that bag she gave me?"

"That thing is gorgeous. She's obviously trying to buy some favor with that gift. Do you even know how much it sells for?"

"Not really. I know it's probably very expensive . . ." I saw him open his mouth probably to tell me the exact amount and held my hand up to stop him.

"Please don't tell me. I already have enough anxiety carrying it."

"Well, don't be surprised if she doesn't expect something in return. That's how she operates."

"I never knew you felt this way about her."

"Ehh!" He shrugged his shoulders. "She's the mother of my best friend. I deal with it and try to keep my distance."

"So, that's why you never come to the parties at their house. I'm guessing you aren't going tonight?"

"I was invited. I haven't decided. I couldn't give a shit whether Senator Davis gets re-elected or not."

"It's not like I care either. But I would love it if you would go so I can have an additional safe harbor. I suspect my new boss will be there to suck up to Drew's dad, and to say that he hates me is an understatement."

"Oh come on. He can't be that bad."

"He is the worst. Just between you and me . . . on the first day I worked for him, he scared me so much that I peed myself."

Max threw back his head and howled with laughter. "Well damn, now I have to go because I have to meet the man behind that story."

I laughed. "Please don't tell Drew. I would be mortified."

"I would never. I can't promise I won't tell Connor though."

There it was. I could drink enough to forget about it for one night but it wasn't going to go away.

"So, you two are getting serious?" I pulled the flower out of the vase and smelled it.

"It's just been a week but I do really like him."

He had the sweetest smile and blushed a little and I knew immediately I wouldn't be the one who crushed that for him. I was going to stay out of this one. Maybe the pregnant girl was his sister? That didn't explain the lying about living in Connecticut or the kissing but I was just going to have to let this one go. I had enough shit to process and deal with at the moment.

I stayed in bed for the rest of the day and alternately napped and plotted out when to make my move on Rena and what exactly I would do. I decided that the Sunday matinee performance would be the best course of action since it would be too hard to get away from the dick face at work during the day and slip the drugs to Rena. I could tell Drew I was meeting Sarah for drinks for a much needed girls' night after dealing with the stuffy fundraiser. That was certainly plausible.

If I was lucky, Max would show up to the fundraiser and he and Drew would go out for drinks, which would make it easier to slip into the hotel unnoticed. From there it was simply a matter of getting invited into Rena's room for a drink, which after our last encounter, I imagined would be easily accomplished. Then I drug Rena. Rena sleeps through the matinee and Sarah gets her moment to shine. It all seemed pretty simple the more I thought it through. If I timed it right, Rena would be drunk as hell before I even got there so it should be a piece of cake compared to taking down the two douchebags. I don't like to brag, but that was pretty boss that I pulled that last minute plan off without a hitch, at Hitches no less. Yeah, I admit that was lame. I can hear you thinking that it is no wonder my comedy career took a dive. Screw you.

The grease, more napping and a long, hot shower made me feel human enough to get through the evening. I went to the Carol-approved section of my closet and pulled out a black strapless dress and a pair of gold strappy high heels. With my hair pulled up and the small diamond stud earrings with matching dainty pendant necklace, I could easily pass for a refined socialite's wife, or at least a very high-priced hooker. It could really go either way.

I pulled out a small gold clutch to carry and slipped the bag of drugs into the small zipper compartment. Adding drugs to my purse probably tipped the scales from socialite over to high-priced hooker. Or maybe not. Maybe the socialites really liked to party and they snuck off to the bathroom to do blow and other drugs to make banging their rich but boorish husbands more tolerable. If I didn't realize that Uncle Benji owned my favorite gossip site, who knows what else I might be missing when I zoned out and spent the entire evening huddled by the shrimp display, hoping no one was keeping count of my intake of shellfish and champagne.

CHAPTER 19

EVERY TIME I STEPPED INTO Carol and Richard's penthouse in the Upper East Side historic district, I felt like the country bumpkin version of Bette Midler and Lily Tomlin in the movie *Big Business*. Even after three years of dating Drew and wearing the clothes picked out by Carol, I always became very self-conscious of my modest, middle class roots and am still irrationally afraid that the snotty saleslady from *Pretty Woman* will show up and announce that I was not allowed to be there.

The first time Drew brought me to his parents' home was the first time I truly appreciated how rich they actually were and what that meant for my relationship with him. I had to fight my initial instinct to preemptively break up with him to spare myself the embarrassment of his parents threatening to disown him for slumming it with the likes of me.

The expansive penthouse took up the entire top two floors of the prewar building and had a large outside terrace where a cellist, violinist and a harpist were playing classical music under the strings of twinkling lights, which were tastefully strewn throughout the potted trees and shrubbery. The terrace was a giant outdoor garden and was the only place in the house where I actually felt comfortable. Large outdoor heaters were strategically placed around the terrace to take the chill off the evening.

There were no political signs or badges or any outward indications that a political fundraiser was taking place or identified the guest of honor. I suspected large checks were being discreetly written and pressed into someone's hand along with a subtle indication of the special interests of each donor. Drew guided me over to his mother who was standing with a short plump woman who I was pretty sure I had met before but I had forgotten her name. I was equally as certain that she had forgotten mine, so I was surprised when she reached for my hand and seemed to recognize me.

"Allison, so very nice to see you again. I'm so glad you were able to make it this evening."

Luckily, Drew came to my rescue. "Senator Davis. It is our pleasure. You know you have our full support."

I squeezed his hand to thank him and he smiled at me. I wondered if Drew had discreetly handed off a check on our behalf.

"Yes, Senator Davis. I am so honored to be here. You are an inspiration."

I had absolutely no idea if Senator Davis had ever done anything at all which would be considered inspirational. In less than two minutes, I had already reached the limit of my party-approved small talk on the subject of politics. I should have at least Googled the woman before coming to a fundraiser on her behalf. Really, I am surprised Drew takes me anywhere. Thankfully, a man appeared at the senator's side who looking like he wanted to engage in what I'm sure was a conversation of some great importance, at least in his mind. I politely excused myself to get a drink. I thought Drew would follow but he stayed behind to listen, so I was left flying solo.

I found a woman circulating the room with a tray of champagne and grabbed a glass. I was hesitant to return back to Drew's side and be forced to fake my way through any further conversation with the senator. I saw Richard off in a corner talking with Uncle Benji and decided to take refuge at their side and not so subtly try to find out some celebrity gossip. I started to make my approach when I had the unpleasant visual of Richard and Elise naked. Nope. I wasn't ready to engage in small talk with Richard with that image in my head. Plus, the two men looked tense and at odds with each other.

I was turning to seek solitude at the shrimp station when I felt a huge disturbance in the force. OK fine, it was really just the fine baby hairs on my neck that prickle when they sense danger. Unfortunately, I didn't heed the warning because I turned too fast, bumped into Tristan-Malcolm who was standing behind me, and spilled champagne on his tie.

He let out an exacerbated sigh upon identifying me as the culprit. "Why am I not surprised? I would think Drew would at least be smart enough to keep you on a short leash out in public."

I wanted to tell him to fuck off and then run and hide in a guest room for the rest of the night. Instead, I heard myself say, "We prefer to keep our leash usage in the privacy of our bedroom, thank you very much."

He sneered down at me and was momentarily rendered as startled and speechless at my brazenness as I was at myself. I had no idea why I again inappropriately blurted out a reference to my sex life. I wasn't doing myself any favors whenever I opened my mouth.

"Shouldn't you be at home working? God knows you don't seem to be getting anywhere on the simple project I gave you."

My fairy godmother with the tray of champagne circled by so I exchanged my empty glass of champagne for a full one. I looked over in Drew's direction to invoke our standard "save me" gesture, but his back was turned to me as he continued to talk to his mother and the senator.

"Are you looking for your boyfriend to come save you, Princess? Whatever would you do without him?"

Oh, just kill a man and drug and scare the shit out of two douchebags. I gained confidence from those memories and the knowledge that we were in the home of my boyfriend's parents, as surreal and unlikely as it seemed.

"I think we both know there hasn't been a damn thing in those notes that are important or in any way helpful in relation to this merger. You just like to throw your weight around and try to intimidate people by growling all the time and twirling your mustache like you're a Bond villain. I'm not even an attorney and even I know that cases about antitrust and debt collection and a bunch of initials and numbers have absolutely nothing to do with Benjamin Mars spending twenty million dollars to purchase a company with absolutely no media presence just for some special technology Richard says Rusk developed. You are just using those damn notebooks to be a bully."

I half expected him to drag me off by my hair someplace secluded and turn me into dinner after I finished my unexpectedly brave tirade. Instead, he seemed more stunned than angry at my words. He opened his mouth to respond but was interrupted by Max arriving at my side.

"Now I remember why I don't come to these events. Could this party be any duller?" He looked up at Tristan-Malcolm and extended his hand, "Hello, I'm Max. Drew's friend."

Tristan-Malcolm looked him up and down, took one last look at me, and then promptly turned and walked away. Max looked quizzically at me.

"That's the infamous new boss." I explained.

"Ohhh. Well, he's rude." We both watched him cross the room towards Richard. "Ruggedly sexy. But rude."

"Seriously? I don't know what is wrong with you or Susan but he is not ruggedly sexy. And I'm probably about to get fired."

"You couldn't be more wrong about both. He is sexy and there is no way in hell Richard fires you."

Drew, who had finally left the senator's side, joined us. "I'm sorry. What did I miss?"

"Just an argument over the degree of sexiness of Ally's new boss and whether or not your dad is going to fire her."

Drew laughed. "I'm guessing you are the one arguing in favor of sexy?"

He turned to me and cupped my chin in his hand, "Babe, I've got your back on the not sexy argument and you know there is no way my dad is going to fire you. He loves you. Maybe he will finally reassign you to work with a non-asshole, but hopefully also one who is as equally as not sexy as the two-named ass face."

He kissed my forehead. Out of the corner of my eye I saw Tristan-Malcolm standing in the corner of the room staring at me.

"Come on. Let's go over and talk to dad and Uncle Benji and you will see that everything is just fine."

The three of us made our way slowly over to Richard and Uncle Benji. They still looked to be in the middle of a serious discussion that I would not have dared to interrupt on my own. Uncle Benji said a polite hello and quickly excused himself. I guess I would have to wait until later to get some inside celebrity scoop.

"Max! Ally!" Richard shook Max's hand and hugged me and planted a kiss on my cheek. I tried not to think about him kissing Elise. Too late. Mental image activated. Gross. "You look as fabulous as always."

"Thank you. You know I owe it all to your wife's good taste."

"Not true at all." He leaned over in a conspiratorial whisper and added, "She just likes to think she's in charge but that's not always the case."

"Better not let her hear you say that, Dad."

"Unlike most people in this room, I've never been scared of her." He looked over in his wife's direction where she was still engaged in conversation with the senator and some new donor who was trying to buy a little slice of power.

"Maybe you should be." Drew's voice sounded a bit ominous and the whole conversation was making me uneasy. His father ignored him and turned his attention back to me.

"So, how are you holding up with Tristan-Malcolm? He hasn't made any complaints so you two seem to be faring well."

I found that hard to believe, especially after I saw him seek Richard out just after our last hasty exchange. I scanned the room and found Tristan-Malcolm leaning against the wall across the room still staring at me. I made sure he saw me. I obnoxiously smiled at him and waived at him. I waited for his trademark sneer of disapproval to glare back at me but he didn't flinch. I turned back to Richard.

"Yeah, it is going much better than I thought it would. I do miss Elise though. I keep sending her texts but she never responds."

I watched Richard's face for any flicker of guilt but his face retained the same soft and easy going smile and the charming twinkle in his eyes. Drew seemed to shift uncomfortably on his feet. Did he know about his father's affair?

"I think we were all startled by her abrupt disappearing act, but we will forge ahead without her. If there is anything I have learned over all these years, it is to never get too attached. Now if you'll excuse me, I should probably go chat with the senator before I get accused of being dilatory in my hosting responsibilities."

He winked at me before turning to start his slow winding path across the room, stopping along the way to slap backs and shake hands with everyone he passed.

"Damn Drew, you could have at least warned us your parents had their daggers pointed at each other before we came." Max grabbed a glass of champagne off the passing tray and handed me one and then grabbed one for himself and Drew.

"Then you would have both feigned ill and I would have been here fending for myself. Isn't family fun?" Drew clinked his glass against both of ours and took a sip.

"I wouldn't know. My parents spend all their time bouncing between Aspen and Saint-Tropez. Not that I'm complaining."

"Well, my parents are probably sitting on the couch watching HGTV trying to come up with some new project for the house, or, if my dad has fallen asleep, then my mom is watching the jewelry channel. She's convinced that this one host is selling stolen vintage jewelry out of a warehouse. She calls me sometimes to turn it on so I can help her look for clues and honestly, I can't say that she is wrong."

My stomach started to growl and I realized I was going to need something to eat if I was going to continue drinking and carry out my plans for later that night. "I'm going to find the shrimp."

"Don't stay there all evening like you did the last time." Drew kissed my forehead.

I circled around the two rooms where most of the guests were located and finally found the food outside on the far end of the terrace. There was no one at the buffet table. I rarely saw people eating at these parties. I stacked a plate with a socially unacceptable amount of mini beef wellingtons, baby quiche, and shrimp. It was more food than all of the women combined at this party would eat. I secreted myself behind a cluster of large space heaters and some topiary trees. There was a concrete bench behind them where no one could see me eat with abandon and I had no fear of judgment. It must be unbearable to have such staunch social graces that you can't even enjoy the food at a party.

I was half way through my pile of bliss when I heard two people begin talking in hushed tones on the other side of the heaters and topiary. They were unaware of my face-stuffing presence.

"Smile and nod your head, people are watching." Carol's voice was low but definitely stern and angry. "Do you have the situation under control?"

"I'm working on it. Once the merger is done it should be smooth sailing." Uncle Benji's voice was low and gravely.

"There is a difference between should be and will be Benjamin. The senator needs to know that this problem has been neutralized."

"Tell Birdie that I'm handling it and for her to cool her damn jets. There isn't going to be a problem."

Shit! I had absolutely no idea what they were talking about but this was not something I should be hearing. I had resolved to stop listening in on other people's conversations. Damn it! Carol would be furious if she knew I was eavesdropping. I considered putting my fingers in my ears to block it all out. I didn't want to know anymore of Drew's family secrets. First, Richard and Elise and now whatever this was with Uncle Benji and Carol. Instead, I sat as still as possible and hoped they would stop talking soon and leave without finding me.

"That's what you said before and we did have a problem. A problem I had to resolve. I expect you to take care of this one. If not, I will handle it myself. I'll be damned if your paranoid idiocy is going to ruin everything."

"Carol, I hope the smile on my face right now is big enough for you. You can go fuck yourself. You and Richard would be nothing without me."

Carol snorted derisively. "Maybe that is true of Richard, but not me. Don't even think of screwing with me."

I heard the click-clack of her heels on the pavement as she walked away. I sat still and waited until I heard the sound of his steps retreat. I wasn't sure if they were still on the terrace so I didn't dare move from my spot.

I finished eating the food while wishing I was at home on the couch watching the jewelry channel over the phone with my mom looking for signs of a criminal enterprise instead of overhearing a vaguely sinister conversation involving the love of my life's mother. I had always only half believed that Carol could be threatening and was not to be fucked with because I only saw her as a benevolent shopping partner. Now? Now, I was legitimately convinced that at some point she would be offering me a cash payout to stop dating her son before his political career got sullied by my uncouth background and behavior. If she were to find out what I had done in the park? What I had done with the two douche-bros? She would destroy me. I got lost playing out all the horrible scenarios in my head.

"Look at you." I jumped and dropped a mini-quiche on the ground when I heard the voice behind me. I knew immediately who it was and wished the night would just end. "Hiding and shoveling food in your face. You really can't be taken out in public"

I stood up and turned to face the sneer. I was out of fucks to give and I wasn't going to endure any more insults.

"I'm not in the mood. You aren't my boss tonight. You can say whatever you want to him but we both know that Richard is not going to fire me. So, take your sneer and find another target."

"I wouldn't be so sure about that if I were you. In this world . . ." He gestured at the grandiose surroundings. ". . . people are expendable. Easily replaced. Whatever hold you have over their son doesn't hold a candle to the power and money they hold over him. They always end up picking power, money, and family."

"Drew's different." I said it more to convince myself since Tristan-Malcolm was giving voice to the fears that were already running through my head.

"You keep telling yourself that if it helps you sleep better at night in the bed you don't own and in the clothes you didn't buy. For your sake, I hope you have a backup plan."

A hand clasped onto his shoulder. Finally, a friendly face appeared in the form of Max.

"Hey, I finally found the place where all the cool kids are hanging out." He winked at me and then looked at Tristan-Malcolm. "I didn't get your name earlier?"

Tristan-Malcolm didn't remove his stare from me. He removed Max's hand from his shoulder. "That's right, you didn't." He turned and walked off. Max was left with a bewildered look on his face after being snubbed for the second time.

"Whoa! What is up that guy's ass? Seriously? You have to deal with that on a daily basis? That sucks."

"Yep. It sure does."

I wanted to tell him that everything sucked. I wanted to tell someone all the shit that had happened, everything I had learned and overheard but I couldn't tell him. He was Drew's best friend. Plus, I wasn't even sure what it all meant. Sarah. At least I could talk to Sarah about the stuff with Drew's parents. She had heard some conversation with a "Burt" on the tapes. Maybe it was Birdie. I remembered her saying that name just before I dropped to the ground in the park. Thinking of Sarah reminded me of my plans with Rena. I could at least salvage this night and do something good for Sarah.

Max must have been reading my mind. "Hey, let's go find Drew and blow this party for something fun before you go meet Sarah for girls' night."

"Good plan." I wrapped my arm in his and we went to find Drew. We passed Tristan-Malcolm on the way out. "So, you still think he is sexy?"

"Would you think less of me if I said yes?" Max grinned.

"Probably." I shook my head and rolled my eyes at him.

We found Drew engrossed in a conversation with his mother and the senator again. I suspected that they were not talking about Uncle Benji's request that the senator chill out while he handled things. Uncle Benji seemed to have left the party, so I missed my chance to ask him all of my burning gossip questions on the off chance he was kept in the loop of all the celebrity sex and drug scandals. It was probably for the best that I hadn't asked since I now knew there was some kind of political scandal brewing. You would never have guessed it though based on how at ease and poised both Carol and the senator appeared.

As we approached, the senator was pulled away by another guest. Thank God. Trying to keep myself composed in front of important people was becoming more difficult by the minute. I didn't trust myself not to randomly blurt the word antitrust in front of her or call her Birdie.

"I found her. You were right, Drew. She was hiding out by the buffet table." Max was all smiles.

Carol seemed to stiffen a bit upon hearing this news and I tried my best not to look guilty.

"He's joking! I wasn't there the whole time. I went to the bathroom first and then got cornered by some boring old man who I've never met who was sure I was his friend's daughter." I was nervously rambling but couldn't stop myself.

"He did catch me piling my plate full though." Please let that be enough to convince Carol that I was nowhere near the vicinity during her conversation with Uncle Benji.

Carol seemed to relax a bit but she kept her eyes trained on me. "Thank goodness someone is enjoying the food. I was out on the terrace earlier and didn't see a soul by the table."

"There was no one out there when I went either. Probably because it's so chilly. I was just out there long enough to grab a few things on my plate before Max found me."

I needed to shut my mouth. I was starting to make myself sound guilty the longer I talked. Max looked at me a bit confused but decided to let the lie go unchecked.

"Carol, as always, it's been a lovely evening." Max leaned in for a chaste kiss on the cheek.

"I'm delighted you came this evening. I know this isn't your typical scene but we will be counting on you to show up regularly when Drew is the guest of honor and running for election. It won't be long now."

Drew kept his head down and avoided eye contact with both Max and me.

"Absolutely. I wouldn't miss it for the world."

"Take care darlings." Carol air kissed me and Drew. "Allison, I do hope you enjoyed the food."

I nodded and grabbed Drew's arm, wanting to get as far away from Carol's piercing glare as possible. She couldn't know I overheard. Could she? I wasn't even sure what it was that I overheard or what any of it meant. Surely she knew I wasn't a threat. I loved her son. I was her life-sized Barbie that she got to dress and try to mold into an acceptable partner for him and the grand political career she had all mapped out. But what if she thought I had overheard the conversation? Worse yet, what if she was stepping up the pace for Drew's political career and had decided I was not an acceptable partner. I looked up at my smiling, gorgeous, loving, and generous boyfriend and heard Tristan-Malcolm's warning about back-up plans.

CHAPTER 20

THE THREE OF US ENDED up at a small neighborhood bar close to home. I limited myself to just one drink. I needed to keep a level head if I was going to carry through with my plan. Twice I considered backing out and just staying in the comfortable presence of Drew and Max. I could have told them Sarah texted and cancelled our girls' night, but then I thought of Sarah and how fabulous she would be on stage. This was a rare opportunity and I could help her. She never needed to know what I did. I had already bought a seat in the upper balcony. I didn't want her to see me or know I was there because I wouldn't be able to explain how or why I had suddenly decided to go to a Sunday afternoon matinee. I would never be able to tell her that I saw her and she had killed it, but I would know.

I was coming back from the bathroom and getting ready to make my exit when I overheard Max say, "You should tell her."

"No. I'm not ready yet."

"She should know."

I felt my heart sink into my stomach and the room started to spin. He was leaving me. Tristan-Malcolm had been right. I stumbled and grabbed the stool behind Drew and he turned around startled.

"Honey, are you OK?"

"I'm fine," I lied. He still called me honey. Everything was fine. Everything had to be fine. I was just letting that asshole get into my head. That is exactly what he wanted to do.

"Are you sure? Maybe you should just have Sarah meet us here?"

"I'm fine." If I kept saying it then I might believe it. Maybe they were talking about something he needed to tell his mother. That is probably what it was about.

"If I didn't know that you could kick someone's ass with a magazine I wouldn't let you go out by yourself this late at night. I worry about you, honey."

He called me honey again. Everything was fine. He still loved me. At least he did for now.

"I love that you worry about me, babe. I will see you later."

He pulled me in close and kissed me. "I will be eagerly waiting for you naked in bed."

"Eww and ick. I'm sitting right here, you two." Max scrunched his face up in mock disapproval.

"We both know you will be fast asleep and snoring."

"You know how to wake me up." He grabbed my hand and put it on his cock. "Promise to wake me up." He smiled and kissed me.

The desire in his kiss reassured me there was nothing amiss between the two of us. "I promise."

IT WAS JUST AFTER MIDNIGHT when the cab pulled up to The Boutique. I glanced through the glass doors and didn't recognize the employee at the front desk, but I still put on my fake glasses and pulled a scarf out of my clutch and wrapped it around my hair. I waited until a group of tourists returned and fell in behind them so I could blend in with a crowd and not stick out. I was more nervous than I had been the other night with the two douche-bros who could have actually hurt me. This should be a cake walk so I couldn't explain my nerves. I got off the elevator at the twentieth floor and took off the glasses and the scarf and returned them to the clutch. I double checked the zipped pocket to make sure the bag of drugs was still there. I'm not sure where I thought they would have gone, but I felt the need for a calming ritual. There was already a small array of mini-bar trash clustered in the hallway. I gathered myself together mentally and lightly knocked on the door.

I didn't hear anything on the other side of the door. Maybe I was too late and she was already passed out. I knocked lightly again and waited. Still no answer. Shit. Maybe she hadn't got back to the room yet and the trash was from earlier in the afternoon. I doubted that Max would not have his staff regularly cleaning up her mess so I knocked a little louder.

This time I heard, "Damn it, I'm coming for Christ's sake." Followed by the sound of the security chain being removed. "I don't remember ordering room service."

The door opened and she was standing in front of me wet from the shower and wrapped in a towel. She looked me up and down.

"I definitely don't remember ordering you, but you'll do." A mischievous smile spread across her face and she let the towel drop to the floor.

Her lack of boundaries should have made me more confident in my plan but instead an alarm in my head was telling me to turn back and go home. I took in the view in front of me. Her hair was wet, her make-up removed and water trailed down her breasts. She looked more beautiful than she had the other night. The absence of heavy make-up gave her a softer appearance which humanized her. I couldn't stop staring at her and she reveled in it. I found myself speechless and unable to move and she made no effort to break the moment. Her eyes suddenly lit up with recognition.

"I remember you from last week."

Shit. Which me did she remember? Did she remember me from humiliating me in front of everyone? If so, this plan was going to derail fast. Or did she remember our moment in the hallway? I worried that a replay of that moment was also going to derail my plan. It had been part of my plan to seduce her enough to get the drugs in her drink but not now. Suddenly, I found myself unwilling to go that route.

"I thought you had been just a figment of my imagination when you didn't come back. Abigail? Right?"

She stepped over the towel on the floor and came towards me. I braced myself for her kiss. Her mouth was warm and caressing. It was a sensual kiss but one that I didn't want and couldn't return. I only wanted Drew. My mind kept replaying the overheard snippet of conversation between him and Max. I faked my way through the kiss. I pulled away. She looked hurt and vulnerable. Maybe she wasn't such a horrible person. Was I making a mistake? No. This was for Sarah. I steeled myself.

"So, are you going to invite me in and offer me a drink?" I had to try to take control of this situation.

"Sure. We can have a drink. I hope that is not all you want."

She walked over to the mini bar and pulled out two full size bottles of Veuve Clicquot. "I finally got that dumb ass of an owner to put grown up-sized bottles in the fridge."

She started to open the first bottle.

"I thought for sure he would pick up on my irritation when I brained one of his staff with a small bottle but nope, I had to hit another dumb ass before he finally got a clue. His ignorant ass doesn't know what the fuck he's doing. I'd have him fired by now if his Daddy didn't own the hotel."

Oh, she sure as hell did not just insult my Max? I shook off all the guilt and doubt I had in my head as I remembered that she was a wretched human being. I had been temporarily disarmed by what I had perceived as vulnerability and humanity, but now that faulty illusion was gone so I could get back on track.

She poured two glasses. She held one out to me and waved it in my direction. "You don't get this until your dress comes off. My room. My rules."

She was going to be much more difficult than the douche-bros.

"And if I say no?"

"No one says no to me."

"Maybe they should."

"You know where the door is if you are going to be a frigid bitch." She sneered and then thought better of it and softened her voice. "I'm pretty sure you came here to screw me, so stop acting coy."

I slowly started to unzip my dress. "I came here to do a lot more than that." She obviously didn't hear the warning tone in my voice since it seemed to please her. She lounged on the settee and watched me undress.

"Keep your heels on." She ordered from across the room. "Everything off but the heels."

I complied. I felt exposed and uncomfortable standing naked before the woman who I had grown up idolizing and fantasizing about being one day. I was the one who was supposed to be in control this evening and so far, I was nowhere close to achieving my goal.

She held up a glass of champagne and as I walked over to retrieve it she poured the contents of the glass on her breasts, trickling a trail down her stomach and between her legs. "Come and get it, love."

Damn. I needed a new plan. This night was not going the way I had planned. I needed to think. I really should have thought this through and come prepared with a bottle that already had the drugs in it. If I was going to spike her drink, then I needed her to drink out of an actual glass. We couldn't just lick champagne off each other all night, which appeared to be her plan.

How in the hell was I going to drug her? A Hail Mary plan slowly formed in my head. If it didn't work, then I was pretty much screwed, in more ways than I had planned.

I ignored the champagne dripping down her body. "So, have you ever tried Special K before?"

She screeched and I couldn't tell if it was an excited screech or whether she was about to call security. "Oh my God! Do you have some?"

I nodded my head and looked over at my clutch.

"Give it to me! I haven't had any Kit-Kat in ages."

I picked up my clutch and fished out the plastic baggie and she quickly snatched it out of my hands and stared at it almost lovingly. Great. Now I was enabling an addict. I was a horrible person. I tried to rationalize that I was not as horrible as her, but as far as I knew she hadn't killed anyone. She had insulted two of my closest friends and pretty much harassed every person who crossed her path. But still, I was giving drugs to a known addict. I was having second thoughts, third thoughts, and fourth thoughts about the whole plan. I could grab the drugs and my clothes and just leave. It wasn't too late.

"You know what. This probably isn't a good idea." I looked over at the clock. "You have a noon matinee tomorrow."

"Fuck the matinee. The tourists that come to a Sunday matinee deserve to see my understudy." She rolled her eyes. "Actually, no one probably deserves to be subjected to my understudy. She's the worst. But they will get a refund. What the hell do I care?"

And just like that my rage button was activated. For her sake, I hoped she didn't have any belts in the room. She already had a trail of the powder on the glass table beside the settee and snorted it up. Damn. I didn't even know you could snort the shit or much less how she did it so fast. I guess that was why she was the professional drug user and I was the girl who can't even figure out how to use Afrin nasal spray when I have a cold.

"I think Sarah is good." I probably shouldn't have said that.

"Who is Sarah?"

She poured out another trail of the powder and gestured over to me. Oh, hell to the no. That is not going to happen. "I'm going to run to the restroom. You do that one. I'll catch up when I get back."

"We are going to have so much fun when this kicks in." She smacked my ass as I walked past her. She was snorting up the second line when I shut the bathroom door. I locked the door. Locking myself in bathrooms seemed to be my new hobby now.

"There's not going to be any left for you if you don't hurry up." I heard her yell from the room.

I started to panic. What had I done? What if she overdosed and died? Was there enough powder in the bag for an overdose? My phone was out in my clutch so I couldn't Google it. This was not the way the evening was supposed to go. What if someone saw me come into her room? What if Drew found out? Or Sarah? Or Max? If she died in this hotel it could ruin Max. If she died, my body count would go up. Who am I that I now have a body count?

"What is taking you so long? You aren't taking a dump are you? If you are, you better shower before you come back out."

Oh dear God. I can't believe I ever idolized this person. She was literally the worst. I didn't want her to die but I was definitely deleting her songs off my iPod.

"I'm doing the last line. You take a dump you lose. I can't believe you are shitting in my bathroom. That is so disgusting."

It seemed it was going to take a while for the drugs to kick in so I turned the shower on. What did I care if she thought I took a dump? Everyone poops. I sat naked on the toilet, not pooping, and let the shower run. I wasn't sure how I thought the night would go down but this was certainly not it. I was trapped and naked in a bathroom trying to avoid the sexual advances of the person I gave date rape drugs. I would have laughed at the absurdity of it all except for the fact that I was worried she was going to die. I waited for what seemed like an eternity.

By the time I went back into the room, Rena was out of it on the settee, singing a song to herself and smiling. She didn't seem to notice that I was in the room. I got dressed and wiped down anything I had touched.

I heard her mumble, "My sweet, sweet Abigail. So beautiful." Then she continued singing one of her own songs, one of her own love ballads.

I leaned down and whispered in her ear, "Your sweet, sweet Abigail thinks that you are a terrible person." I started to get up and leave but then changed my mind and continued to hiss in her ear.

"You don't have to be so nasty to everyone around you. The staff here is just trying to do their job. Sarah and the rest of the cast are doing a great job and not only can you not acknowledge that, but you insult them repeatedly and for no reason. Have you ever considered that if you were nicer, then maybe you would have friends? Maybe you wouldn't be drinking alone in your room after the show every night. You used to have everything in the world at your fingertips. Millions of girls around the world wanted to be you or be your best friend. I was one of those girls. Not anymore. No one wants to be you or be your friend anymore because you are a horrible excuse of a human being."

She continued singing, unfazed by my words. I am sure I wasn't the first to tell her she was a terrible person and I was certainly not going to be the last.

"I hate you, but please don't die," I whispered before I left the room. As the door closed and locked behind me there was no turning back. There was nothing I could do if she overdosed. I couldn't call down to the front desk and tell them because I would risk being identified. I had made the decision to leave her there. I rationalized that she was the one who chose to do all of the drugs, but I couldn't rationalize away the guilt that I was the one who gave them to her. That was on me.

CHAPTER 21

IT WAS PAST THREE O'CLOCK when I finally got home and crawled into bed with Drew. He was sleeping so soundly that I didn't want to wake him up, but I had promised him. I slid my hand underneath the covers and gently took hold of his cock and started to slowly stroke it. I felt it harden and then I heard a murmur from his side of the bed. He rolled over towards me. I tightened my grip and found a slow and steady rhythm.

"God babe, I love it when you wake me up." He leaned in and kissed me.

"I'm glad, because I love waking you up."

He rolled over on top of me and mounted me and all thoughts of Rena left my mind.

The next morning, I found a note from him on the kitchen counter with a stack of freshly baked blueberry muffins letting me know he was going to be at the library studying all day. I again convinced myself the stack of text books that were still collecting dust on the kitchen counter must not be relevant to what he was studying. Maybe they were books from his last semester he hadn't recycled yet. We didn't exactly have a formal library and neither of us were the tidiest of people. The good news was that I could go watch Sarah in the play and not have to lie about where I was going. I still hated to lie to him, so every lie I didn't have to tell him felt like a win to me.

I got dressed and dumped the contents of my clutch from the evening before on the bed to transfer everything back over to the beautiful red designer bag that I definitely did not deserve. The cats jumped on the bed and decided to help. The two of them slowly and deliberately batted tubes of lip gloss off the bed, followed by the fake purple glasses. They began wrestling for possession of the scarf, each trying to drag off their end in opposite directions.

"I don't have any idea what I'm doing any more or what kind of a monster I'm becoming, but at least you girls still love me. Right?" They were too busy with their game of tug of war to pay attention and I wasn't saying any buzz words that interested them like "treats" or "wet food," but I kept talking to them. Maybe if I said the words out loud they would stop thundering through my head all the time.

"I killed a man in the park. I didn't think I could get any lower than that, but at least I could tell myself it was an accident. Drugging those two assholes and choking the one out with the other's belt. That was definitely not an accident."

I sat down on the bed and petted Daisy, who had curled up on her end of the scarf, effectively ending the game of tug of war with the heft of her body. ZuZu was oblivious to the insurmountable obstacle and continued to attempt to pull the scarf in the opposite direction.

"I do at least think what I did was necessary for the good of society, or at least any future poor unsuspecting women, but it was definitely not how a normal person would have handled it. A normal person would have gone to the cops. I doubt the cops would have done anything though, just based on what I had heard. And I don't really want to be anywhere near the cops after the whole park incident. I'm definitely not a normal person anymore. I am afraid I'm turning into a monster."

Daisy licked my hand. "At least you seem to still love me . . . but I haven't lied to you. I have lied so much lately that I don't even know what my own truth is anymore. I don't deserve Drew or any of this. I gave drugs to a struggling train wreck of a pop star with a known drug addiction and left her for dead all in the name of helping a friend. A friend who would be furious if she found out."

I grabbed ZuZu against her will, putting an end to her futile mission and hugged her tight against my chest. She relaxed into the hug and I started to cry. "You two and Drew are the only things that matter. I have to get my shit together. I can't keep going off half-cocked and ready to fight every time I feel the slightest injustice. I just need to keep my universe intact. Fuck Conner. He's not my problem. Fuck Richard and Elise and whatever the hell that was about. Fuck Tristan-Malcolm and this merger. I don't care anymore. I'm done. I've done too much damage already. I'm done."

It felt cathartic to unburden myself, even if it was only to two cats who didn't care what their human did as long as the wet food, treats, and belly rubs were still delivered. I grabbed the red handbag and headed off to watch the fruits of what would be my last meddlesome act.

THE LINE OUTSIDE THE THEATER doors was already beginning to snake down towards the end of the block when I arrived. I had never been more excited to see a show. I was bubbling over with pride for my friend. As soon as I took my place in the crowd I started to overhear snippets of angered conversations from up ahead.

"Are you kidding me? This is bullshit." One woman in her mid-forties practically yelled.

An usher walked past her trying to keep a smile on his face as he walked a few more feet with a roll of tape and stack of papers in his hands. He parted through the line and began taping up the sign announcing that the starring role of Sugar would be played by Sarah Diebold during the matinee.

"I didn't pay my money to see a nobody. I paid to see Rena!" The woman behind me yelled. The low murmurs of rage started to grow in volume as the usher made his way down the line posting the announcement.

"Who the hell is Sarah Diebold? I want my money back." Angry proclamations about wanting a refund began to ripple down the line.

It hadn't occurred to me that there would be this much rage or that it would be directed at Sarah. Shouldn't it be directed at Rena for failing to show up to work? Although, in reality the rage should be directed at me. What if everyone demanded a refund? What if the show didn't actually go on and Sarah didn't get her chance? It did always go on, right? That is what performers are always saying, "The show must go on." What if the crowd booed Sarah the entire time and hated her? Panic and regret started to overwhelm me. What had I done?

The doors opened and people began making their way inside. A large faction of the crowd began to form a new line at the ticket counter demanding refunds, but others filed to their seats, deflated and angry. They were most likely from out of town and had spent a substantial amount of money to come see the pop sensation Rena and now they were going to have to return home and tell their friends how they had to settle for a performance by an understudy. I slid down in my seat in the very last row and tried to tune out all of the angry conversations around me. There was no bubbling excitement out in the crowd as usual. Just anger and disappointment and sadness, all of which must certainly be seeping its way back to the performers. To Sarah. Was she scared? Was she excited? I wondered what was going through her mind ten minutes before the curtain call. I took my phone out of my purse to turn it off and saw a missed text from her.

Shit! The bitch got seriously hammered last night and can't function this morning. I have to go on. I'm not ready for this.

My heart fell into my chest. She was scared. I had faith in her though. I believed in her. I wouldn't have done this if I hadn't. So why did I suddenly feel like throwing up?

I texted back, *OMG! I wish I was there. Break a leg! Call me tonight and tell me everything.* I had to keep up appearances. I couldn't let her find out about my involvement.

The sound of the chimes made everyone quiet down and wait for the curtains to rise. I noticed that there were more than a few empty seats in the normally packed theater.

I was not used to sitting so far back from the stage and it was a different perspective from being so up close and personal in the front row. It was less intimate but I knew from the moment Sarah stepped on the stage that she was nervous. Her first few notes started out pitchy and unsteady. The silent hostility of the crowd seemed to shake her confidence. I had done this to her. She wasn't ready. I hadn't listened to her. I listened to strangers on a subway and clandestine conversations about political shenanigans but I hadn't really listened to my best friend.

I saw her close her eyes for a few bars of the song and when she finally opened them again, the fear and uneasiness were gone and she was again the fierce friend who I knew could embody the role of Sugar. I cried tears of joy and pride through the show as I watched her slowly but surely win over the crowd with her performance. She was gritty and wry and sexy and sarcastic and the audience responded to every emotion and rewarded her with a standing ovation at the end. The woman behind me exclaimed to her husband, "She might have been a nobody when we came in, but I suspect we might have seen a breakout star today. We're still coming back to see it again when Rena returns."

I wanted to run back stage and hug her and take her out to celebrate but I knew I couldn't. She could never know I was there. I checked my phone again and with the timing of her text to me and my response back there was no feasible timeline by which I could have made it on time to the show. As I was leaving I bumped into the back of an usher who had seated me several times for other performances and I quickly ducked my head and hastily made it out of the theater. Outside, I carefully removed one of the posted notices announcing Sarah as the lead role and folded it up and put it in my Playbill.

I was still giddy when I got home and Drew was still out. I opened a bottle of champagne and toasted the notice and Sarah. I drank and waited for her to call. I hoped she would suggest we go out and celebrate together. She had done it. She worked her ass off all those years and she finally got on the stage and brought the house down. We could drink all night and laugh and talk about how far she had come and I would just skip work the next day. Because screw everything, my best friend had just killed it on stage and she was going to be a star.

I finished the bottle of champagne but still heard nothing from her. I figured she was probably caught up celebrating with the other cast members. I decided to switch to water because I didn't want to be too drunk to meet her when she finally texted. Three hours later still no word. I decided to text.

How did it go?

I got no response from her.

Drew came bursting through the door, "Did you hear about Rena? Max texted me this morning freaking out. They thought she was dead when they first found her."

"What?" I didn't really have to pretend to be surprised because in my excitement for Sarah, I had momentarily forgotten about Rena.

"I mean . . . I got a text from Sarah that Rena had gotten hammered and that she was going to have to go on, but I didn't know it was that bad."

That was a lie. I hadn't ruled out her death as a possibility when I left her drugged out of her mind the night before.

Drew came and sat beside me on the couch.

"She was apparently zonked out on something pretty harsh because she wasn't moving and just kept saying 'I'm sorry sweet Abigail. I'll be a better person.' Super weird. Her manager refused to let them call an ambulance because they didn't want the press to find out. The official story is food poisoning."

"Whoa! That is crazy." I tried to make myself feel better about being the one who drugged her by rationalizing that maybe she would try to be a better person and it would be a win-win for everyone. I doubted it. I didn't feel better. I was a monster.

"How did Sarah do?" He pulled me into his arms to snuggle.

I desperately wanted to tell him that she was fabulous and she brought down the house but I couldn't. "I have no idea. I've texted her but I haven't heard from her. I'm guessing it's just utter chaos there. I'm sure she will call tonight."

But she didn't. I checked my phone repeatedly to make sure it was charged and turned on. I felt desperate and despondent, like a girl who had just lost her virginity and texted her boyfriend that she loved him and got no response back. I couldn't believe that she didn't contact me to include me in her celebration.

CHAPTER 22

I STILL HAD NOT HEARD from Sarah by the next morning when I got up to go to work. My feelings were hurt that she didn't at least call to tell me how it went. I considered texting her but assuming she had been out all night with her cast mates, I decided not to wake her by sending her an early morning text. That would just be rude and you can say what you want about me, but I try not to be intentionally rude. Plus, early morning texts waking me up from hangovers are right up there with texting and walking in my wheelhouse of what some might consider possibly irrational rage triggers.

I sat on the subway with Fiona Apple's "Criminal" blasting in my ears to avoid the possibility of overhearing yet another conversation that would rage-trigger me or worse yet, give me another secret to keep from my boyfriend. I replayed the conversation between Uncle Benji and Carol in my head and convinced myself I was being overly dramatic and it was probably some banal politician "problem" they were discussing that involved boring paperwork or the accidental snub of an important donor. I had just been tired and hungry and nervous about what I was going to do with Rena when I overheard the conversation so it probably sounded more dramatic in my head. But there was that weird taped conversation Sarah had overheard about Birdie taking care of something for Uncle Benji. I was going to have to ask Sarah about that when she finally got around to calling me.

I was filled with my usual dread as I turned on my laptop and waited for my daily email insult to boot up. I was surprised and somewhat disappointed that there was nothing in my inbox other than spam. I'm not sure what I have searched for on the Internet that has resulted in my daily enticements about Russian brides, penis enlargements, and garage floor coating.

I started my daily grind of fruitless squinting, typing and saving. I kept alert for any chicken scratch that might possibly allude to Birdie or Senator Davis. I briefly considered looking back at the stack of notebooks I had already finished to see if there were any such references that I might have missed, but decided that could wait until I finished. So, I briefly teetered on the edge of being a thorough and responsible employee, but reasoned myself off that crazy ledge. Let's not pretend I suddenly morphed into the employee of the month. We all know that wasn't going to happen.

I kept waiting for my daily insult email, but by lunch, I had still not gotten one. I let myself fantasize that maybe Tristan-Malcolm went to complain about me to Richard and rather than me getting fired, Richard turned the tables and gave him the ax. I leaned back in my chair and savored that thought for quite a few moments. My phone rang just as I had gotten to the good part of the fantasy where I got to watch Tristan-Malcolm walk forlornly out of the office with his precious few belongings in a box while I twisted my imaginary mustache. It was Sarah. Finally!

"I'm outside your building. Get your ass down here."

"Yay! I can't wait to hear everything. Let me get my purse out of its protective nest. Where do you want to eat?"

"You don't need your purse because we aren't going to lunch." Huh. She sounded kind of snippy. She must be super hung over and the thought of food must make her sick.

"I'll be down in a minute."

I WALKED PAST THE SECURITY guard and could immediately tell that she was pissed. She was pacing frantically back and forth in front of the door. When she saw me through the glass she stopped and her eyes narrowed in anger. Oh fuck! She knew. I considered just backing up and running past the security guard to the safety of the elevator where she could not legally get to me without a visitor's badge. I knew that would only make matters worse. So, I sucked it up and went out the door.

"What the fuck did you do?" She yelled at me as soon as I got outside. "Tell me what you did."

"I'm not exactly sure. What do you think I did?"

Wrong move. Her face managed to contort even angrier and her voice got louder.

"What do I think? I think you drugged Rena and almost killed her so you could play fairy godmother and in doing so, you almost ruined my career."

I was not prepared for this much anger. I took a deep breath. "Sarah, that's not fair . . ."

"Don't even try to play hurt and innocent to get out of this. I am so furious with you right now. I can't even look at your dumb ass face. I'm out." She turned and started to walk away from me.

I panicked and called out to get her attention. "I didn't drug her . . ." I have now lied to everyone that I loved.

She whipped around and the look on her face dared me to lie one more time.

"I might have provided the drugs but she took them willingly."

"Oh! Well that makes it perfectly OK then. Forgive me. I didn't know that little detail so everything is all good now." The sarcasm and anger amplified her voice louder.

"I was just trying to help. You deserved a chance and she is a horrible person. And you were so good."

"Don't you dare!" She walked back over to me and put her finger in my face.

"You are not allowed to talk about whether I was good or not. I didn't ask for your help and I didn't want it. I told you that I wasn't ready. It wasn't up to you to make that decision. The theater lost money because of you. Do you even care how many tickets had to be refunded? If Rena were to ever find out that her 'sweet Abigail' was my friend, I could be out on the street with a reputation that I would never be able to outlive. Do you even understand that? Did you even think of that?"

I hadn't. I was immediately ashamed. I felt horrible and I had no words to say other than, "I'm sorry. I thought I was helping."

"Well, you didn't help. I don't even want to know how you got your hands on those drugs."

No. She definitely did not want to know that story.

I pleaded with her. "I don't know what to say other than I'm sorry. How do I make this better? What can I do? I'll do anything. You are my best friend." I was now openly sobbing on Fifth Avenue.

"I don't know what to tell you. I don't want to see you and I don't want to talk to you for a while. Stay the hell away from me because right now I think you are way ahead of Rena in the competition as to who is the worst person in the world."

"I'm sorry. I'm so sorry." There was nothing else that I could say.

She turned and left me crying on the sidewalk. Everything managed to get even worse when I saw that Tristan-Malcolm had been standing behind her and had been watching the whole scene unfold.

I slid down the wall and curled into a ball. Tears ran down my face and I wished I was invisible. I was in no shape to hear the nastiness that was going to come from his mouth although nothing he could say would cut as deep as Sarah's words.

I was an idiot to get involved. She was right. I was a horrible person.

The ugly sobbing started and I could tell people were staring at me out of the corner of their disinterested and yet simultaneously judgmental New York City eyes.

"Oh, for Pete's sake. Blow your nose and get off the ground."

He waived a white handkerchief back and forth in front of my face. I took it from him.

"Get up. You look like a four year old having a meltdown because they've just been told they can't have ice cream."

He extended his hand and helped me to my feet.

"Thank you. It's just that. . ."

"I have no interest in hearing your sad story. I'm sure it is tragic enough in your mind to warrant this display but I'm not interested. I don't need people to see a psychotic woman having a breakdown outside of our building."

He held the door open for me and I followed him in, deciding for once that I should keep my mouth shut and accept the small gesture of kindness being offered without calling attention to it.

WE RODE IN THE ELEVATOR in silence. When I got to my floor I whispered, "Thank you," and rushed off and headed straight to the bathroom to finish my cry in private.

I sobbed. I realized that I had been stupid and reckless. I never even thought Sarah could get branded as a Nomi from *Showgirls* if they believed she was involved with my plans to sabotage Rena. I was shortsighted and arrogant and it might have cost me my best friend.

There was not a single person who I could talk to about it. Drew would eventually start to wonder what happened if it took too long to patch things up with Sarah. I didn't even know how to start to fix things with her other than to leave her alone and give her time.

I'm not known for my patience and my instinct was to go full throttle and throw myself into a shameless spiral of constant texting and desperate voicemail messages begging for forgiveness. I was certain that would have the opposite effect based on my recent attempts with Elise. Although in fairness to Elise, she might not have received any of my messages since she skipped town and left her phone.

I lost track of time sitting in the bathroom stall and crying. I was becoming way too familiar with the feel of a hard toilet seat on my ass lately.

Several women came and went but no one asked if I was alright or made any attempt to invade my privacy. I wasn't the first person to cry in the bathroom in this office and I wouldn't be the last. They most likely assumed it was Tristan-Malcolm-related and would have hushed conversations about who had today in the office betting pool as my quitting or firing day. Secret squabbles would break out over my chair. They would be completely off base, but at least I wouldn't have to explain to anyone what had really happened.

I splashed some cold water on my face and went back to my desk.

I had a voicemail message from Richard asking me to come to his office when I had a moment. My heart sank. Maybe someone was going to win the office pool today after all. Richard never called me or asked me to come to his office. All of the work that I did for him went through the lower ranked attorney on the case.

Tristan-Malcolm had finally won. My public meltdown must have been the last straw.

I got my makeup out of my purse and attempted to do some damage control to the mascara streaks that I missed when I washed my face. I dabbed some concealer over the redness of my nose and tried to cover up the dark and puffy circles forming under my eyes. There was nothing I could do to hide the redness of my eyes. I could feign allergies but I suspected that I would be crying again within a few moments of entering Richard's office, so what was the point?

Today was just a disaster and it only seemed to be getting worse. At best, I hoped I could get through the day without accidentally killing someone.

I took some deep yoga breaths and got up from my chair. I saw my phone and noticed a missed text from Drew that simply said "love you" with a heart emoji. I could feel another set of tears bubbling to get up to the surface. I wasn't sure I would ever get another text like that from him again after my meeting with his father.

As I passed by Susan's cubicle, she stopped me and whispered, "Hey, I can tell you have had a rough day. I'm sending you something special to your inbox. I'm pretty sure you will like it, but honestly, if faced with it in reality, I think it would put someone's eye out."

In spite of everything that happened and was about to happen, Susan's commitment to trolling the internet for pictures of naked men made me smile.

"Thanks. I can't wait to get a load of it." I said.

"Ha! I see what you did there." She laughed.

CHAPTER 23

I MADE MY WAY TO the elevator and rode the eight flights up to Richard's penthouse office. Richard's life was a series of penthouses. I imagined that it must be nice to always know that you are on top of everything and safe from everything crashing in around you. So secure in the belief that your world would never fall apart. I'd never know that feeling. My life was teetering on the edge of disaster and there were more than one pair of hands on the rug ready to pull it out from under me. And every pair of fancy shoes that I owned was ready to drop.

I got off the elevator and his secretary waived me into the great expanse of his office. It was almost larger than the home Drew and I shared. He was sitting at his desk looking out at the skyline when I entered. He was probably trying to find the words to tell me that he had to let me go. He had probably already alerted Drew.

"Ally!" He jumped from his seat and came around the desk to hug me. Well at least maybe he wasn't planning on having me erased from the family. Just the firm.

"Come sit with me." He led me over to a grouping of overstuffed, leather chairs that looked out over the city. I obediently followed and sat in the chair beside him.

"It's a beautiful view isn't it? I never get tired of looking at it." He nodded towards the window.

"Yes, it is a fantastic view." Oh God. Just fire me already. Don't make me look out at a view of a life that I will never be able to obtain on my own. This is just cruel.

"You know, I started this firm with practically nothing. I was a solo practitioner. Hell, I couldn't even afford a secretary when I first 'hung out my shingle' as they say. I had a small office with no windows in a rundown building in the Meatpacking District of all places."

I had never heard this story before and wasn't sure what his point was in telling me all of it just before firing me. Was I supposed to draw some inspiration from it? Was I supposed to go to the Meatpacking District? Is that where all the answers to life are hidden? Was the answer 42?

He continued. "We are a far cry from the Meatpacking District now though, aren't we?" He again gestured to the view.

"It was before I met Carol. Before I met Benji." He got up and walked over to the bar at the other end of the room.

"You know, I grew up in Hoboken, New Jersey. Middle class family." He poured two glasses of water and walked back to his chair and handed me a glass as he sat. "My family was a lot like yours, I suppose. I had big dreams just like you. I could see this office, every detail of it, in my mind. Every day and every hour that I worked in that windowless office I could see this place and knew what I was working towards. I actually lived in that office for most of the first year. I ate most of my meals down the street at Redling's Dinette."

He sighed and looked out at the horizon. I was really hoping he would just cut to the chase and give me the ax.

"I've eaten at some of the best restaurants in the world and I don't think I've had a croissant as buttery and flaky as the ones Shey would make. She was the owner. We'd drink whiskey at the back table and listen to Frank Sinatra and talk about our dreams. I was going to take over the legal world and she was going to move to Paris and bake and paint."

He seemed to temporarily get lost in this memory. "I wonder if she ever made it to Paris."

I continued to sit awkwardly beside him, not sure of why my presence was needed for his trip down memory lane. He finally stopped staring off into the horizon and turned to look at me. I was getting uncomfortable with the maudlin tone of the conversation, so I shifted in my seat and looked out at the horizon myself.

"We are a lot alike, the two of us. You moved here to follow your dreams. You are working your ass off to make it as a comedian but still putting in the hours here."

I turned to look at him. He was smiling so sweetly at me. I thought this had to be the oddest and most longwinded way ever to fire someone, but I appreciated that maybe he was as uncomfortable with the situation as I was, although, I was technically the one losing my job. I wasn't sure what I was supposed to say.

"I had never thought of it like that but I guess we are." Please let this bonding moment end and just get to the firing already.

"I'm concerned about you Ally. I hope your work here is not keeping you from achieving your dreams. I don't want to hold you back."

Ahh! So that is how he is going to play it. He's doing it for my sake so I can follow my dreams. Well, at least we were getting close to the cord cutting, Band-Aid ripping off moment. Soon, I could go down and pack up all my shit and congratulate the winner of the office pool. Funny, how earlier in the day I had wished this exact moment on Tristan-Malcolm and yet here it was happening to me. Karma is a bitch and she seemed to work pretty fast.

"I understand that you have to let me go, Richard. It's OK."

"What?" Richard seemed genuinely startled. "Ally, certainly you don't think I am firing you."

"You aren't?" Then what in the hell am I doing in your office? And why am I listening to your origin story?

"Why would I do that? You've been working harder than ever lately. I've noticed the late hours you've been keeping here. Drew told me you've been taking work home. I'm worried about you."

He inched closer to my chair and put his hand on my knee and for a brief uncomfortable moment, I feared he was looking for a replacement for Elise in his extracurricular life.

"Stop letting Tristan-Malcolm get under your skin and boss you around. He's not your boss."

"It kind of feels like he is though."

"Well, sometimes he needs reminded of whose name is on top of the firm letterhead. Tell me what he has you working on and I will decide if it is important enough for you to be staying here at the office working so hard all the time."

Tristan-Malcolm's warning about never going over his head rang through my ear. But sitting in the penthouse with Richard and being comforted by him reminded me that there was nothing Tristan-Malcolm could do to me. I calculated that there was only a sixty percent chance he would kill me and eat me. I found myself feeling relieved for the first time in days.

"Umm, he has me deciphering Elise's notes that he found in her office so he can get up to speed on the merger. There are a lot of notes and her handwriting is hard to read."

"And have you found anything important in them? What is it that he has you specifically looking to find?" That seemed like a weird question. Doesn't Tristan-Malcolm give him updates?

"Well, I don't think I have found anything, but then again, nothing makes any sense to me. I'm sorry. I shouldn't admit to my boss that I don't understand this merger at all."

He laughed. "You don't need to understand it. I've got it all handled. I've been doing this job a long time. So, did he find the notebooks in the office or did you find them?"

"Well, he found them, but really a blind person could have found them. They were stacked everywhere. Her office was a complete disaster."

He laughed again, "She was quite a slob." For a flicker of a moment I could have sworn I saw a wistful smile cross his face followed by a trace of sadness just before he regained his usual easy going smile.

"And so the notebooks are the only thing that he has you working on? Nothing else? He didn't mention finding anything else in her office that he needed you to work on?"

"No. Just the notebooks."

It suddenly felt like the friendly chat was turning into an interrogation. I thought of the tapes and my stomach suddenly got queasy. I hoped my face was not physically turning red, even though I could feel the nervous blush blotching its way up my cheeks. I had to fight the urge to fidget in my seat.

I knew I should tell him about the tapes, but I couldn't tell him since I didn't exactly have access to them at the moment. I thought about the conversation between Uncle Benji and Senator Davis, which was on one of the tapes. I couldn't admit I had provided confidential information with potential political scandal ramifications to someone not working for the firm, even if that someone was my best friend. Well, possibly my former best friend.

No. I had to wait until I got them back from Sarah. I could just casually say that after we talked I later remembered the box of tapes I found and had thrown in my desk drawer. I will just tell him I had forgotten all about them in the midst of all my notebook transcribing. That could work. I could make that work. Getting Sarah to talk to me long enough to give me back the tapes would be much harder than convincing Richard that I had forgotten about them.

"Are you ill? You don't look well." He asked.

Shit. So, apparently the flush was noticeable.

"I'll be fine. I think that street vendor shawarma is not sitting well on my stomach." I patted my stomach and scrunched up my face. If I have learned anything over the years, it is that nothing will bring a meeting or a conversation to an abrupt stop like a subtle reference to potential explosive diarrhea.

"Oh dear." Richard instantly stood up to indicate the chat was over. I don't mean to sound cocky after the disaster of a day that I'd had so far, but I was confident that maneuver would work. I will take a win no matter how small.

I stood up to leave and he hugged me. "Don't work too hard on those notebooks. No more staying late at the office or taking them home."

He walked with me to the door. "Elise had a habit of writing down everything she read because she said it helped her remember things. I doubt there is a single thing in any of those notebooks that Tristan-Malcolm needs to know. I've brokered this deal and he is just in charge of writing up the documents. You got that?"

I nodded. "Thank you."

He smiled. "I'm glad you are part of the family, Ally. You make Drew very happy. I will see you on Thursday for dinner as usual and I want to hear all about how your set went the night before. Never stop chasing your dream, Ally."

"I won't." I had, but he didn't need to know that right now.

I was so relieved I hadn't gotten fired that I actually smiled on the elevator as I returned to my desk. The smile faded when the elevator stopped at Tristan-Malcolm's floor and he got on.

He looked at me accusatorially. "Were you just up in Richard's office?"

"I was. Are you just full out stalking me now?" My meeting with Richard had definitely increased my confidence.

"What were you up there discussing? Was it the merger? Did you find something and go over my head?"

I wanted to use the opportunity to tell him that Richard had just confirmed that he was just a scribe on the whole merger deal and was as useless as a third tit, but the elevator door opened on my floor.

"It was personal." I walked off and didn't look back. I was done taking his shit. His power over me was gone and it felt pretty fucking awesome. My confident smile returned as I returned to the safety of my cubicle.

I opened Susan's email image and agreed with her assessment that the cock attached to the man in the picture could definitely put someone's eye out. Other than losing my best friend, the day was starting to improve.

My cell phone rang. It was Carol which was odd but not completely unheard of, I assumed she must want to shop.

"Allison, darling. How are you doing?" Jesus. What was up with everyone suddenly caring about my well-being? I mean, given everything I had done in the past two weeks, my mental status was somewhat suspect, but I thought I had done a pretty decent job of hiding my murdering, vigilante justice, and potentially psychotic ways from everyone. Obviously, I had not.

"I'm doing great. How are you?" Great was a bit of an overstatement.

"Richard has to work late this evening so I thought I would invite you over for dinner."

"Sure. I will text and check with Drew to see what time he can be available."

"Let's just make it a girls' night. I feel like we barely get to talk just the two of us anymore unless we are shopping."

"Oh. Sure. Sounds great." I felt the prickle of the fine hairs on the back of my neck. One-on-one interactions with both of Drew's parents on the same day seemed a bit out of the ordinary. I couldn't recall Carol ever wanting to share a meal with me just to chat. Oh God, what if she had figured out that I had overheard her conversation with Uncle Benji at the fundraiser? Did I have to steel myself for another inquisition?

"Great. I will see you at 8 o'clock at my place. I will have the cook prepare something special for you."

"I will see you then." It was weird, but maybe I was overthinking it. Maybe she did just want to bond. I was currently in the market for a new friend given Sarah's recent shunning of me and I never turned down a good meal.

CHAPTER 24

"JUST GO INSIDE THE HOUSE and have dinner. You will be fine and it will be over sooner than you think." Drew was trying his best to give me a pep talk over the phone as I stood outside his parents' building.

"But it's going to be weird. At least when we are shopping we have the clothes to talk about. You know I'm not good at polite chit chat. I'm going to say something wrong and offend her. I just know it."

He laughed. "She could use a good offending every now and again. Don't worry about it. Try to have fun."

"Well, I think we both know that fun is not on the table for me tonight. I want to be home with you and the cats."

"We will be here when you get home. Go eat, maybe try not to say 'fuck' too many times, and then come home and I will make it up to you."

"What do you mean don't say 'fuck' too many times? Has she said something about that? Oh my God, if I have to worry about how many times I say 'fuck' this is going to be the worst meal ever."

"No, she hasn't said anything. I was trying to be funny. See, this is why you are the comedian and not me. My jokes aren't funny."

"Fine. I'm going in. I can do this."

"You've got this. Love you."

"Love you." I put the phone back in the red bag. I felt a twinge of ungratefulness that I was so reluctant to share a meal with the woman who had gifted the beautiful bag to me. I braced myself and entered the building.

"ALLISON, HOW LOVELY TO SEE you." Carol greeted me at the door. She immediately embraced me and kissed my cheek. I really was an ingrate. My mother would be ashamed of me for acting like such a petulant child over having dinner with the mother of my boyfriend who so graciously treated me like a daughter.

"Here, give me your coat and handbag. I'm so glad you are carrying it. I was worried that you would stick it in a closet and not use it."

I handed them over and she placed them on the ornate chair in the foyer. "It is beautiful. Thank you again for giving it to me."

"You are very welcome dear. Come, I've had dinner set up out on the terrace. I know how much you love to eat out there."

My feet froze in place and my heart stopped. She knew. She knew I had been out there and overheard her. This was not going to be fun at all.

She turned to me, "I remember the first time you and Drew came over for dinner and you raved about how much being out on the terrace felt like dining at home in your backyard."

Oh! Maybe I over reacted just a bit and she didn't know. The past couple of weeks had made me jumpy. I told myself to relax as I followed her outside. The lights were twinkling and I could hear the faint melodies of music playing over the outside speakers. Loud enough to hear but not too loud to make conversation impossible. Of course, Carol would know the exact proper volume to play dinner music.

The table was set and dinner was on the table waiting for us with an open bottle of wine in the center. She motioned for me to be seated and she poured me a glass of wine before sitting opposite of me.

"I gave the staff the night off after the chef finished the meal. You know, sometimes I just like being in the house without people hovering around all the time."

"That was very thoughtful of you to give them the night off. Drew and I are practically the cats' staff and they never give us a night off."

She didn't laugh at my joke.

"But, I can imagine that it would be irritating to always have people hovering about trying to do things for you."

That came out wrong too. If I kept talking I was going to make it much worse. I took a large sip of wine and hoped that she would just start talking. Maybe she would tell me some long winded story about the good old days like her husband had earlier this afternoon.

"I hope you enjoy the meal. I know how much you like to eat." She waived her hands across the table as if to present the meal as a prize I had won on a game show.

My internal alarm bells went off again, but she wasn't wrong, I did love to eat. I had to actively conceal the horror on my face when I looked down to see that dinner was an autumn salad with seared tuna. What the fuck? This woman doesn't know me at all. I was expecting some kind of red meat and some potatoes. This was literally the worst dinner that could be served to me outside of maybe monkey brains or bull testicles.

Well, at least there was a bread basket. I reached for a piece of bread and a dense brown seeded concoction that was shaped like bread but would need an entire tub of butter to be palatable. I searched the table and there was no butter in sight. This night was already leaps and bounds worse than I had ever imagined it would be. I flashed her what I hoped was a sincere enough looking smile.

"It looks great." I picked up the fork and started picking at the salad and wondered if I could get away with nonchalantly dropping the food into the potted topiary near my chair rather than trying to choke it down.

"You are so fit. How do you manage to stay so tiny while eating and drinking as much as you do?"

What the hell? I could almost physically feel the sting from the backhanded nature of the seeming compliment as it smacked me up the side of my face.

"I work out a lot." The food and the conversation were on equally unpleasant footing at the moment.

"Oh, that's right. The firm does pay for a gym membership for its employees."

At this point, I wasn't sure if that was meant as a jab at my financial situation as well but I decided to play dumb and not take notice if the remark was meant to be malicious.

"Yeah, it is great that they do that, but, I mostly just run in the park nearby." Running is free bitch. I admit that I might have been getting a tad sensitive at this point in the conversation.

"How lovely." She continued to smile at me and I wasn't sure what to expect next. I just chewed the disgusting dry bread and chased it with wine and thought about the pizza that I was going to eat when I got home before I fucked her son seven ways to Sunday. We ate in silence for a few moments.

She placed her utensils down and stared across the table at me. "You know, I underestimated you when I first met you."

I waited for the sting of another backhanded compliment that was sure to follow such a statement.

She continued. "When it became apparent that Drew was apparently smitten with you, I resigned myself to working with you and trying to mold you into at least a respectable match for him out in the political world. I could vaguely see how I could spin your background to our favor to win over the lesser educated and rural voters of New York . . ."

Wow. Not backhanded at all. That was a forward serve straight to the face.

And here comes the large cash offer to leave her son. I shouldn't have been surprised. Although I had joked about it, I always knew there was a distinct possibility that it would actually happen. I began mentally searching for the right words to tell her to shove her money up her stodgy ass along with her goddamned salad and sawdust bread.

She continued to stare at me, ". . . but I never considered that you could be useful to me."

What? Useful to her? How the hell could I be useful to her?

"You see . . . I know what you've been up to, Allison."

My mouth suddenly felt drier than the bread.

"I know that you haven't performed at a comedy club for months now, let alone been 'killing it' as you so eloquently put it."

My heart started racing as I listened to her words. She knew one of my secrets. Was she going to tell Drew? How did this make me useful to her? My mouth opened to say something but there was nothing I could say that would help me.

"While you haven't been 'killing it' . . ." She actually made air quotes with her hands, which seemed out of character for her, but then again, this whole conversation had come quite out of left field. ". . . you have actually killed before, have you not?"

I dropped the fork that I had been using to push the field of grass around on my plate. The clamor it made as it tumbled off the plate and onto the ground matched the clamor of thoughts tumbling through my brain. She knew. How did she know? What was I supposed to do or say? How much did she know? Did I hear her right? Maybe I misheard her.

"Allison, are you alright dear?" She extended a hand across the table and patted my hand which was now griping the edge of table. "You seem upset that I mentioned your past killer career success."

I had no idea what she was trying to insinuate or if she was trying to insinuate anything at all. Maybe she didn't know. Maybe she had just heard Drew and I say killed it so many times that she was trying to be hip and speak in our vernacular. My head was spinning, trying to decide what she meant and how to respond and what my actual level of panic should be in this situation.

"I . . . how did you find out that I haven't been doing shows?" That was the safest response that I could come up with to avoid possibly confessing to a murder that she might not actually know about.

"Oh, darling. I can always tell when someone is lying. It's a skill you must develop when dealing with politicians. I was concerned you were cheating on my son. I simply can't have that come up to bite him on the ass in a campaign, so I sent out an investigator to the comedy clubs in the area. I was quite relieved when I discovered that you were merely sitting at the bar and drinking alone. I can at least work with the recovered alcoholic angle."

"I'm not an alcoholic."

I was less confident in that statement than I should have been, but I had only been drinking more these past few weeks because of the circumstances. I might like to drink and I have a particular weakness for champagne, but I was in no way an alcoholic. My fear started to recede just a tad as anger began to trickle into its place. How dare she call me an alcoholic while also offering me wine? Way to be an enabler, Carol. I was also sick and tired of hearing about her micromanaging Drew's life into a political career that he didn't even want.

"I'm getting a bit off track. The point is, I do believe that you love my son and for whatever reason he seems to love you, so I'm going to have to work with what I have got in front of me and make use of it."

Well, wasn't that just lovely. Fuck this. I was done. I moved to get up from my chair.

"Sit down. I'm not done yet." Her voice was stern and commanding. It was the first time I had ever seen her break from her well-born, ladylike demeanor. I reluctantly sat back in my seat. I had no idea what she was going to say next.

Her voice returned to her normal dulcet tone. "As I was saying, I have determined that you can be useful to me. In exchange for me not revealing to Drew that you have been lying to him for months, which you know will just devastate him, I'm going to need you to do me a favor."

Max had been right. The purse definitely had strings attached to it. And yes, I will call it a purse. I don't care if Carol insisted that it be called a handbag or not, it was a goddamn purse.

"And what is the favor you need me to do?" I relaxed a bit since it seemed that at least for now, I would not be getting a buyout check and shown the door. I would do her favor and then find the right time to come clean to Drew and get out from under her control. I had watched enough television and movies to know that blackmail didn't stop at just one favor.

"Sadly, after thirty-five years of marriage, Richard has become a bit of a loose cannon and a problem. He needs to be handled."

Oh shit! She must have found out about his affair with Elise. I don't know how the hell she thought I was supposed to handle the situation though. I wondered if there had been other women and Elise was just the last straw.

"Is this about Elise? I doubt my sitting him down to have a stern talking to about it would really cause him to change his ways."

"Oh, I don't want you to talk to him. I want you to kill him."

If I had another fork in my hand, I would have dropped it too. Instead, I heard myself laugh out loud because it had to be a joke. There was no way my boyfriend's mother was seriously asking me to kill his father.

"Oh God, I almost thought you were serious for a second and that suddenly I was in the middle of a Lifetime movie of the week scenario."

For some reason I could not stop laughing. I should have been mad at her for playing such a cruel joke on me. The whole evening must have just been a farce, right down to the food she had served. Well played, Carol. I didn't know you had it in you. She continued staring at me very seriously and was not ready to break the scene.

"I don't watch Lifetime so I don't get your reference. Frankly, I don't get half of your references and it is something we are going to have to work on if you end up on the campaign trail with Drew. Grownups don't always reference everything back to random bits and pieces of entertainment, Allison."

I stopped laughing. I knew she never got my jokes but now this one of hers was starting to go too far. This spontaneous roast of hers needed to come to an end.

"Allison, I am quite serious. Richard has become a problem and I'm going to need you to take care of the situation for me. You take care of me and I take care of you. That is how the real world operates."

I had heard the words "problem" and "taken care of" before on this terrace. Just a few days ago. I suddenly started to fear that it wasn't a joke at all but that she was actually serious. The fear must have been apparent on my face because she again reached over to pat my hand across the table.

"I know. It is all a bit startling. A completely untoward affair to be sure, but sadly it has to be done and you are the only one that I can trust to do it."

Trust? I think the word she was looking for was blackmail. If she was serious, she was sadly mistaken to believe that I would do such a thing.

"Carol, this is crazy. You want him dead because he cheated on you with Elise."

She sneered. I had never seen Carol sneer before. It was alarming. "Don't insult me. This is not about Elise. As if I could care less about who he sleeps with at the office. I am not going to tell you the reasons that I need him dead but I certainly won't have you think it is over something as stupid as one of his never-ending string of affairs."

"Look, I still think this is all one big fucking joke, but I will play along. You are asking me to kill my boyfriend's father, your husband, and you don't think I have the right to know why? Fuck you."

I got up from the table and threw my napkin on the plate. "Fuck all of this. Fuck this goddamn joke of a meal. Fuck your insults. Fuck you for this asinine joke. And if it is not a joke, then fuck you for asking me to do it."

She grabbed my arm as I passed her chair on my way toward the door. "He took something that doesn't belong to him and won't give it back. That is all you need to know and that is all that I'm going to tell you." She tightened her grip on my arm. "You have until Thursday to make up your mind. The consequences of your refusal will be swift and unpleasant."

"Whatever, bitch. I will take my chances with telling Drew the truth. Next time you try to blackmail someone you should have something a little more damaging. Like I can't spin my story and then suck your son's cock until he forgives me."

She laughed. An actual laugh, not a polite chuckle.

"Oh darling, eloquent as always. It is like you have forgotten that I have friends in very high places. Governors, senators, police chiefs, . . . and people with a more enterprising background. People who I would normally have dispense of Richard, except this time I want it to be personal and painful. I know how much Richard adores you and so I want him to feel that moment of bitter betrayal just before he dies when he realizes what you have done."

I tried to squirm my way out of her demented grasp but she tightened her grip with her surprisingly strong hand.

"Haven't you asked yourself why Elise just up and disappeared without a trace? It's unsafe out in this city for a woman. Terrible things can happen. You should be careful."

My stomach pitched forward and if I had actually eaten any of her terrible food, I would surely have vomited. I wrenched free from her arm and ran out the door.

"You have until Thursday." She called out to me as I ran towards the door. I grabbed my coat and the purse of deception and ran.

My head was spinning. I managed to make it two blocks before my legs gave way on me. I dropped to the ground just like I did at the park, but this time I didn't have Sarah there to help me. I had no one to help me. I crawled over to the steps of a nearby brownstone and sat down to gather myself together. Nothing made sense anymore. Drew's parents were apparently worse than aliens. Richard was apparently an adulterous thief of some sort and Carol, well she was just a monster in a Gucci dress and Louis Vuitton shoes.

What could Richard have stolen that would make her want to kill him? My brain tried to sort through all of the information that I had been inundated with over the past few hours, actually the past few days. I thought back to the overheard conversations, the references to a problem that Birdie was going to fix for Uncle Benji on the tapes that Sarah was listening to for me. The tapes that I had found in Elise's office. Was she hiding them for Richard or from Richard?

A guttural cry that I didn't quite recognize as my own escaped my own mouth as I realized Elise was probably laying in a morgue somewhere as an unidentified Jane Doe. Maybe she was lying next to the body of the man I had killed. Did the police know what I had done? Was it just a matter of time before they came knocking at my door?

I willed myself to get up and steady my legs so I could make my way home. Home to Drew. I couldn't stop to think about what all of this meant to our relationship and whether he would still be part of my home. I just had to get to him and crawl into his arms. I had until Thursday to figure out a solution.

CHAPTER 25

WHEN I GOT HOME, I was greeted by the smell of bacon and Drew in the kitchen.

"Hey babe, how was dinner with my mom?" Drew was removing the bacon from the skillet and toast popped out of the toaster.

I put the purse down on the table and walked over and kissed him. I had been preparing for this question the entire cab ride home. I couldn't say it was great or he would know that I was lying and ask questions. "It was about as uncomfortable as I thought it would be, maybe actually a little worse."

"I'm so sorry, honey. She has good intentions but she can be overbearing." He proceeded to stack the bacon, tomato and lettuce onto toast and cut the sandwich diagonally.

Love his heart, as we say back home. He had no idea that his mother was a monster who wanted his dad dead and likely had Elise murdered.

"I know she probably had the chef make something that you hated. So, tonight I went with something simple that I know you have loved since childhood. No mayonnaise. See? I listen."

He put the plate on the table and proceeded to make another sandwich for himself.

"You are too good to me." I had no appetite after the events of the evening but my stomach growled to let me know that I did in fact need to eat.

"Not possible. You are the best thing in my life."

I wanted to believe that would still be true after Thursday. I could tell him about the lies. I could tell him I hadn't done a show in six months because of stage fright and how embarrassed I was to admit that to him. He would forgive me. He might be disappointed, but he would forgive me. Unfortunately, that didn't seem to be the only card up his mother's sleeve. She was smarter than me and had more time to perfect how to make other people bend to her will. She ran with the big dogs and I only had cats.

I thought about Tristan-Malcolm's warning that I should have a back-up plan and how people like Drew always chose the money and power of their family. I couldn't imagine Drew choosing sides with his mother if he knew her plans, but I also couldn't tell him. He would think I was crazy. I needed proof. A back-up plan also wouldn't hurt.

"What if we just ran away?" I blurted out.

His mouth was full so it was a few moments before he responded. He humored me. "Sure. What are we running away from, honey?"

"Just everything. The tedium of work, law school, a political career that you don't really want, all of it. Let's just leave and not look back."

"And where are we going?" He took another bite of his sandwich.

"I don't know. Somewhere far from here. I would say the Bahamas but we have to take the cats." I leaned down and petted Daisy on the head as she wove between my feet, hoping a small crumb of bacon might fall her way. "Don't worry baby, I wouldn't leave you and your sister behind."

"So we are taking the cats and running away somewhere. What about your comedy career? And then there's the small detail of my parents cutting me off, so what do we live on?"

"Love and sex." Even I laughed out loud at the absurdity of my response.

He pulled my chair over beside him and put his arms around me. "Honey, I would love to run away with you and live on love and sex."

It was clear he wasn't taking me seriously since he had no real reason to think I wasn't joking.

"I'm serious. Let's just run away. You know, since you never let me pay for anything around here even though I have repeatedly tried, I have close to $200,000 in savings and retirement. That is plenty of money to fund a getaway."

He hugged me tighter. "Dinner with my mom was that bad, huh?"

I tucked myself closer into the safety of his arms. "I just want to run away."

I held back the tears as I realized that by Thursday, I might have to run away by myself. It might be the only solution. No matter what Carol threatened me with, there was no way I was going to kill his father. Maybe it would be better for everyone if I just left. Then again, if I left, I was pretty sure Carol would still have Richard killed. Drew would still lose his dad and would get sucked even further into the vortex of his mother's evil world. I needed to come up with a better plan.

CHAPTER 26

I SAT AT MY DESK holding my phone, willing it to light up with a notification that Sarah had responded to my text begging her to forgive me. I not only needed to salvage our friendship, but I also needed to get those tapes back. The tapes were my only shot at fixing things. If I gave them back to Richard, then he could return them to Carol and she would call off the whole crazy murder plot. It was so simple. I don't know why it took me so long to think of it. The shock of finding out that Carol was not a benevolent wardrobe fairy but rather a horrible Machiavellian lunatic might have played a small part in delaying the obvious solution from materializing in my head.

It had been an hour and Sarah still hadn't responded to my text. I waited to send it until after 10 o'clock so I would not wake her up, but my courteousness was apparently not enough to gain her forgiveness. I hadn't mentioned the tapes in the first text because I didn't want her to think the tapes were more important than patching up our friendship, even though the tapes were kind of a life or death matter. I put the phone down and contemplated how long to wait before sending out a second text. Although it was urgent that I get in touch with her, I also didn't want to be that crazy person who sends seventeen unreturned texts. And yes, I realize I was that crazy person when it came to texting Elise when I was merely dealing with the not entirely rational threat of being turned into a stew and eaten by Tristan-Malcolm. Who knew that I would look back on the past few miserable weeks as the halcyon days?

I sat and stared at my computer. I hadn't picked up a notebook since the talk with Richard. There had been no morning email waiting for me in my inbox from Tristan-Malcolm. It was possible he had just decided to give up on bullying me. I thought back on the talk with Richard and his questions. He was obviously trying to find the tapes. There had to be something on those tapes worth murdering over since Elise was gone and Carol wanted Richard dead. Since I had feigned ignorance and mentioned that Tristan-Malcolm had been in Elise's office before me, there was a slight chance Richard might think Tristan-Malcolm had the tapes. An unexpected wave of panic flooded my body as I imagined Tristan-Malcolm dead somewhere because I might have accidentally implicated him as having possession of the damn tapes. Sure, I had gleefully fantasized about his death for weeks now, but not like this. I hadn't been serious about wanting him dead. I had enough blood on my hands.

I grabbed the phone and dialed his extension. It rang five times. I hung up before it went to voicemail. I waited five minutes and dialed the number again. On the third ring he picked up.

"Why are you bothering me? What do you want?"

Oh, thank God, he was still alive. Still a dick, but also still alive. I was caught off guard by him answering since I was convinced he was dead and hadn't thought of an excuse for the call. "Just checking in on you. I got worried when I didn't have my insult of the morning waiting on me in my inbox."

Click. In a strange way, his hanging up on me gave me some odd reassurance and feeling of normalcy. At least some things remained the same. The entire world had not spun off its axis. Just mine.

Despite my earlier resolve, I spiraled down the rabbit hole of sending endless texts to Sarah. Each one a tad bit more desperate than the last. I tried calling her but it went straight to voicemail. I left an embarrassingly desperate apology and begged her to call me. I considered going to see her at the theater but was afraid I would run into Rena, which would make everything even worse. I didn't want to even imagine what worse could even look like at this point. I got no work done and I didn't care. I just sat in my cubicle and stared at my phone, waiting. Waiting and thinking up places to run away to if getting the tapes back wasn't enough to keep Richard alive.

I was restless and stressed by the end of the day and no closer to a solution to my Carol problem. I wasn't ready to go home because I was afraid I would break and blurt everything out to Drew, and that would only make things worse. I needed to run. It had been a week since my last run. It would help to get some fresh air and some miles logged. I would just steer clear of the reservoir. I pulled the red purse out of its nest in the file drawer and grabbed my phone.

I called Drew. I wanted to hear his voice to soothe my nerves. I got his voicemail. "Hey honey, just wanted to let you know that I will be home a little late. I'm going to head to the gym and take a run in the park."

I sat on the bench in the locker room, dressed and ready to try to burn off some stress. I checked my phone one last time for a message from Sarah. There was none. I tucked the phone into my purse and closed the locker.

I ran over to the park and kept to the main paths and instinctively ran in the opposite direction from "the incident," which is how I now mentally referred to it when it popped back into my conscience. I resolved to switch back to my regular purse in the morning and throw the gorgeous bag into the back of the closet. I didn't need the constant reminder of Carol's manipulative attempts to control me. In fact, I would only wear clothes I had bought myself. I was no longer going to be indebted to her. I was done. I felt stronger and more confident as my run progressed. This would be my independence day.

I would go home and tell Drew about my failure as a comedian. I could weather that storm. It wasn't the only hold she had on me, since she had alluded to Elise's death as a clear threat to my safety, but I could at least take one lie off the table and declare a small moral victory.

I would show up at Sarah's unannounced and get the tapes and give them to Richard. Carol would back off. It would be frosty and uneasy between us but I wasn't leaving Drew without a fight. I didn't have all of my problems worked but as I approached the end of my run, everything felt a bit more manageable.

I was standing at the corner waiting for the light to change so I could cross over to the gym when I heard a voice behind me.

"Allison Brown?"

"Yes?" I turned and saw two uniformed police officers standing close behind me and peed myself just a little. The perspiration on my forehead from the run covered the panic sweat that I could feel begin to drench my face and the hair on the back of my neck.

"We're going to need you to come with us to the station." One of the officers pointed in the direction of their patrol car parked a few feet away.

"I don't understand. What is this about?"

"Just come with us, ma'am. We will explain at the station."

This couldn't be happening. I suddenly realized I was wearing the clothes from the night of the incident. Fuck! Why didn't I burn these clothes or throw them away? Instead I had just washed them. It was no wonder they caught me. This was it. Everything was over and I was going to jail. I should have read Drew's criminal procedure book that had been sitting on the counter and prepared for this moment. I searched my knowledge of law learned through television and movies and tried to remember if I had any rights that I could assert and not go with them. Or did that make me look guilty?

"Ma'am? You need to come with us."

"Do I though?" Oh shit. I just sassed an officer. Perhaps not the smartest move. "I'm sorry. I just don't know what this could be about and my boyfriend's father is a very well respected attorney and I'm certain I must have some right to know what this is about before agreeing to go with you."

One of the officers grabbed my arm and started pulling me over to the car. People were stopping to watch. I considered screaming for help but realized the futility of someone coming forward to save me from two police officers. I saw someone put their phone up as if they were recording the incident. The last thing I needed was to become a viral sensation for resisting arrest. Was I being arrested? I hadn't been read my rights. Maybe they were waiting until we got to the station. I let myself be led into the cruiser but resolved to say nothing. The door slammed shut and as the officer started the car, it occurred to me that my purse, with my identification and most importantly my phone, was still in the gym locker.

"Officer, I need to get my purse the gym from across the street. If you don't mind. I really need to go get it."

The officer responded to my plea by driving down the street. At the station, I was escorted up the elevator and into a room that looked like every interrogation room I had ever seen on film. I was left alone for what seemed like an eternity but was probably no more than five minutes. My clothes were now drenched in panic sweat and the slightest bit of pee. I hoped the sweat and previous washing had been enough to eliminate whatever DNA or trace evidence I might have left behind or picked up at the scene. I tried to console myself that I wasn't put in handcuffs and that I hadn't been read my rights so I was not yet under arrest.

A red haired woman in a pantsuit entered the room. "Ms. Brown. I'm Detective Jackson. How are you this evening?"

She smiled at me and extended her hand. I assumed she must be good cop and I wondered how long it would be before bad cop arrived.

"I would like to make my phone call now."

She smiled warmly at me. "Ms. Brown, you aren't under arrest so that is not necessary."

"If I'm not under arrest then it shouldn't be a problem for me to make a phone call. I would have already made one with my cell phone but the officers who picked me up didn't permit me to get my purse."

"I apologize, Ms. Brown. That should not have happened. I will talk to the officers about their behavior."

"That would be great. Now, I'd like my phone call." As I kept insisting for my phone call, I realized that without my cell phone I had no idea what anyone's phone numbers actually were, other than my parents', and there was no way I was calling them.

"That really isn't necessary ma'am. We just want to ask you some questions as to your relationship with Elise Newman and what you might be able to tell us about her disappearance."

A wave of relief flushed through my body. Oh thank God. They didn't know about "the incident." It was only about Elise. I might be able to get through this after all.

"When was the last time you were inside Ms. Newman's apartment?"

That's a weird question. My sense of relief might have been premature.

"Excuse me?"

"We found your finger prints inside her apartment and we are just trying to get a sense of when you were last there and last saw her. We are just trying to put together a timeline as to what happened before she disappeared. Unfortunately, her phone is locked so we can't retrieve any information from it."

I tried to steady my breath and not reveal any signs of stress and panic. She had to be mistaken. I had never been inside Elise's apartment. I didn't even know where she lived until Susan told me a few days ago. Suddenly, Carol's warning about having friends in high places, including police chiefs, echoed through my brain.

"Detective Jackson, trust me when I say this, Elise was my friend and I want to be as much help to you as possible in finding out what happened to her. Here's the thing. Obviously, you know who I am and that my boyfriend's father, Richard Stephens, is a highly respected attorney in the city, and that his mother, Carol Stephens, is friends with the police chief. So, please, again with the upmost respect, I ask that you allow me to make a phone call before we continue this discussion."

"Ms. Brown, there is no reason for you to make this so difficult. Elise's life might be in danger."

"I understand, Detective. Again, I'm not trying to be evasive and difficult. I'm simply asking for a phone call that I'm absolutely sure that I'm entitled to make. I feel that both Richard and Carol would be very upset if they learned that I wasn't allowed to make it."

Even I recognized the irony that I was using Carol's reputation in an attempt to get out of a situation that I had no doubt she had specifically placed me.

"I understand. Follow me." I could tell by the tone of her voice and body language that her tenure as good cop was close to ending and that she really wanted to switch over to bad cop. Maybe she and her partner could flip coins while I was on the phone to see who got to try to intimidate me when we got back to the interrogation room.

Detective Jackson led me to a small nook in the lobby with a phone and a tattered phone book.

"Dial 9 to get an outside number." She turned and walked down the hallway approximately fifteen feet and leaned against the wall to wait for me.

I stared at the phone and contemplated who to call. My options were limited since I didn't have my phone. Even if I did have my phone, Sarah wouldn't answer if I called. I couldn't call Drew. I didn't want to get him involved and he would just call his dad. I could call Richard, but given his affair with Elise and the tape situation, I wasn't exactly sure I could trust him not to turn on me and use me as a scapegoat. I could call the hotel and ask for Max, but he would feel obligated to tell Drew.

If the detective was telling the truth and someone had planted my fingerprints in Elise's apartment, I was possibly in a lot of trouble. I had to call someone.

I really only had one option. It was a horrible option but the only one I had. I opened the phone book, found the number I was looking for, and dialed. It rang three times. I started to panic that there would be no answer. Finally, the phone pick up after the fourth ring.

"Hello, this is Tristan-Malcolm."

CHAPTER 27

"IT'S ALLY. PLEASE DON'T HANG up on me. I am down at the Central Park Precinct. The police are asking me questions about Elise." I blurted the words out in a hushed whisper and as fast as I could. I was desperate to get enough information to him to know that it was urgent but also I did not want to give away anything to the detective who I was sure was trying to listen. Hell, for all I knew the phone was tapped.

He let out one of his trademark disgusted sighs. "What have you done?"

"I haven't done anything. I swear. Please come help me." I remembered how he helped me outside of the building under the pretense of not wanting to ruin the firm's reputation. "Someone from the firm should be here since it involves Elise."

Another disgusted sigh. "Fine. Don't say a word to anyone until I get there."

"One more thing." I lowered my voice so hopefully the detective couldn't hear. "Please don't tell Richard. Not until we talk."

There was a silent pause on the other end as he considered my request. "I will be there in fifteen minutes. Keep your damn mouth shut. I know how hard that is for you."

I hung up feeling relief that help was on the way even though I suspected I had just sold my soul to the devil. I turned to the detective and flashed her one of my friendliest smiles. "They are sending someone over from the firm since this involves a former employee. I'm supposed to wait until he gets here."

She shrugged. "If that's the way you want to play it, Ms. Brown. We just had a few questions."

She led me back to the room and shut the door, leaving me alone with just my thoughts and my panic. I tried to keep a neutral face and relaxed body language because I was convinced someone was on the other side of the mirror watching me. It could be Carol for all I knew. I wasn't going to let them see me sweat. Well, they had certainly seen me sweat when they picked me up and I was drenched in it, but you know what I mean.

Not having my phone for the duration of the wait felt like torture. How did people sit in waiting rooms anywhere before cell phones were invented without killing themselves out of boredom? Surprisingly, the police station didn't keep old issues of *People* or even *Reader's Digest* for their suspects to peruse while waiting for their counsel to show up. I'm sure the slow torture of silence and boredom has led to at least one hasty confession just to break the monotony. I wondered if Drew had texted and was worried about why I wasn't home yet since I hadn't checked in after my run. What if I had missed a call from Sarah? Maybe she was finally ready to talk and forgive me.

The door opened and Tristan-Malcolm came in. I had never been happier in my life to see someone. I never would have imagined those words would formulate in my brain. Even the scowl on his face was a welcomed relief. He shut the door behind him.

"What the hell have you gotten yourself into? Do you realize the damage you have potentially caused the firm?"

My feeling of relief had been premature. I tried not to wilt under his glare. This might have been a huge mistake.

"Can you please just sit down and listen to me?" I begged and against all my survival instincts I pointed for him to sit in the seat next to me. "Is the detective coming back in?" I looked nervously at the door.

"Not yet. I asked for a few moments with you before she began." He walked over and sat down. "Explain yourself and make it quick."

I leaned over as close to him as possible and whispered. "Is the room bugged? Can they hear us?"

He sighed. "Oh dear lord. Please don't make this so dramatic. What did you do? Did you get drunk and assault Elise?"

He rolled his eyes as I scooted my chair closer to him in order to close the distance between us. I cupped my hand to his ear and whispered, "Elise is missing. They think I have something to do with it because someone planted my finger prints in her apartment but I have never been inside it.

I think Carol had her killed."

"That's enough. I don't need to hear any more." He got up and left the room. My mouth dropped open. I had just blown my only chance to get out of this mess. What had I been thinking? I should have held back on the Carol bombshell. He thought I was crazy on a normal day.

The door opened again and this time Detective Jackson was with Tristan-Malcolm. I wondered if he had convinced her to place me on a mental hold. Could he do that? Although, would that really be so bad at this point? I wouldn't have to deal with Carol's assassination attempt while in a psych ward, and there would probably good drugs and pudding.

"As I was saying, my client will fully cooperate with any investigation . . . "

No! I wanted to scream that he wasn't my attorney and that I had not consented to cooperate. This was worse than being committed to a mental hold.

". . . as soon as you provide evidence that there is an actual crime to investigate which, so far, you have not done. You admitted that you were following up on an anonymous tip and that there were no signs of struggle at her apartment. In all likelihood, Ms. Newman is on vacation sipping a tropical beverage with a tiny umbrella. Neither the firm, nor any of its employees will subject themselves to harassment until such time that you actually know what you are investigating. Any further attempts to make communication, with not just Ms. Brown, but any of the firm's employees, without the presence of counsel will be met with the filing of a protection order with the judge."

"Sir, we are just doing our job . . . but in the future, I will coordinate any further discussions with your office, as instructed."

"Ally, get your stuff, we are leaving."

I leapt up from my chair. I wanted to hug him but I felt sure that would not be appreciated. I followed him to the elevator.

As the doors shut and we were finally alone, he leaned over and in a hushed voice said, "Don't say a word until we get to my place."

He believed me! I had no idea why he would believe me but I didn't care. I would ask questions later. For the moment, I was just relieved to no longer be alone. Once outside we got into the waiting town car and rode in silence. The ride seemed to take forever. I looked out and we were leaving the city. Oh God! What had I done? What if Tristan-Malcolm was working with Carol? Was he taking me somewhere to silence me? Panic sweat started to drench my clothes again. At the next stop light, I would leap from the car, that is if the doors weren't locked. I would run to safety. Not that running had been leading me to safety lately, but there had to be a first time that something would go right. I should have been suspicious that he agreed to come down to the station so easily. I was never going to see Drew again. Or the cats.

I was on the verge of tears when the car came to a stop. Before I could grab the door handle and make a run for it, the door was open for me by the driver.

"We're here." Tristan-Malcolm announced.

His place turned out to be a brownstone in Carroll Gardens, Brooklyn, which was why the drive had taken so long. Fine. I might have overreacted a tad bit. But, can you really blame me?

CHAPTER 28

HE LED ME INTO HIS study, which was filled with rich leather furniture and dark wood covered walls. It suited him - unlike the sharp modern edges of his office. I could imagine him sitting in the room, smoking a cigar while contemplating how to make me and everyone else around him miserable, which was clearly his hobby since he excelled at it. He turned on the gas fireplace and went to the bar and poured us each a glass of bourbon. I wasn't sure if I was allowed to talk yet. If I squinted and tilted my head, I might just be able to make out the rugged sexiness that both Susan and Max seemed to see. Maybe it was because he was in his natural habitat, but it was more likely because he had at least temporarily saved me from Detective Jackson and hadn't hand-delivered me to Carol, or my death.

"Why did you believe me?"

"Would you rather that I hadn't? I can have the town car return you to Detective Jackson, if you would like."

He handed me the glass of bourbon. I took a sip. "Do you have any snacks?"

"Are you four years old? You can have a snack later. You need to tell me what you know or what you think you know."

"How do I know that I can trust you? You could be working with Carol for all I know."

He snorted. "The day I work for Carol is the day Hell will finally freeze over. I always assumed you were her puppet."

"That doesn't answer my question. How do I know that I can trust you?"

"If you called me, then I suspect that you don't really have a lot of options right now. You retain me as your attorney and then you can trust me. If I breach your trust, feel free to sue me." He took a seat in one of the giant chairs beside the fireplace.

"Put it in writing that you are my attorney and I will tell you what I know." I sat down in the chair opposite from him.

"Do you think I just carry contracts around with me?"

"Humor me. Get a notepad or a cocktail napkin and write up a paragraph that you are my attorney and we will both sign it."

"This is ridiculous. I just got your ass out of jail."

"I'm getting ready to tell you all the details I know about a possibly huge conspiracy. So, how about you humor me?" My voice raised louder than I intended it but my nerves were shot.

He stared blankly at me for what felt like an eternity. Finally, he stood up. "I might have some paper in the kitchen."

"Dude, what's your deal with paper? I have Post-it notes stuck all over the place."

"That doesn't surprise me. Wait here."

After he left, I got up and started pacing the room and looking at the pictures on the shelves. The first shelf had a picture of Tristan-Malcolm and another man about his age who was ridiculously handsome. They were both smiling. I had no idea Tristan-Malcolm's mouth could even form a smile. His brother must have gotten all of the charm and personality. There were more pictures of the two of them together in various vacation destinations, arms draped intimately around each other, all smiles. By the time I got to the picture of the two of them in tuxedos in a side hug with their heads touching just ever so slightly, it dawned on me that Susan did not have any chance whatsoever with him. How odd to think of him having a personal life and being in love? I was still staring at the picture when he returned with the hastily drawn up contract and a pen.

"Are you married?" I asked. "Is your husband going to be coming home soon? Is it safe to talk here?"

He ignored my questions and handed me the paper and pen. "All you have to do is sign here and it will be official and you can tell me everything. I, on the other hand, don't owe you any explanations or discussion about my personal life."

The look on his face told me not to push him on the issue. "Fine." I took the paper and signed it.

"Tell me what you know." He sat back down in the big leather chair and began stroking his mustache while waiting for me to proceed.

I sat down. I had contemplated how to start the story during the silent ride over in the town car, but the mustache stroking mentally sent me back to day one in his office.

"First, promise you won't get mad, kill me, and turn me into a stew."

"I don't even know how to respond to such a ludicrous request other than to say, start talking or I will rip up that contract and hand-deliver you back to Detective Jackson."

I blurted out everything I knew. Richard and Elise's affair. Uncle Benji and Senator Birdie. Carol and Uncle Benji's conversation at the fundraiser. My meeting with Richard. Everything Carol had said during our dinner from hell. I ended with the police picking me up on the street. The only thing I didn't tell him was that I had given the tapes to Sarah. I wanted to keep her out of it.

He listened silently while I talked and didn't even interrupt me with an exacerbated sigh or well-timed eye roll. He occasionally got up to refill our glasses. At one point during my story, two calico cats wandered in the room and one jumped up and curled into his lap. I almost lost track of what I was saying as I tried to process that he was a cat person. It was actually more shocking to me than the fact that he might have a husband.

"So, I'm seriously fucked, right? I have no moves here other than to give the tapes to Richard and hope he gives them to Carol so she will call off killing him. Right?"

"That story is quite a lot to process." He pinched the bridge of his nose between two fingers and closed his eyes. He was quiet for a few moments and I was grateful that he at least wasn't stroking his mustache and staring at me. He finally opened his eyes.

"For now, I'm going to gloss over the fact that you didn't tell me about the tapes immediately, but trust me, I will most certainly be revisiting that issue."

"But you believe me?" I could deal with being reprimanded later. I just needed to know someone would believe me.

"It will take me a bit to get my head around Carol killing Elise and wanting you to kill Richard. Maybe she is lying to you. Maybe she has another end game. But I will agree that she has certainly never been trustworthy and neither has her brother."

He got up and paced the floor. "I'll admit something has felt off since Elise left. Richard has been acting odd and has not been giving me very much information about the merger. The night of the fundraiser, you said Richard told you that Rusk Communications was being purchased because of technology. But Richard told me the company was being purchased because of its market share and certain web content that it produced, which was of particular popularity with adult male youths. Now, I didn't research the company because I assumed he was subtly trying to tell me it was an online porn conglomerate. I didn't really care about their product because I was told to concentrate on getting the paper work solid and airtight."

I fidgeted in my chair. "Please don't ask how I know, but Mars already has an online porn division and a gossip division."

He shook his head and sighed. "It certainly doesn't surprise me that you know that." If I had a dollar for every time I made him sigh and roll his eyes, my escape fund would allow me to live a life of luxury.

"I also couldn't understand why all of Elise's notes were about antitrust cases which had nothing to do with this merger. Honestly, I thought you were just messing with me and making shit up."

"That would have taken a lot of effort on my part just to mess with you. It's a pretty brilliant idea though, so I kind of wish I would have come up with it myself instead of squinting my way through those damn notes."

He lowered his eyebrows into a scowl, stroked his mustache as he leaned against the fireplace.

I backpedaled. "I mean . . . I obviously wouldn't have done that to you. You scare the shit out of me with that whole cannibalistic vibe you give off. You really need to learn to tone that down."

"Please stop talking nonsense while I'm trying to figure out how to save your bacon."

"See right there, you are stroking your mustache and talking about me and bacon. It's very creepy. I mean really you look like you want to eat me. Speaking of which, can we please have some snacks now? I'm starved."

"I think I have some leftover pizza in the fridge." He started toward the door.

"You eat pizza?"

He stopped and turned around to look at me quizzically, "Why in the world wouldn't I eat pizza?"

"I don't know. I didn't think you would be a cat person either. You just give off more of a super villain/cannibal vibe." I held up my hands. "I'm sorry. I'm just being honest here."

"Don't mistake my help in this matter for us being friends all of a sudden." He left me and went to the kitchen. He returned a few minutes later with a box and napkins and plate.

"So, what are your cats' names?" I took a huge bite out of a slice.

"That isn't germane to what we are discussing. It's getting late. Drew is probably worried about you and we don't need him asking questions while we try to figure out a solution. I'll have the town car take you home. Nothing is getting solved tonight."

He was right. Drew was going to ask a lot of questions. I would have to lie again. It felt nice to talk to someone and tell the truth. Even though we hadn't figured a way out of my predicament, I still felt like a burden had been lifted off my chest. Not all of it though. There were still a few burdens I had to carry.

"Can I ask you something?"

"I've never been able to stop you from running your mouth before, so why should I try now. If it's something personal, then I won't be answering."

"Does the attorney-client privilege cover anything that I say to you?"

"Absolutely. Is there something else about the merger or Carol that you haven't told me? I need to know everything."

"It's not about that. It's just that . . ." I inhaled a deep breath and then slowly exhaled. "I think I killed a man in the park." I started crying. I don't know why I told him other than it had felt so good to get everything else off my chest. "It was an accident. I was running and I was alone and I thought he was going to attack me. Although, to be fair, I attacked him first for running and sexting and knocking me down. Things just got out of control and I panicked and I left and. . . ."

"Oh my god, Ally . . ." His voice sounded more dismayed than angry. He handed me a napkin to blow my nose.

"I didn't know what to do. It was an accident."

"When did this happen?"

"My first day working for you. It had been a really shitty day. I thought he was going to hit me and I just flipped him in self-defense and he must have hit his head on a rock. There was just so much blood."

"Did you feel for a pulse? Are you sure he was dead?"

I shook my head. "I was too scared and he was on the other side of the railing by the reservoir."

"I will see what I can find out."

"I can't tell anyone. I'm not turning myself in. I can't go to jail. I would lose Drew. I can't lose him."

"I'm not asking you to turn yourself in. We have more pressing issues right now, so we will come back to this later. For now, just go home."

"Thank you. I'm sorry I told you. I shouldn't have told you."

"It's fine. It seems like you have been carrying quite a bit of stress on your own these past couple of days." He pinched the bridge of his nose again and took a deep breath. "Which makes it harder for me to tell you this, but since you trusted me enough to tell me what you just did, I feel obligated to tell you."

"Tell me what?"

"I tried to warn you at the fundraiser to have a backup plan. I knew you wouldn't listen to me based on all of our prior interactions, but I meant that as a sincere gesture. My ex . . ." He pointed towards the pictures on the wall. "He came from a family a lot like Drew's, very powerful and wealthy and politically savvy. His father never approved of us, but while his mom was alive, she was able to keep his dad under control. As long as we stayed discrete. When she died, I was banned from attending her funeral . . . Let's just say, I know from experience they always chose power and wealth over love."

My heart actually ached for him, something I never thought possible. But his story wasn't the same as mine.

"Drew's not like that though. We can find some way to fix this without Drew leaving me."

Tristan-Malcolm hung his head and then looked back up at me with soft, weary eyes. "Ally, I saw Drew going into Elise's office the night she supposedly quit or disappeared or whatever happened to her. I saw him carry a box of her things out. It seemed weird to me at the time, but given what you've told me tonight . . ."

"No. You must be mistaken. That's not true."

"Ally. It was him."

CHAPTER 29

THE WHOLE RIDE HOME FROM Brooklyn, I was preoccupied with rationalizing why Drew would have been at Elise's office on the night she disappeared. I thought of a dozen different ways Tristan-Malcolm could have been wrong and mistaken someone else for Drew or had the night wrong. It just wasn't possible Drew could be involved. I refused to believe it. It was after midnight when I got home. I had to knock on the door since my keys were in my purse, which was still at the gym. It took several knocks of increasing loudness before Drew finally opened the door all sleepy-eyed.

"Why didn't you just use your key, babe? What time is it?"

"I'm sorry. I ended up having to work late and I forgot my purse at the office." I convinced myself this wasn't a complete lie. I had been discussing work.

"How did you get home without your purse?"

"The two-named asshole had a moment of humanity this evening and let me use his town car. Honestly, I think that's what confused me and made me walk out in a daze without my purse or phone in the first place." I walked back into the bedroom to change into my pajamas and hoped that would put an end the interrogation.

He followed me and crawled into bed and waited for me. "That was nice. Maybe there's hope for him."

"Well, let's not get crazy just yet. He might have just had a high fever." I crawled in beside him.

He smiled and pulled me close to him and encased me in his long arms. My safe harbor. At least, I thought it was until tonight. Now, I wasn't so sure.

"I still wish Elise would come back."

I waited to see if his body tensed or flinched at the mention of her name. There was no reaction.

"Did you have any idea Elise was going to leave? Did your dad ever mention her or did you talk to her?"

I had to know that Tristan-Malcolm was wrong.

"I know you miss her, honey. No, Dad never mentioned anything. I can't even remember the last time I actually talked to her . . . maybe at the firm's Fourth of July party? You know I would have told you if I had any warning she would leave, especially if I knew Dad would make you work with the bearded ass. Maybe once the merger deal is signed and finished on Friday he will ease up or you can start working with someone else."

I had no idea the merger was going through on Friday. "How is it that you always know more about my work than me? Are you sneaking into the office and talking to your dad about cases without coming down to see me? You are in so much trouble if you do that." I playfully swatted at his leg.

He laughed. "I promise. I would never come to the office without coming by to see you."

"You should come to see me more often. Maybe lunch one day and a quickie somewhere discreet. I can't even remember the last time you were there, can you?"

There was a long pause and I wished we weren't spooning so I could see his face.

"It must have been months ago. You need to get some sleep. You've had a long day."

He kissed me on the back of the neck. "I love you, Ally Brown."

"I love you, Drew Stephens."

I closed my eyes, but I didn't get any sleep because I knew he had just lied to me. I could feel it in my bones.

CHAPTER 30

I WAS LATE GETTING TO the office the next morning. I scrounged through the purses in my closet to find enough money to get a new metro card to get to the gym and finally retrieve my purse and phone. The phone battery was dead so I still didn't know if Sarah had tried to contact me. Once I got to my cubicle, I plugged the phone into the portable charger and waited for the phone to finally flicker to life. When it did, I was disappointed to see that she had not responded. There had been several missed calls and texts from Drew worried about me. I should have felt comforted by that, but it did not relieve the anxiety of believing that he lied to me. I still couldn't bring myself to believe he was involved in whatever happened to Elise.

There was a message from Tristan-Malcolm waiting in my inbox:

To: Allison Brown

From: Tristan-Malcolm Reynolds

Subject: Your work

Please come to my office as soon as you get here.

TRM.

Well, at least we had maybe gotten past the morning insults and he did use the word "please." I was counting on him to come up with a solution to my problem. I certainly hadn't found one. In fact, I had pretty much stopped thinking about anything other than why Drew would lie to me. I'd felt something was off, but I had always chalked it up to insecurity or projection on my end because of my own repeated lies to him.

I took my phone with me to his office on the off chance that Sarah might respond.

"CLOSE THE DOOR BEHIND YOU." He was looking at his computer screen and hadn't bothered to look up. For the first time, I wasn't absolutely terrified walking in to face him.

"Did you bring the tapes? You haven't given them to Richard yet, have you?"

I suspected I was about to have reason to be terrified of him again. "Yeah, umm, here's the thing. I don't actually have them."

That got his attention. He looked up from the screen. "What? You said you had them last night. You told me that you had listened to some of them."

Shit. This could get ugly. I suspected I might need to use my backup pair of underwear from the purse.

"Well, umm, I sort of gave them to a friend and had her listening to them because I was so busy with the notebooks and . . ."

"You gave confidential work information to someone outside of the office? What the hell were you thinking?" His fingers went immediately to the bridge of his nose, which I was starting to figure out was his stress tell.

"I know. If you could try to keep things in perspective. I wasn't exactly in the best frame of mind at the time I made what I will admit was a very poor judgment call."

"A poor judgment call? Is that what you want to call it? I have some completely different words altogether that I would use. This is unacceptable. Call your friend and have her bring them here immediately."

"Yeah well . . ." Deep breath. "There's a slight hitch in that area at the moment."

"A slight hitch? What pray tell is the slight hitch?"

"Ummm, remember the scene outside the office? That's the friend who has the tapes and she's not exactly taking my calls or texts at the moment."

He stared at me not blinking. "Every time you open your mouth, things keep getting exponentially worse. I have honestly never witnessed anything like it."

I grimaced and was not sure what to say in response because he was right.

"Give me her number."

"What?"

"Give me her number. I'm calling her."

I pulled my phone out of the pocket of my dress and read him the number. "She's not going to pick up. She hasn't answered any of my calls and it is really early in the morning. She's going to be super pissed about being woken up."

He ignored me and dialed her number on his cell phone and waited. "Hello, this is Ally's boss Tristan-Malcolm. I'm going to need you to bring those tapes that she gave you to the office immediately or Ally is going to be fired."

I mouthed, "What the hell, dude?"

He listened to her speak for a few minutes. Her voice was so loud that I could hear it from where I sat, but I couldn't make out the words.

He continued. "Well it seems we both want the same thing in that regard, but I'm afraid if you don't return them, I will have you arrested for possession of stolen property."

He listened again for several minutes and I could only imagine the profanity he was being met with on the other side of the conversation. "Yes, I agree with you completely, she is meddlesome and selfish and doesn't think anything through at all, but that doesn't change the fact that I need those tapes."

I hung my head while he continued to listen to her tirade on the other end. It was obvious she was never going to forgive me.

"I understand. I will send a town car for you after the show." He hung up the phone.

"I don't know what you did to her and I don't want to know, but she is not your biggest fan at the moment."

"I kind of got that. You didn't have to join in and agree so much with her."

"She made some very valid points. She will bring the tapes to you tonight after the show. I would prefer to have them now, but given her temperament at the moment, I suppose that is the best we can do. Make sure you get the tapes in your hand before you open your mouth and screw things up even worse."

"Ha ha. I get it. I'm a fuck-up. You have made that perfectly clear on several occasions."

"Well, you were at least smart enough to finally get me involved, so I will grant you that. We don't have a lot of time. So put your hurt feelings aside because I'm going to need you to get some actual work done today. I'm researching any cases that Senator Davis worked on when she was a judge that could have in anyway involved Benjamin Mars and antitrust issues. I need you to spend the day finding out as much as you can about Rusk Communications and just read through the notebooks and see if you see any mention of Senator Davis or Rusk. I don't need you to type them up. Just flag anything important with one of those goddamn Post-it notes you love so much and we will talk again later this afternoon."

"Is it OK if I ask for help on researching Rusk? Susan, who works downstairs with me, she can find practically anything on the internet." He didn't need to know the exact details of her skills.

"First, let me congratulate you on making progress by actually asking me before going off and doing something half-cocked on your own. Do you think you can trust her?"

"Absolutely. She doesn't ask questions when I ask her to find me things. She just does it. Although, there is this issue of her wanting me to figure out your dating status."

"Excuse me. What did you just say?"

I held my hands up. "I know. I don't understand why she seems to think you are ruggedly sexy either. It's a complete mystery to me."

"My dating status is off limits as a topic of discussion. How dare you . . ."

"Settle down. I'm not going to tell her about your ex-husband. I've got this."

"That is not in the least bit reassuring to me." Disgusted sigh. "Go get your work done. We'll talk later."

"Yes, sir." I saluted him, which I immediately regretted after seeing the scowl on his face. He was still holding firm to his desire not to be amused.

I LEFT HIS OFFICE AND immediately sought out Susan. If anyone could find out what Rusk Communications actually had to offer in this merger, it was her.

"Susan, I need your help. Well, actually Tristan-Malcolm needs your help."

She swiveled her chair to face me.

"You've got my attention. I'm listening."

"Can you find out everything there is to know about Rusk

Communications?"

"Is that a real question? Are you seriously doubting my abilities?"

"I would never. I have a very special folder on my computer proving your research skills. Tristan-Malcolm needs this done ASAP and I told him you were the perfect person for the job."

"Thanks for the recommendation. Do you have any other news to report on that front? Is there a girlfriend?"

"I'm still working on that, I promise. Today was the first day he hasn't yelled at me, but it's not even noon yet so that could blow up at any time."

"Got it and I'm on it. I'll have you a full dossier by the end of the day."

"You are the best. I'm taking you to eat wherever you want to go after this damn merger is finally finished."

"Sounds good. It's going to cost you. Now, leave me alone so I can impress Tristan-Malcolm."

I sat down at my desk and got a text message from Sarah. *Seriously? You had your boss call me? That was a bitch ass move. I'm bringing the tapes tonight but that's it. We aren't discussing anything else.*

I responded with a simple, *I understand.*

I picked up the stack of notebooks and started combing through them to see if I could find anything that was useful. At least it went faster not having to type everything word for word. About an hour had passed by when I felt a shadow at my back.

"Did you find something?" I turned expecting to see Susan but was met by the icy smile of Carol.

"Hello, Allison darling. Come have lunch with me, will you? We have things to discuss."

"But it's not Thursday. I thought I had until Thursday."

"Come along dear." She grabbed my arm in what would appear to any onlookers as an act of assistance in getting up but in fact was a steely grip that defied me to resist her. I stood up and she led me to the elevators. She was smiling and laughing her dainty wealthy lady laugh as we walked past all the other employees. They all probably hated me, seeing what they thought was me getting preferential treatment by having lunch with the main partner's wife, when by all accounts I should have been fired by Tristan-Malcolm already. The office firing pool must be in a chaotic tailspin of confusion.

CHAPTER 31

I DIDN'T SAY A WORD as she practically dragged me down to the town car or on the drive. I had no idea where she was taking me. Maybe she had decided to kill me herself.

"You are so quiet today, dear. Something troubling you?"

I glanced at the driver's refection in the rearview mirror, trying to determine if he had the face of a killer, but not exactly knowing what features I thought would divulge that information. Maybe a huge scar down his face? No, that would be too cliché.

"Fuck you." I muttered under my breath.

"Still so salty. I would have thought your visit with Detective Jackson would have settled that down your attitude."

I was right. It *was* her who had sent the police after me. What a bitch. The town car stopped and I realized we were at The Club. I hadn't realized they were open for lunch. Fred greeted us and opened the door. "Mrs. Stephens and Ms. Brown. What a lovely surprise! I didn't expect to see you two lovely women until tomorrow night."

The Club was empty when we got there. It was strange seeing the room without the crowd, alive with political and business chatter and the clink of bar glasses as they made agreements to scratch each other's backs at the expense of society at large. Frankly, it lost all of its grandiose charm when it was empty and quiet. It seemed so very ordinary. Louis appeared and sat us at our usual table. He was also the one who brought us our water. He appeared to be the only one working.

"I will bring your salads out whenever you are ready." He nodded at Carol and left. Great, another salad. If she really wanted to convince me to kill someone, she needed to learn to lead with better food.

"Thank you, Louis." He left the room and it was just us.

"Well, aren't you special that they opened this place up just for you." I tried to hide my fear behind sarcasm. It was always my go-to cover.

"I am actually. It appears I'm going to have to do a little more to convince you just how powerful I can be when I set my mind on something."

"No, I get it. You can have me picked up by the police and blamed for a murder I didn't commit. Very cute."

"It was clever, I agree. I needed you to understand that you can't just pack up and run away with my son."

Louis peeked out the kitchen door and she nodded, indicating he could bring the food. She waited until after he placed the huge pile of rabbit food in front of us before speaking again. To add insult to injury, there wasn't even a bread basket. I didn't even make an effort to pretend to eat the pile of grass. I kept my hands folded on my lap.

"So, hopefully you have accepted that you have no other choice but to take care of Richard. It must happen tomorrow."

I was taking a sip of water and nearly choked, "I thought I had until tomorrow to make up my mind."

"No darling. Your listening skills leave a lot to be desired. You have until tomorrow to kill him." She stabbed a piece of her salad as she said the word "kill" to give it emphasis.

I just stared at her. How could she just eat a salad while discussing having her husband killed? I wondered how many similar conversations had taken place at this illustrious club.

"Well, I can't do it. I won't do it."

"But you will. And frankly, I've already done all the hard work and the planning for you. It's very simple really."

"Oh, is it? Tell me how simple it is to kill my boyfriend's father."

She nonchalantly picked up her glass for a sip of water as if she wasn't plotting her husband's murder. "Stop being so sentimental. Drew will survive."

"Has anyone ever told you that you lack maternal instincts? You are talking about killing your son's father and your own husband as if you are deciding what wallpaper to put in the bathroom."

"Wallpaper in the bathroom? Oh dear, what kind of home did you grow up in?" She touched a hand to her chest to express her horror at my droll upbringing.

"A home with parents who weren't psychopaths. It was actually rather nice."

"How pleasant for you darling. Now, I need you to listen to me. This is what you are going to do. Tomorrow night, The Club will be closed down for some remodeling work so we are going to have our normal family dinner at our house."

Interesting that Fred didn't seem to know The Club was going to be closed down. I guess he didn't know the most powerful woman in the world, or at least in her mind, had determined it was going to be closed. What dirt did she have on Louis or whoever had the pull to make that decision?

"During our cocktail before dinner, I'm going to need you to put this in Richard's drink." She slid a small vial across the table towards me.

"What is it?"

"It's merely some crushed up Ambien and Xanax from his own prescription bottles."

"And that is supposed to be enough to kill him?"

I didn't touch it. The vial didn't seem big enough to contain a lethal dose, not that I had any prior knowledge about lethal doses of Ambien or Xanax.

She let out an exacerbated sigh. "No, that is not enough to kill him. It's just enough to get him drowsy so you can kill him. I am really going to need you to listen to me because I'm not going to tell you all of this again."

I kept my mouth shut and let her keep talking. There was no way I was going to go through with it but I figured it was better for me to know the whole plan.

"Once the drugs take effect and he is sufficiently groggy, I will suggest that he go lay down in the study while we finish our meal. Before dessert, you will excuse yourself to go to the bathroom and follow him. In the top drawer of his desk, you will find a syringe filled with enough insulin to kill him. He has a large freckle on the right side of his neck which is where you will inject him. Just after you inject him, I'm going to need you to make sure he is awake enough for you to explain what you did to him and tell him he should know better than to steal from me. You pocket the syringe and return to the table. Please wear something with pockets. I suggest that marmalade dress with the matching cardigan. You return to the table. After we have dessert, we'll retire to the study where we all are horrified and saddened to find him dead. Voila! It is all very simple."

I listened to the whole description in horror. She was really not fucking around. She'd planned everything, including my outfit. "So, here's the thing, Carol. First, I know how much you loathe it when I make pop culture references, but I think you have probably watched *Reversal of Fortune* too many times. Second, there is no fucking way that I'm doing it. Third, if it is so simple then you can do it yourself."

"Darling, I've already explained all the reasons why I want you to do it. And you will do it or I'll tell Drew everything and you get visited by Detective Jackson again."

"Tell him. I don't think me missing some comedy sets will be fatal to our relationship. But killing his father, yeah, that probably would be the end of us. Second, I had nothing to do with Elise. Planting my fingerprints in her apartment means nothing. It is not nearly enough to get me convicted." I really hoped that was true.

"It's not just the fingerprints. Had you not called Tristan-Malcolm, which was a rather unexpected turn of events, I must say, then you would have found out there was an eyewitness that heard you pounding and screaming on her door and threatening to kill poor Elise."

"That happened way after she went missing."

"Are you sure about that? I've heard the witness is a bit of a drinker and easily confused. I suspect she will remember it differently after a little nudging."

"Bullshit. That's still not enough to convict me." Again, I was wishful thinking but I wasn't going to let her see me waiver.

"Oh, Allison. I was hoping I wouldn't have to be so crass as to bring up your other extracurricular activities, but it appears your sheer stubbornness and thick-headedness is forcing my hand."

My stomach tightened. "I don't know what you're talking about." She couldn't know. There was no way that she could know.

"I think you do. That poor man in the park, those two random men at the bar, and Rena. Does that help jog your memory?"

No! No, no, no. She couldn't know about any of that. My mind tried to work out how she could possibly know. I had not left any traces behind. I had been careful.

"I know everything, Allison." She pushed the vile of drugs closer to me. "So, if you aren't going to finish your salad then take this . . ." She slid the vial closer to me. "I will see you tomorrow night. You can use the walk back to the office to come to grips with your fate."

I stood up, grabbed the vial, and shoved it in my pocket. "You are a monster."

She threw her head back and laughed. "I'm sorry, but you trying to take the moral high ground in this situation is just ever so quaint."

"Fuck you." I left the table.

She called out to me just as I got to the door. "Do tell your new bestie Tristan-Malcolm hello for me."

CHAPTER 32

I WAS FURIOUS AS I stormed into Tristan-Malcolm's office, "You told her! You told her everything! I trusted you. You signed the contract. You were supposed to be my attorney and you told her everything!"

Tristan-Malcolm stared at me like I had gone mad, because in all honesty, I had. I had built up quite a lot of steam on the walk over as I figured out the only way she knew about the man in the park was because Tristan-Malcolm had betrayed me.

"Who? What are you yammering on about now? Shut the damn door before you go saying another word and simmer your ass down."

I slammed the door so hard it knocked a picture off the wall.

"I knew better than to trust you. You were in on it this whole time."

"Sit down!" He barked at me loud enough that my Pavlovian fear of him caused me to immediately sit.

"Now, tell me in a calm voice what you are talking about because I haven't told anyone anything."

"Carol. You told Carol. She took me to lunch to give me specific details on how I'm supposed to kill Richard tomorrow night. I refused to go along and she pulled the ace out of her sleeve. She knew about the man in the park. She knew all of it. She knew about the two douche-bros that I drugged at the bar and she knew that I gave drugs to Rena. She knew all of it."

I was starting to fall apart as I realized just how much jail time that I was looking at.

"Wait a minute. You told me nothing about drugging two so-called douche-bros, whatever the hell that means, or Rena. Are you talking about the pop star who is on Broadway? Why would you give her drugs? What else have you gotten yourself into? Is it possible for you to go a day without making some huge mistake or committing a crime?"

I was about to break down into tears but I stopped myself. "You are right. I didn't tell you about them did I?"

"No, and frankly, at the moment, the less I know about all of that, the better."

"How did she know?" I got up and started pacing his office trying to piece it all together. "How could she possibly know? I haven't told anyone. Sure, Sarah knows about Rena, but there is no way she would tell that monstrous bitch anything. I don't care how mad she is at me. Sarah wouldn't tell her. And the douche-bros didn't know my name. How did she know? And she knew you had come and bailed me out."

"Well, if she is working with Detective Jackson or anyone else in the police department, then that was easy for her to find out."

"But everything else." I thought back on her words and everything she said at lunch. "She told me I couldn't just run away with her son. I talked to Drew about running away from everything the night before I was taken into the police station. I doubt Drew would tell her that, so how did she know about it."

I stopped in my tracks. "Oh my God! It can't be possible . . . but it's the only thing that makes any sense. I confessed everything to my cats. That has to be how she knows."

"What? Well, now I know you've lost your damn mind."

"It's the only possible way. I think there's a bug in that goddamn purse!" I slumped down onto the chair. "That bitch has been listening to everything."

"Where is this purse now?"

"It's down in a filing cabinet drawer. It all makes sense now. She ambushed me at my desk and got me on the elevator so fast I didn't have time to get it. She took it from me and put it in another room when we had dinner that night. She didn't want to be caught on any recordings asking me to kill him. I'm going to throw that fucking bag into the goddamn river."

He got up from his desk and came around and sat in the chair beside me.

"Stop and think for a minute. We've got the upper hand on her now. We just have to figure out how to use it. In the meantime, just make sure it is nowhere near you when you are talking to anyone about anything important. Now, think. Have you said anything about the tapes out loud? Is there any way she knows you have them?"

I searched my memory and shook my head. "I can't think of anything I would have said. She hadn't given me the purse yet when I gave the tapes to Sarah. The next time Sarah and I talked about them we were out jogging, so I didn't have it with me. I've only sent Sarah texts the past few days except for one voicemail message, but I didn't mention the tapes."

"Well, that is at least a bit of good fortune Let's just stick to the plan. I haven't found anything connecting the senator and Benjamin yet, but I'm sure it's out there."

"Well, hopefully we find it soon, because we are running out of time."

I WENT DOWN TO MY desk and yanked open the filing cabinet drawer. I flipped the purse off while mouthing the words, "Fuck you, Carol." Then I slammed the drawer shut.

After my mini-tantrum, I went back to reviewing the notebooks. It felt futile but there was nothing else I could do other than stew in my hatred and berate myself for confessing everything out loud to my cats. What had been only mildly cathartic was now contributing to my downfall. I thought of how careful I had been about everything else but I had never stopped to consider someone was listening to me. I really should have been alerted to that possibility when Sarah told me about the tapes and the burrito debate. Taping people without their knowledge must be a family tradition. That must be how Uncle Benji's gossip site got such good scoop. He probably gave people gifts that were bugged or maybe he cloned their phones. I suddenly felt a tinge of guilt for reading all of the salacious details that were probably illegally obtained.

I was flipping through pages of random initials and dates and numbers that only Elise would have been able to cipher when I saw what I had initially interpreted as "Reva 10-08 T12 SA 14:02." Total nonsense. Now looking closer at it, I wondered if it was possible that Elise meant Rena instead of Reva.

I realized I could be grasping at straws, but I pulled up Google and searched Rena and October 2008. The second search result was a story on GTrendz about a rumor that Rena's mom had sold Rena's virginity to an Arabian sheik for millions of dollars. I remembered scoffing at that story when it hit the tabloids. At the time, Rena was dating Miles Mickelson. He was a hot young actor so there was no way she would have had sex with some sleazy old geezer and not Miles. What didn't make sense was why possible references to a piece of gossip would be in Elise's notes?

I pulled up my typed version of the notes and scrolled down to where I had transcribed the random lists and for the first time noticed a pattern. "T12 SA 14:02" was followed by "T12 SB 6:04" and then "T13 SA 8:10." I hit my hand on head. Of course. Elise was making a log of the recordings on the tape. I printed off the pages and furiously started highlighting and flagging every entry that could possibly be read as being either Birdie or Davis. Along the way, I noticed several that could be read as "Richard" or "Stephens," and I highlighted those as well. The hours flew by as I felt like I had finally cracked Elise's secret code.

I made sure the file cabinet drawer with the purse was shut all the way before picking up the phone to call Tristan-Malcolm.

"What? Did you find something?"

I whispered, "Elise was making a log of the tapes. Text me your phone number and I will text you the dates that are beside the entries that look like they could relate to the senator."

"Why don't you just email them to me?"

"Because it will be on the computer system and I don't want Richard to possibly see it and find out we know about the tapes. I promise I'm not going to prank call you or text you a bunch of funny cat pictures. Although, I do have some really good ones. Just give me your number."

He exhaled loudly to emphasize how much he did not want to comply, but then ultimately gave it to me. I was about ready to hang up when he cleared his throat and said, "That was a good catch, Ally. This could really help. Great job." He hung up before I could say anything else.

I stared at the phone in my hands and for the first time in days, a genuine smile appeared on my face. I had done something right and it was acknowledged and it felt really good. The smile was short lived when I remembered that I had less than one day to come up with a way to save Richard's life and not go to jail. Susan came by my desk and handed me a purple folder.

"This is everything I could find. I hope it helps. There wasn't that much out there."

"Thanks, you are the best."

"Good luck on your show tonight." She left and I realized that it was after six. I wasn't even going to pretend to do a show tonight. I had no time. Plus, I had to wait on Sarah to come over with the tapes. Drew would be at his study group, so I decided to take Susan's folder, my highlighted notes, and the last few notebooks home and work while I waited for Sarah. I didn't want to lose track of time and miss her. I flipped the purse off again as I pulled it from the drawer and headed out.

On the elevator, I thought again about Tristan-Malcolm's claim to have seen Drew carry a box of Elise's stuff out on the night she went missing. I had to tell myself she was just missing and not dead. It was the only way I could concentrate on getting through this whole ordeal. I would have plenty of time to grieve later. Maybe while rotting away in a jail cell.

"Hey, Ms. Brown. Glad to see you are getting out of here at a decent time tonight." Greg checked me out of the building.

"Me too. Sorry about the game last week. That was harsh."

"We were so close. I feel good about this weekend though."

I wished I could say the same. I was almost out the door when I stopped. I put the purse down on the ground and covered it with the notebooks and folder. I walked back over to Greg with my phone.

"Hey, can you help me settle an argument with my boyfriend?"

"Probably, if it's about sports."

I laughed. "No, it's not about sports, but I still think you can help. Our anniversary was a couple of weeks ago and he claims that he didn't forget and that he came to the office with a box for me and I wasn't here. I think he's just trying to cover his ass because he forgot and didn't get me anything until two days later."

"Well, now I don't want to get anyone in trouble."

"Oh, he won't be in too much trouble, but he will owe me a steak if I can prove him wrong. His name is Richard Stephens, III and it would have been on October 18th."

He looked on his computer for a few minutes and then looked up. "I'm sorry to tell you this ma'am, but you will not be getting a steak dinner. Looks like my boy remembered your anniversary after all." He grinned up at me.

"Are you sure?" I pulled out my phone and showed him a picture of Drew. "Is this who you saw?"

"Oh, yeah! I remember him. Nice fellow. Gave me a tip for opening the door for him because he did have a big box in his hands. I don't usually get tips."

It felt like my world had collapsed in on itself. I had suspected that he lied, but now I had proof. What else did he know about everything that had happened? What else had he lied about? I thought about the untouched law books, all the time he spent with his mother, how long he had talked with both her and the senator at the fundraiser.

"You alright, Ms. Brown? You look a little pale."

"I'm fine. Just really shocked that he was actually here." That wasn't a lie. "Thank you for your help, Greg."

I walked over and picked up my belongings and headed out the door. I briefly considered just walking into the traffic.

CHAPTER 33

I WAS IMMEDIATELY GREETED INSIDE by the two cats when I got home. I wanted nothing more than to scoop them up and curl up into bed with them and never leave again.

"Hey babies, do you want some wet food?" I headed to the kitchen and threw everything on the kitchen counter.

"Ally, honey is that you?" I heard Drew calling out from the bedroom. Shit! Why was he home. I heard him coming down the hall. "Ally?"

I grabbed the purse and quickly threw it in the refrigerator. I did not need his mother listening to my conversations with Drew. I wondered how often she might have overheard us having sex. Gross. Well, if she did, then it was her own damn fault.

"Hey honey, what are you doing home? Shouldn't you be at your study group?" I turned and leaned up against the refrigerator door and hoped that he wasn't thirsty. It would be hard to explain why the purse was in the fridge.

"I'm running a little bit late. I can cancel and stay home and cook dinner if you want me to since you are here."

He backed me up to the fridge and kissed me. Normally, kissing him made all of the shit from the day melt away. Not tonight. Tonight all I could think about was his lies. His possible involvement with what happened to Elise and his mother's plans for his father. It felt like I was kissing a stranger and I found myself unable to turn off all the questions in my head.

He pulled his head back. "Is something wrong? Why you aren't going to do a set tonight?"

"Just a long day at work." I continued to lean against the fridge, afraid that if I moved, he would open the door.

"You look like there is something wrong."

I wanted to scream that it was because I was living with a liar, but I knew I was far from guiltless in that regard.

"Did you know?"

"Did I know what?" Drew's face was perplexed.

"Did you know about Elise?"

His perplexed face turned to stone and I could practically see him mentally choosing his words carefully before they came out of his mouth. "I knew about my father and Elise, but I didn't find out until the day she left the firm."

"The day she left. You mean the day you went and cleaned her office out? Is that the day you are talking about?"

"Shit honey, I'm sorry." He ran his hands through his hair. "I should have told you. I was just trying to respect my mom's wishes and keep it private. It was very embarrassing for her."

I laughed. "I find that hard to believe."

His face hardened, "Ally, this is my mother we are talking about. I love you, but please have some respect. Her marriage is in a crisis right now."

Oh, if you only knew, I thought. Maybe he did though. Maybe he was firmly "Team Mom" even if it meant killing his dad.

"You could have told me. You saw how upset I was when she left. You should have told me. And why did you take everything out of her office? That doesn't make any sense."

"I know I should have told you. I almost told you last night when you asked but I didn't want to betray my mom's trust."

He sat down at the table and put his head in his hands.

"She asked me to clean out Elise's office so Elise wouldn't make a scene by coming to the office to pick everything up. Mom and Dad had a huge fight when she found out about the affair. He ended things with Elise. She was angry and didn't take it well. So, Mom gave me Dad's key to Elise's apartment and asked me to clean out her office."

I sat down at the table and tried to convince myself he was telling the truth.

"She wasn't home when I dropped everything off so, I didn't lie when

I said I hadn't seen her since the Fourth of July party. It wasn't the whole truth, but it was a lie. I'm sorry."

He grabbed my hand across the table. "I'm sorry. I shouldn't have lied to you. I won't do it again. I love you, honey."

I loved him so much that I resolved I couldn't continue lying to him either. Everything was going to blow up tomorrow anyway. I took my hand from his and looked away. I didn't want to see his face when I told him. He would be so angry but I was going to pull at least one Band-Aid of guilt off and unburden myself.

"I've been lying to you too for a while now . . ." I stared at my feet and searched for the way to tell him.

"I haven't done a set in over six months. I lost all of my confidence and my creative voice . . . and I'm not that funny, fierce woman you fell in love with anymore. I'm a pathetic loser who can't even be honest with the one person who I love about how scared I am. I was so upset over you lying to me about Elise and thinking that you knew something about her death, when really it was me who was lying all the time . . ."

"What did you just say?"

"I know. I'm so sorry that I've lied to you for so long about it. I was just so scared . . ."

"No. Back up. Why do you think Elise is dead and why the hell do you think I would know something about it?"

God damn my blurting. I hadn't meant to say that, but it was too late to take it back now. I finally looked up at him.

"Last night. I wasn't working late. I was at the police station being questioned about Elise. They think I had something to do with her disappearance because someone planted my fingerprints in her apartment. An apartment that I have never been inside. And I will give you one guess who planted them there and who had me picked up by the police. Your poor, embarrassed and hurt mother who is suffering a marital crisis . . ."

He slammed his palm down on the table with such force that a juice glass left on the table from breakfast, fell off and shattered. His face was red with rage. I had never seen him so angry. I wanted to slide under the table and cower, but my natural instinct was to bend down and start picking up the glass so the cats wouldn't walk through the mess and cut themselves.

He got up from the table and walked out the door without saying a word. I was left behind, shattered in as many pieces as the juice glass. I cleaned up the mess with tears running down my face. I had fucked up once again. Tristan-Malcolm was right. Drew wasn't different. He would choose his family and all the wealth and power that came with it. That was perfectly clear from the look of rage on his face when I confronted him about his mother. If he wasn't willing to believe me about Elise, then he would never believe his mother wanted me to kill his father. I had been a fool to believe there was any scenario out of this clusterfuck in which Drew and I remained together. There was no scenario which didn't involve me going to jail, probably for the rest of my life.

I grabbed a bottle of vodka and went back to the bedroom. I ripped off my work clothes, which had been bought by Carol. I threw them in a heap on the floor and stomped on them a few times for good measure while screaming, "Fuck you Carol!" I put on yoga pants and a T-shirt and crawled into bed with the cats at my feet and the vodka bottle in hand. I eventually stopped crying and just laid on the bed in a state of numb surrender. I was done. I had no moves left.

Eventually, my silent staring was interrupted by repeated banging on the door.

CHAPTER 34

I LOOKED OVER AT THE clock. It was 10:45. Great. Now I had to endure an awkward exchange with Sarah, who would probably be openly hostile to me. Not that I didn't deserve it. I took a swig out of the vodka bottle and shuffled to the door.

Bang! Bang! Bang!

"I'm coming." I swung open the door with one hand and took another swig out of the bottle with the other.

"What the hell? Ally? What is going on with you?" Sarah actually looked concerned instead of angry.

I turned and looked at myself in the hallway mirror and saw I had streaks of mascara down my face and my hair was sticking up in mats. My nose and eyes were red and swollen from crying.

"Want a drink?" I offered the bottle to her.

"No." She took the bottle away from me. "And I think you need some coffee. You should know I got a text from that asshole boss of yours. Thanks for giving him my number by the way. He plans on meeting us over here."

"Super. That's just super." I tried to grab the bottle back from her but she had a firm grip on it.

She grabbed my hand, lead me into the kitchen, and directed me to the sink. "Wash your face."

Sarah started the coffee while I washed my face in the sink. She asked, "I'm assuming you have some of your ridiculous flavored creamer in the fridge?"

She opened the refrigerator door before I had time to stop her. She stared inside for a few seconds then pulled out the chocolate-caramel creamer container. She shut the door and turned to face me. "There's a ten thousand dollar Hermès handbag in the fridge. Exactly how much have you had to drink? What is going on with you?"

I made sure the door was shut. "It needs to stay in there."

"Ally, tell me what is going on? I was still pissed as hell at you this morning, but now I'm legitimately concerned since you apparently have put a handbag in timeout."

"You won't believe me if I told you and I don't want to get you involved." I leaned against the sink. I should be happy that she wasn't mad at me, but I was really just numb. I just wanted everything to be done and over.

"Bitch, you better sit your ass down and start talking." She poured a cup of coffee and plunked it down on the table in front of a chair.

I grabbed a spoon from the drawer and the sugar container. I sat down and concentrated on getting the sugar and creamer to coffee ratio just right. I didn't even know where to start. I started with what happened in the park and the rest started pouring out. I told her everything that had happened and everything I had done over the past few weeks and ended with Carol and her threats and blackmail. While I talked, she kept refilling my coffee cup. I distracted myself with reestablishing the cream and sugar ratio when I got to the hard parts. I never looked up at her. Not even when I was finished. I was afraid I would see the same rage that had been in Drew's eyes. Or worse, disappointment.

"Holy shit! Ally. Holy shit!" She was rubbing her hands on her face and shaking her head in disbelief.

"I know. I'm the worst person in the world." I slumped down in the chair and wished for a sinkhole to appear.

"Hey, don't talk about my friend that way." She reached over and grabbed my hand.

The tone of her voice softened. "You could have told me in the park that day."

Fresh tears welled up in my eyes and I shook my head. "I couldn't tell anyone. I didn't want to burden you with what I had done."

"Hey, I will always have your back. You know that, right? I might have been pissed about Rena, but I do know what you did came from a good, although very misguided, place in your heart. You aren't a bad person."

I wiped my eyes, "I'm a terrible person. The dead guy in the park called me a crazy bitch and I'm not so sure he was wrong."

"Screw that guy in the park. You don't know what he would have done to you."

"I started it though. It was my fault . . ."

There was a knock at the door. "That's probably Tristan-Malcolm." I started to get up.

"Sit down. I'll get it."

Tristan-Malcolm was standing in my kitchen helping me through a crisis. A week ago, I would have imagined it was more likely for me to sashay down the catwalk at a Victoria's Secret fashion show than him being my ally.

"You look like a disaster." He frowned at me. I saw a touch of concern in his eyes.

"It's good to see you, too."

"Where's the purse?" He whispered.

"Oh, she put it on ice. It's in the fridge." Sarah nodded in the direction of the refrigerator.

"I'm assuming you have a TV in the bedroom based on all the television nonsense you constantly spout. Why don't you go put it in front of the TV and shut the bedroom door? We don't need Carol getting suspicious that you have figured out there is a bug."

"There's nothing wrong with the amount of TV I watch. Everyone needs to stop judging me about how much I reference pop culture!"

I saw the two of them exchange a look and shrug their shoulders as

I snatched the purse out of the fridge and stomped back to the bedroom.

"God, this day has sucked. I need some Captain Tight Pants in my life," I announced loudly as I turned on the TV, pulled up *Firefly* on Hulu and hit play. "Fuck Fox." I instinctively added my ritualistic response to seeing the Serenity ship on my screen.

By the time I got back to the kitchen, Sarah had a laptop open and was showing something to Tristan-Malcolm.

"What's going on? I thought we were going to listen to the tapes."

"We are." Sarah pointed to the laptop. "The guy at RadioShack, which does still exist by the way, was very helpful. He suggested that in case I had to listen to the tapes more than once, I should go ahead and buy the equipment and convert them to digital recordings. So that's what I've been doing. I have all of the tapes on my computer." She waived her hands slowly and dramatically in front of the camera as if she was displaying a potential prize in the showcase showdown on The Price is Right.

"Based on what I heard, I also made several copies of the files on thumb drives and have them hidden in various places." She looked over at Tristan-Malcolm. "And your ass better reimburse my expenses."

I looked from the computer to her and back to the computer. "You did all of this for me?"

"Bitch, I told you I had your back. I should have told you sooner but I was too busy being mad at you. I would have given it to you sooner had I known you had all this other crazy shit going on. Speaking of crazy, there's a lot of weird ass shit on these tapes. Who is this creepy dude?"

She hit play and Uncle Benji's voice boomed out of the computer speakers talking about cigars.

Tristan-Malcolm responded, "That's Benjamin Mars. He's Carol's brother and he owns Mars News and Media."

"He must be paranoid as hell because he records every conversation he has with anyone. Even his damn dentist appointments are recorded for posterity. The noise of the drill gave me such a migraine and I wasn't sure I was going to be able to perform that night."

She turned the recording off. "And the taped phone calls of all the celebrities make me very happy I haven't exactly hit the big time yet."

She turned to me, "Ally, remember that rumor about Rena's v-card being sold to the highest bidder? Totally happened. This dude had a recording of Rena's mom sealing the deal. I felt so bad for her. Her mother talked about her like she was just a piece of property. I can totally see why Rena's such a raging bitch now, so I'm trying to be nicer to her."

She paused, "That's why I got so mad at you over what you did to her."

I reached for her hand. "I'm so sorry. I wish I could go back and change everything, even though you were so amazing up there on the stage."

"Really? When those lights came on I was so scared. I thought I was going to throw up, but then I just closed my eyes for a minute . . ."

Tristan-Malcolm interrupted, "Ladies, I'm sure this is a very heartwarming moment that you two are sharing, but can you maybe put a pin in it for later. I need to listen to any recordings that are relevant to the senator."

Sarah shot him a look that made me warn him that he was in grave danger. As scared as I was of him at times, I would put all my money on

Sarah if these two were to ever come to blows.

"Hey there, Mr. Two-First-Names. Settle your ass down and I will get to it. Would you have this sweet set up without me?" She scowled at him and pointed at the computer. "Yeah, I don't think so. So, a little appreciation would be nice."

Things were about to get really ugly. I slid further down in my chair so I would be out of the line of fire.

To my surprise, he ignored the barb and calmly responded, "I think you did a great job. Thank you for your help. Unfortunately, time is running out and we are trying to find a way to save Ally's ass."

Sarah's face relaxed and I was relieved that for now, the tension had been defused.

Tristan-Malcolm said, "I think I have finally found the ruling the Senator made in favor of Mars News and Media and I would like to know whether there is any proof on the tapes that the ruling was obtained in exchange for a favor."

He pulled out a small notebook from his coat pocket. "It was in the fall of 2008, Mars was trying to take over a large internet company and there were rather significant antitrust concerns in that case. Public opinion was against the merger and there was an outcry for the government to intervene. Senator Davis was on the committee that was rumored to be investigating the merger when suddenly the investigation stopped and the merger went through. So, is there anything in that time range?"

"I think there was. Give me a second." She scrolled through the index.

"Ally, what did you find out about Rusk Communication?

Anything useful."

"Oops. I kind of forgot about that during my meltdown. Sorry." I got up and went to the counter and grabbed the purple folder that Susan had given me and opened it.

Sarah pushed play and Uncle Benji's voice blasted through the kitchen.

Now Birdie, you owe me this one. You're like family. You were Carol's college roommate.

I recognized the senator's voice from the fundraiser when she responded. *This is too high profile now. I'm going to be up for reelection in two years. I can't just drop the investigation or the public will have my head on a goddamn platter. Certain factions get nervous when they fear one company will control not only a major source of the news on television and print, but also the internet.*

That's bullshit, Birdie. The people who care aren't even your bread and butter voters. They aren't going to vote for you even if you do stop this merger.

The Senator replied. *It's about the optics of it. It's just too risky. I've given you a lot of help over the years, but not this. I have higher aspirations and I don't want this to come back and bite me in the ass.*

I know all about your higher aspirations, Birdie. I hear about them every damn time I talk to my sister. I don't give a shit if you want to be Vice President or President. All I'm asking you to do is drop this one investigation and let my merger happen. The public will completely forget about it as soon as some starlet gets outed or goes on a booze filled rampage. You know I can make sure a story like that floods the airways and drowns out any noise about the merger. The public cares more about who celebrities are sleeping with than they care about who controls the media.

And what's in it for me? I'm putting my professional reputation on the line.

How about a Super-PAC for your reelection, to be run by whoever you chose, funded with ten million dollars?

That's chump change for what you are getting if the merger goes through as planned. It's insulting that you would even make such an offer.

So, thirty million?

There was a long pause on the tape. *I want to see confirmation of the funding by the end of the week.*

Always a pleasure doing business with you, Birdie.

The recording cut off. I had been listening to the illegal exchange while flipping through the papers Susan had given me. It looked like Rusk Corporation was a subsidiary of a corporation which was a subsidiary of another corporation and so on and so on. There were more than a dozen corporate names going up the channel of ownership but two stuck out. Shey Specialty Corporation and Redling Unlimited.

"Hey, you guys? I think I have something here. Look at the names of two of these companies." I spread the paper on the table for the both of them to see. "Richard was telling me a long-winded story about this woman he used to know before he met Carol. I'm pretty sure he was in love with both her and her croissants. Her name was Shey Redling."

Tristan-Malcolm picked up the papers and leafed through them. "All of these corporations were incorporated on the same day. It's a shell game to hide the owner."

"It has to be Richard, right?" I questioned. "Oh my God, he was using these tapes to blackmail Uncle Benji. That is why Carol wants him dead before the merger is final on Friday."

We had been so caught up in listening to the recording and figuring out Richard's plan that we hadn't heard the front door open.

"What the fuck is going on?" The voice startled us and we all turned and found Max standing in the kitchen door.

CHAPTER 35

"OH MY GOD, ARE YOU cheating on Drew with this asshole?" Max pointed at Tristan-Malcolm accusatorially.

"Really?" I lifted my hands up the in the air in the universal signal for "what the fuck" and rolled my eyes at him. "Yeah, that's exactly why the three of us are standing around a table and staring at papers and a computer. We are about to have the world's most nerdy and awkward threesome ever. Not to mention the fact that he's gay."

"Ally!" Tristan-Malcolm snapped at me. "How many times do I have to tell you to keep my personal life out of this."

I shrugged my shoulders. "Sorry. Drew is mad enough at me. I don't want Max telling him something that would make things even worse."

Max stepped closer to me. "You know I just heard you talking about Carol wanting Richard dead right? I don't see how things can get worse than that at this point."

"And yet, you still went straight to accusations of an affair." I shook my head in agitation and disbelief. "What are you even doing here?"

"I got worried. Drew didn't show up for his shift and he's not picking up his phone or answering my texts."

"His shift? What are you talking about? Tonight is his study group."

Max looked anxiously at the other two and started to open his mouth and say something but then closed it again.

"Max, what shift?" I stepped closer to him and jabbed my finger in his chest.

He backed away from me. "Shit. He was supposed to tell you . . . I don't think I should be getting involved in something this personal."

"Too late. You already know about Carol's plot to kill Richard so tell me about this goddamn shift that Drew didn't show up for tonight." I backed him up against the counter and could feel my rage started to rise over the fact that Max and at Drew were keeping secrets from me. Yes, I do see the irony of it all.

Max put his hands on his head and let out a huge sigh. It was clear he didn't want to betray his best friend. "He's been working a few shifts at the hotel restaurant as a chef, just to see if he liked it. Something you said to him renewed his interest in it . . . You can't say anything to his mom."

"His mom wants me to kill his dad, so I think you can be assured that I'm not telling that bitch anything."

Tristan-Malcolm finally spoke up. "Ally, do you think it's wise to include him on this? We don't know that we can trust him."

"Excuse me?" Max stepped past me and toward Tristan-Malcolm. His nostrils flaring. It was now Tristan-Malcolm's turn to have an angry finger jabbed in his face. "I've been friends with Ally a lot longer than you."

He got even closer to Tristan-Malcolm and their faces and chests were almost touching, "So back . . . the fuck . . . off with your judgment on whether or not I can be trusted. Out of everyone in this group, you would be in the lead for most likely to ratfuck all of us."

I finally stepped between the two men and put my hand on Max's chest in an attempt to calm him down.

"Stand down. Tristan-Malcolm has already proven himself trustworthy when he got me out of the police station."

Max let out a derisive snort. "No wonder you wouldn't tell me your name the other night. Two first names. How very pretentious of you."

He looked down at me concerned. "Wait, why were you in the police station?"

Tristan-Malcolm glared at Max. "Does he really have to be here? We don't need him for anything."

I continued to play peacemaker and shot Tristan-Malcolm a pleading look that I hoped he interpreted as "play nice."

"Actually, I think we can use his help. Sarah, can you take Max into the living room and get him up to speed on what is going on with the merger and Carol situation?" I hoped she got the hint not to tell him about the man in the park or anything else I had done.

"Got it." Sarah smiled at me and nodded. I was pretty sure the amount of vodka and coffee I had consumed had given me telepathic powers at this point.

Once they left the room, I walked over to the counter and grabbed a bottle of Wild Turkey and two glasses.

"Let's sit for a second." I sat at the table and poured out a drink for both of us and slid his across the table. He sat down across from me. I looked at him. Again, bemused that he was in my kitchen and helping me. "You said earlier today we should use what we know to our advantage."

I spun the whiskey around in the glass.

"Well, what if we turn this situation on its head. I want everything . . . Drew, this condo, the money, Carol in jail. Hell, I even want you to get the law firm out of this. I think I can find a way to make that happen, but I'm going need your help. We both know my judgment can be questionable at times . . ."

He chuckled softly at the understatement of the century.

" . . . and that I have a tendency to bend the boundaries of the law on occasion. What I need to know is, how flexible are you?"

He took a drink and leaned back in his chair.

"What are you thinking?"

He stroked his mustache while he listened to me explain the plan, which had started formulating in my head from the moment I learned Richard was using the tapes for blackmail. I finished laying out my plan and waited for him to tell me I was crazy and any other number of insults he might decide to throw my way.

He stared at me and continued stroking his mustache while he tapped his finger on the rim of his whiskey glass. For once, I was not concerned he was contemplating how to make me into a delicious meal during the painfully long pause.

Finally, he announced, "It could work. It needs a few tweaks, but it could work. I have to admit that I'm a little afraid of you right now . . . but you'll notice, somehow I managed to not piss myself." He flashed me a wicked smile.

My face immediately flushed with embarrassment. "How in the world do you know about that?"

"The janitors talk." He shrugged and took a drink. "Get the other two back in here. We have a lot to get done."

I called Max and Sarah back into the room. Tristan-Malcolm got up from his chair, walked over to Max and extended his hand. "Truce."

Max took his hand. "Truce."

"Since you all seem to have a problem with my God-given name and we are going to be working closely together, I suppose you can call me Mal." He smiled at me for a second time in one night, something I could never have imagined would have happened. "My cats' names are Zoe and Wash. You were right, fuck Fox for canceling *Firefly*. It was a damned good show."

I squealed and jumped up out of my seat. "I kind of want to hug you right now."

He held out a straight, right arm in my direction. "But you won't."

"Nope. I wouldn't dare." I went to the cabinet, grabbed two more glasses, and poured out a round of drinks for everyone.

"Let's take this bitch down." We all clinked our glasses as if planning to take down two of the most powerful people in New York was just a normal occurrence worthy of a toast. Mal and I began to fill them in on their roles and what needed to be done. The first hurdle involved Max getting Conner in the loop, which I hated, but I could see no other way because I was pretty sure what I needed was beyond the abilities of Sarah's RadioShack connection.

He exited the room to make the call. He was distracted and agitated when he came back.

"So, can he help us?" I asked.

"Yeah, he can. He'll text me back with the details." His voice had a hint of sadness to it and he looked distant.

"What's wrong?"

"He just seemed kind of hostile that I called 'at this time of night.' It's barely midnight. It's the first time I've called him. We usually just text. I don't know. . . he just sounded weird . . . but we've got bigger problems to deal with now. I'm sure it's fine."

My heart broke for him because I knew that it wasn't fine, but I couldn't tell him. Not only because I had resolved to stop meddling, but for the more selfish reason that I needed him to have his head in the game and not be distracted.

"He was probably just sleeping and crabby. You should hear how Sarah talks to me when I accidentally wake her up."

"I'm sitting right here. Don't even start with me." Sarah laughed and elbowed me hard in the arm which made Max laugh and his mood seemed to lighten once again.

We spent the next hour tweaking the plan and brainstorming. Mal kept bringing up every way it could backfire and everything that could go wrong. At first, I was annoyed as hell at his constant Debbie-downer interruptions, but I finally admitted his concerns were valid and that they forced us to consider how to compensate should something go wrong. I wasn't used to having feedback on my plans since they were usually half-cocked and fueled by rage.

Mal offered Max a ride back to his hotel in his town car, so it appeared that whatever male territorial pissing contest that had taken place earlier was officially put to bed. I took Max aside before they left.

"I'm sorry that so much of this rides on you." I put my hand on his arm. I was worried I was asking too much of him and possibly risking his friendship with Drew. "Drew is the wildcard in this whole thing and you are going to be the only one he trusts. Please find him and try to calm him down. He has to show up to the family dinner tomorrow for this to work and he has to be under control. He's the key to everything."

Max flashed me his most charming of smiles. "I've got this. Everything's going to work as planned. He will calm down and understand. I will get him there."

"But what if he doesn't understand or won't show up?"

"I've known him all of my life. He loves you. He will show. I can handle him. Get some sleep." His phone beeped.

"Connor can be on the first flight in from Vermont and will meet you here at 9:30 to give you what you need."

I tried not to flinch. I knew for a fact Connor was not catching a flight, but would just be walking down the street to meet me. I once again wished there had been some way to avoid Connor's involvement.

"Thank you. I don't know how to thank you enough."

"You are saving my best friend from being under the thumb of a horrible woman. We've got this." He kissed me on the head and headed out the door. I heard him and Mal laugh about something as they walked down the hall and wished I was that confident.

Sarah was determined to stay the night with me despite my protestations that she go home.

"I'm not leaving you alone." We curled up on the couch to sleep, leaving the evil purse from hell in the bedroom. I had gone in earlier and turned the television off so it would appear that I had gone to sleep. I wrapped the purse in several blankets and put it in the back of the closet and shut the closet door and the bedroom door just in case any sound from the living room drifted within range of the microphone.

"Am I a terrible person?" I whispered even though I was pretty sure the purse was out of range.

"No." She paused. "You just don't tend to think things all the way through before acting. You have good intentions. Most of the time."

"What if this doesn't work?" I was nervously twirling my hair into tangles.

"Then we figure out another plan. You *Heather*-ed two douche-bros all on your own. At least this time you have help."

"Thank you."

She grabbed my hand to stop the hair twirling. "You know, it was pretty amazing."

"What was?" I couldn't think of one thing I had done that could be described as amazing.

"Playing Sugar. It's not how I wanted to finally get to play the role, but it was amazing. Thank you." She squeezed my hand.

"You were so damn fierce up on that stage." I squeezed her hand back.

"I was, wasn't I? We are two badass fierce bitches."

I couldn't sleep at all that night. I replayed the plan in my head and worried about Drew. What was he thinking? How much did he hate me right now for betraying his trust? Would he ever forgive me? Did he believe what I said about his mom? Had I crossed a line that could never be undone? If he left me, would he fight me over who got the cats? There was not a question or anxiety too insignificant that failed to cross my mind to keep sleep from washing over me and giving me even a few minutes of peace.

At 2:30 a.m. my phone alerted me to a text. I lunged for the phone hoping it was from Drew. What I wouldn't give for one of his silly heart emoji texts at this point. It was Max. *He's here. He is super fucked up and drunk off his ass, but I've seen him in worse shape. I've got this.*

CHAPTER 36

I SAT AT THE TABLE with my coffee and a muffin waiting for Connor to arrive. Sarah was still asleep on the couch and snoring. I savored every bite of the muffin, believing it to be the last thing I would ever eat that Drew would cook for me. How did I get here? Could I have avoided it all if I had just not gone running that evening? What if I hadn't lost my temper with the man in the park? Or the douche-bros? Or Rena? I tried to pinpoint the exact moment when I sealed my fate. What if I had just asked Mal about those damn tapes? Would all of this still be happening? Or, would Carol still be trying to kill Richard and I would just be none-the-wiser, an innocent bystander at the funeral watching Drew grieve.

The knock on the door roused me from my maudlin thoughts.

LULU SMITH

I opened the door and found Connor looking nervously up and down the hall. He was biting his lower lip and swiveling his head wildly from side to side, obviously worried that someone he knew might see him.

"Is Max here?" He practically bolted in the door both to avoid being seen and no doubt also excited to see Max. I felt for him. No doubt he had made some hard life choices that weren't necessarily in his own best interests. I could certainly never judge someone for making bad life choices.

"No. He's got something more important to do." Hopefully, he was plying Drew with coffee and talking him off the ledge.

Sarah let out a loud snore which caused him to jump and alerted him that we were not alone. Now that he knew Max wasn't here, he seemed anxious to get the exchange over with and out of any potential exposure.

"What exactly do you need this for? It's an unusual request. I'm only helping because Max sounded so desperate. Is he in trouble?"

"No. Not him. But someone he cares about." I couldn't tell him it was me or he would bolt out the door in a heartbeat.

"Do you have it here with you?" He asked looking around.

"It's in the fridge." I nodded into the kitchen. I had brought it out of its cocoon while I was making coffee so it would appear to whomever was listening that everything was normal on my end. I made sure to talk to my cats and bitch about my day in its presence. I shoved it back in the fridge a few minutes before Connor arrived.

"Let's see it."

I fetched the purse out of the fridge. He felt carefully around the bag and pointed to let me know that he thought he found it. I used the scissors

308

and as quietly as possible, cut a small incision in the interior liner. It felt like an extreme act of vandalism against such a beautiful bag, but it was necessary. Connor removed the bug. Even upon seeing it, I still couldn't quite believe that I was right and the purse really was bugged. He put the bug back in the purse and I put the purse back in the fridge."

"I brought five. That should be enough." He handed me a small black bag. "They are noise activated. I just need to sync them with a computer."

I walked him into the kitchen where Sarah's computer was sitting on the table. He began typing in that fast paced rhythm of a person actually experienced with a computer's use, which always fascinated me. Hell, there were times when Word could send me into a fit for hours with its penchant to default to a font, spacing, and paragraph margins that no one on the planet has ever voluntarily used.

"And it will record?" I asked.

"Yes. That's kind of what they do."

"And you can edit it, if needed?" I leaned over his shoulder watching his fingers fly effortlessly over the keys until finally a screen popped up that looked like a digital soundboard.

This request seemed to make him uncomfortable. "I can. I'd prefer not to, but it can be done. I'm going to send a link to Max so he can also tap into it from his computer. I would have preferred to have seen him and done it for him, but I can talk him through it if he has any problems. That way you will have two recordings. A backup is always a good idea."

He made a final few clicks on the computer and then nodded at the small bag of bugs on the table.

"This is a test . . . testing 1, 2, 3." Connor spoke in a normal toned voice standing a few feet away from the table. He walked back over to the computer and showed me there was an entry on the screen with a play button beside it. He pushed the button and the computer played his test message.

"Thank you." If he had been anyone else, I would have hugged him for coming through for me in such a big way.

After he finished sending a link to Max, he followed me out to the hallway. His demeanor had relaxed and he was not as nervous as he was when he first arrived. "Don't forget to use the backups. I wouldn't try to place them anywhere in the room. Just drop them in pockets if you can. The microphone is strong enough to pick up sound through fabric. All the recordings will come to that computer and Max's computer."

"Thank you. It means a lot to me that you helped me." I paused not sure if I was going to continue. Hadn't I promised myself not to interfere? But I knew I had to say something. "Even after I was kind of a jackass to you in Starbucks that day. I'm sorry. It was a really bad day. Actually, that was just the beginning of it all. It got so much worse after that."

His face flinched and then tightened. "I don't know what you are talking about."

"Connor. I know." I took my phone out of my pocket and showed him the picture.

"Oh my God! Are you blackmailing me? After all I just did for you? That takes some nerve." He raised his voice and his face was red with anger.

I held my hands up as if to surrender. "I'm not. I promise." I deleted the picture off my phone in front of him. His body was trembling probably more from the fear of being outed than anger.

I lowered my voice hoping to calm him down and reassure him. "Look. Max is a great guy. I just don't want to see him hurt. It's not my place to tell him and I won't . . . but if you really care about him, then I'm asking you to do the right thing."

Connor's face switched from anger to sadness. "I never wanted to hurt him. I just . . ."

I apprehensively reached out and touched his arm, not sure if he would swat it away. "I'm not judging you. Trust me. I'm in no position to judge anyone. Just don't hurt him."

He nodded. "I understand."

I could hear the heartbreak in his voice. I felt a similar breaking in my own chest when I thought about Drew.

After Connor left, I went back inside and grabbed the wretched purse and put the small bag of friendly bugs inside. I left Sarah a note that I would meet her at lunch and made my way to the office. I sat on the subway and listened to Eminem's "Lose Yourself" on a loop to psych myself up for the day ahead. I had one shot, one opportunity to get this right. Yo!

CHAPTER 37

AFTER I GOT TO THE office, I shoved the multi-bugged purse into its file drawer nest for the last time. I hated that I still had to carry it but I knew that everything had to appear normal so that Carol didn't get suspicious.

I made a bee line to Susan's cubicle. "Susan, the work you did was awesome as always. Can you do one more thing for Tristan-Malcolm? It's a rush job."

She turned her chair to face me with a large, satisfied smile on her face. "Sure. At this rate, the dinner you are buying me is going to be phenomenal."

"Trust me. It will be fabulous. I need you to find out everything you can on Shey Redling, including where she is currently living, whether she's married, single, dating, divorced. I need it by noon. She used to run

Redling's Dinette down in the Meatpacking District about thirty years ago. She loves to bake and wanted to move to Paris. That's all I've got to go on."

"Oh! This sounds fun. I'm on it." She tapped her fingers together as if she was partaking in some devilish plot.

"In case I don't say it enough, you are the best."

"I know. It's good to be told though. Now get out of here, I have work to do." She swung back to her computer and began typing fast and frantically.

I left her cubicle and went up to Tristan-Malcolm's office. I mean Mal's office – I still haven't quite gotten over that shocker. His hair was ruffled and he was wearing the same clothes from the night before. He didn't look up, but it was not out of rudeness this time. He was engrossed in what he was doing and there were actual papers on his desk.

I knocked lightly on the side of his door. "How is everything going? Can I get you anything?"

He looked up. "I'll be done in time. And on your end? Did you get what we need?"

"I did. I've got Susan working on the last piece."

"Do you think she can find it in time?"

"She can find a naked picture of a man in hard black shoes, a top hat and a monocle in under ten minutes."

He shook his head perplexed, "I can't tell if that's a yes or a no, and for the love of God don't explain to me why you know about those particular skills. I've been up all night."

"It's a yes. Can I get you a coffee?"

"I'm fine. Go finish what you need to get done." He waived me away towards the door.

I turned to leave, hesitated and turned back. "Thank you. Thank you for everything."

"Don't get sentimental on me and don't thank me yet."

I returned to my desk and picked up the phone and called Richard's assistant and made an appointment to meet with him at three that afternoon. She initially told me that he wasn't available. For the first time in my three years of working at the office, I pulled rank as his son's girlfriend and made her put me on hold and ask him personally. She sounded pissed when she got back on the line with me and confirmed Richard would meet with me as requested.

I picked up my phone hoping to see that I had missed a text or a call or some contact from Drew, but there was none. I was desperate to see one of his silly emoji's blowing a kiss. I was pretty sure I was never going to get one of those ever again.

I did have a message from Sarah waiting on me. *Got everything on my end. See you at lunch.*

I was fidgety and nervous because there wasn't anything I could do for a few hours. I typed out and then deleted at least a dozen apology texts to Drew. I searched online for a cottage to rent in Parry Sound, Ontario. Most people wanting to flee the country to hide would head down south, but not me.

My family vacationed in Parry Sound every year growing up. For a month, I would swim in the lake, fish with my dad, and flirt with the bag boys at the grocery store. I was happy in the land of 30,000 islands. I could use the peace of the Georgian Bay right about now. Most importantly, Canada allowed domestic cats to cross the border with just proof of a rabies vaccine, so I could disappear there with my girls. I might lose Drew, but I was not going to leave my cats behind. They were mine. They were one of the few things that were mine. I had adopted them from the shelter. I would need only the smallest of cars to transport stuff that was actually mine. I hated that I was preparing for a life without Drew, but I had to accept that was almost certain to occur. Mal was right. I needed a back-up plan.

My planning was finally interrupted by Susan popping by my cubicle with another one of her purple folders.

"Found her. She lives in Paris, owns a bakery. A widow. I even found pictures of her."

I jumped out of my chair and hugged her. "You really are the best."

"I know. I am going to spend the rest of the day picking out exactly which restaurant you will be taking me to repay me and every course of the meal."

She walked away and I opened the folder. She was every bit the opposite of Carol. Her face was glowing with a large welcoming smile. She had traces of wrinkles at the edges of her warm eyes that hadn't been surgically smoothed out to mask her age. She had silver gray streaks in her dark hair that she hadn't bothered coloring. She was beautiful in a way that Carol could never hope to be. I realized I would not have Drew in my life without Carol, but I was sad for Richard and the life he could have lived had he chosen differently. He might not have lived the high life, but just by looking at Shey's face, I was pretty sure he would have had a life filled with love instead of blackmail and lies and a wife that wanted him dead.

I slid the folder in my top desk drawer. I grabbed my wallet, my phone, and the piece of paper that I printed off the computer earlier, and left to meet Sarah for lunch. I left the purse in the filing cabinet.

I WAS LATE GETTING TO the restaurant and Sarah was already seated at a table in the farthest corner away from the door. Seated beside her was Rena, in sunglasses and a scarf wrapped around her hair.

"So, I guess your name was never Abigail?" Her voice was bitter and strained.

I sat down. "I'm sorry." I was full of regret about what I had done to her and I needed her to know that, but I wasn't sure what else to say.

"You should be." She took off her sunglasses and stared at me with hard eyes, but then they softened ever so slightly. "But I guess I needed a wakeup call. I was slowly throwing away my one chance to reclaim my career. I was a train wreck waiting to happen. You obviously accelerated the hell out of it . . ."

"I'm so sorry. Sarah didn't know anything about it. I should have never brought the drugs out in the first place. I'm very sorry. Please don't blame Sarah. It was all my fault." I tried to reach for her hand but she pulled away from me.

"I wouldn't be here if I blamed her." She leaned back in her chair and relaxed into it. "She has actually been a good friend to me the past few days and put me in touch with a sober coach. I can see now why you defended her so vigorously and tried to help her." She looked at Sarah and smiled genuinely without a hint of condescension. "I realize I was more than a nightmare to people, but after hearing my mother on the tape, maybe you can understand how I might have developed some . . . issues."

"I'm so sorry about what happened to you. I was one of your biggest fans." I immediately felt guilty for the use of the word "was" instead of "am."

Rena waived her hands as if shooing away an annoying gnat. "Well, let's both try to get a fresh start, shall we? We seem to be in a position to help each other. You give me the recordings about me and I will sue the fuck out of Mars. Give me a list of the other celebrities illegally recorded and I will get them involved and we will take this perverted eavesdropping asshole down."

"Thank you for helping me." I had said "thank you" so much in the past 24 hours that I felt like I was a doll where you pulled the string on the back and those were the only words I could say.

"I'm mostly doing this for myself." She put her sunglasses back on.

"I understand."

She reached across the table, took my hand and a wicked smile flashed across her face. "But I'm partly doing it for my sweet Abigail. She was a great kisser and had a killer body . . ."

I could feel the blush as it crept up my cheeks, turning them beet red.

". . . and she told me some harsh truths even when she was screwing me over. I will miss her."

"I will miss her a bit, too."

I handed her the piece of paper. "If anyone asks, this is a project we have been working on together."

She looked down and read it. "Not bad. Needs some edits, but I can make it work." She smiled at me.

As I got up to leave, Sarah stood up and handed me a gym bag. "Everything you need is in here. Don't worry. Everything is going to work. It's a good plan."

She hugged me tight and I believed her.

CHAPTER 38

AT TWO O'CLOCK, I WENT back up to Mal's office. He managed to look even more disheveled than before and the stacks of paper on his desk had grown bigger. I knocked lightly on the side of his door.

"I got you something." I said it in a sing-song voice. I saw the immediate crinkle of annoyed disapproval ripple across his brows. I walked in and put the large, thin box on the corner of his desk that was still paper-free. "I figured you probably hadn't eaten, so I ordered you a pizza."

He stopped typing, looked at the box and then back up at me. "This is from the place near my house . . . in Brooklyn."

I nodded my head and smiled smugly. "I remembered the name from the box of leftovers you fed me the other night. Turns out if you offer them the right amount of money, they will bring a pizza into the city."

He opened the box and took out a slice. "Thank you. You didn't have to do that."

"Well. You don't have to be doing all of this for me and yet, here you are. I mean you are even using paper - so shit must be getting real." I laughed. Rather than return the laugh, his face grew serious.

"Close the door and sit down for a minute." He motioned to the seat across from the desk. It was an invitation as opposed to the barked command from my first meeting with him.

After I sat down, he stared at me and stroked his mustache for a few moments before he started talking. Again, it was just like the first day I met with him, only this time I wasn't afraid he was going to eat me. He finally spoke.

"The man in the park. You don't have to worry about that anymore. There are no open homicides relating to any death in the park from that night."

Of all the words I might have expected him to say, I was not prepared for these.

"I don't understand . . . how did you find out? . . . are you sure? . . . Wait what exactly does that mean "no open homicides?" Is he alive? Is he dead? Has someone else been charged? Do they think it was an accident?" My brain was trying to process that maybe I was a slightly less horrible person than I thought.

"I have friends. I made some inquiries. It means there are no open homicides and you don't have to worry about it." He took another bite of pizza. It was clear he was not going to give me any details.

"He could still come after me for assault though, right? I still have to worry about that happening."

He put the pizza down and stared at me again. "No. You don't. He's not going to be coming after you." His tone sounded a bit ominous and for just a moment I wondered if maybe he had eaten the man in the park.

"But how do you know? I don't understand."

He put a hand up to indicate that I needed to stop asking any further questions. "I've handled it. Again, there is not an open homicide case. I feel like I'm speaking English but for some reason you are incapable of comprehending it. Just put the whole thing behind you. Just drop it." The last command was said forcefully enough that my Pavlovian response to obey him kicked in once more.

I sat there staring at him, not knowing what to think. Part of me didn't believe him. Was it possible he was lying to try to make me feel better and ease my conscience? And if he was, would it be so horrible for me to accept his offer of atonement? If he was telling the truth . . . maybe I really wasn't a killer but the way he kept saying "no open homicide case" made me uncertain. If I simply chose to believe him and not question him, then the man in the park would be like my Schrodinger's cat or something like that. Could he be both dead and yet not dead at the same time? I haven't watched enough "Big Bang Theory" to fully understand that paradox. I thought about how I was sitting across from a man who just weeks ago I thought hated me and wanted to turn me into a Bolognese sauce. Now, he was now looking at me with an almost parental warmth in his eyes and half-smile. In that moment, I decided to accept that just maybe the man was alive. No questions asked.

"I want to hug you right now." I bolted up out of my chair towards his desk and was immediately greeted by a stiff-arm creating a barrier between the two of us.

"Well, you aren't going to do that now. I should clarify that you aren't going to do that ever." His smile broadened. I could get used to him smiling. "Thank you for the pizza. Carry on with what you need to do. I will have the paper work done in time."

I returned to my desk and waited for three o'clock. I sat staring at the picture of a sunset over the Georgian Bay, a lone pine tree swaying in the wind on one of the small islands. A few days ago, I was that lone pine tree, but now, I had moss and rocks and a whole support system. Minus Drew.

I checked my phone and there were still no messages or missed calls from him. I had no idea how he was going to react when he saw me at dinner or if he would even show up. That would be a wrinkle I would have to work out on the fly and then I would know that Canada was definitely my immediate destination. I called the nearest rental car place and reserved a car just to be on the safe side. If shit went sideways, I could have the cats and my stuff packed and be on the road in less than an hour's time. Hopefully, that was fast enough.

At 2:45, I pulled the purple folder out of my top drawer, dropped one of the bugs in my pocket, and made my way to Richard's office.

CHAPTER 39

I WALKED PAST THE STILL pissed off secretary and into his office. He looked up from the papers on his desk.

"Ally, I'm so happy to see you. Surprised, but happy. I'm sure that whatever you wanted to talk about could have waited for dinner tonight, but I will always make time for you."

He got up from his desk and walked around to hug me. I hugged him back tightly. Regardless of how he had managed to get into this mess, I knew he genuinely cared about me.

After he pulled back from the hug and looked at my face his expression changed to one of concern. "You look so serious. Is something wrong? Let's sit down."

I followed him over to the big chairs where we had sat just days ago. It was hard to believe it was not long ago that I was naïve enough to believe my only fear was of being fired. I had been completely oblivious to the fact I would soon be blackmailed by his wife to kill him and falsely accused of being involved in Elise's disappearance. I shifted uncomfortably in the chair and stared out the window. This was going to be a difficult conversation to start. Finally, I gathered my courage and turned to face him.

"Thanks for making time for me. I've been thinking a lot about our last conversation in these chairs. And the thing is . . . I lied to you that day."

I noticed his face tense up just ever so slightly before returning to his usual ever-present smile. "Ally, what are you talking about?"

I found a crease in the arm of the chair and focused on nervously running my finger across it. I dropped my voice to almost a whisper. The whisper of a child confessing to their mother that they broke the antique vase they had been warned not to touch. "Well, there was something else I found in Elise's office after she left."

His face tensed up again.

"I found these boxes of old tapes. Now, at the time I didn't know what they were or how important they were, so I just kind of set them aside since I was working so hard on the notebooks . . ."

The tension in his face was replaced with relief. "You found the tapes! That's great. I was worried Elise had accidentally taken them home. I couldn't find them in the file." His voice was casual. I could tell he was trying his best to downplay their importance.

"You should have brought the boxes up with you. Were they too heavy? I'll just have a runner stop by your desk and bring them up to my office." He picked up the phone on the small table by his chair.

I took a deep breath. "Please put the phone down, Richard. They aren't at my desk." This was so much harder than I thought it was going to be, even after rehearsing it all night with Sarah.

"Where are they?" He looked at me confused.

"Richard, you have been so good to me all of these years . . . which is why this is so hard."

His mouth tensed and his eyes hardened.

"You have to believe that I wasn't aware of how important the tapes were at the time we talked. Then, after my dinner with Carol the other night, I found out what was on them and the role they played in Elise . . . leaving the firm."

His face grew pale. "You talked to Carol? About the tapes? Ally, if she knows you have them, you are in danger. Elise didn't just leave the firm . . ." His voice caught on her name.

"Carol doesn't know I have the tapes. I know about Elise. I know she's . . . dead."

I put my hand on his knee in some small attempt to comfort him. It took all of my focus to not cry.

He slumped over and put his head in his hands. "I shouldn't have gotten her involved." He looked up at me. "You shouldn't be involved. We've got to get you out of town. She will have you killed next."

I was touched that Richard was one of the rocks surrounding my lone pine tree and so willing to help me, which made what I was going to say next even harder. "Here's the thing. It's not me she wants dead. At least not yet . . . It's you."

"What? How do you know?" His face managed to get even paler.

I took a deep breath. "Because she thinks she has blackmailed me into doing it tonight at dinner."

He shook his head in disbelief. "I don't understand. She asked you?" He continued to shake his head and stare at me perplexed. "Why would she ask you?"

I shrugged my shoulders because I still wasn't exactly sure of her reasons. "She wanted it to be personal and for you to feel gravely betrayed in your final moments. She's a sick bitch, Richard. I don't know why you married her."

He let out a small chuckle. "Trust me. I've asked myself that question more times than I can count over the past three decades. Drew was the only good thing that woman has ever done and even now she is trying to slowly suck him into her corrupt world."

He motioned to the view outside of his window. "This view here. I sold my soul to get it. I told you about my little windowless office but I didn't tell you how I got here, did I? I was hustling hard for work at the time. Just dying to get rich." He got up and walked over to the bar and poured out a shot of whiskey and slammed it down before coming to sit back down. The perks of being the big dog at the office. You can openly drink alcohol if you want, meanwhile, I still hadn't gotten my stealth bottle of desk vodka which really could have come in handy over the past few weeks.

He continued, "I spent what little money I had on one very expensive suit. I crashed parties and hit all of the best clubs and bars with my business card just hoping to strike up a conversation over a scotch and cigar that I could never really afford. One night, it finally paid off and I met Carol and Benji. Carol was so unbelievably beautiful. She had money and class. She was everything I wasn't and everything I aspired to be and I was desperate to impress her. A few days after meeting them, Benji called my office and wanted to meet. I thought I had finally made it and I was going to be a legitimate corporate big shot."

His voice broke, "Instead, what Benji wanted was a legal front man for all the scams he was running. He needed someone with legal letterhead to threaten people into paying money that they didn't owe him. He wasn't content with the money he got from his family and he wanted to build his own empire. This was back in the days when people had to rent VCRs and movies because they were so expensive." He half-heartedly chuckled and looked over at me. "I know you can hardly conceive of such a thing since you can watch a movie on your phone now. Life has changed a lot since then."

"Benji opened up chains of rental stores and he preyed on the people who rented from him. He had this grand idea to claim a majority of the machines returned be declared damaged and he wanted me to pursue the damages fees that were written into the rental agreement. So, with every rental he got, he also got a damage fee."

He rubbed his hands on his legs and looked down. "The poor bastards would get a letter from a lawyer threatening a lawsuit and they would always fork up at least half the money just to make the whole thing go away. Now, this was obviously well before the internet so nobody could start a blog or leave a Yelp review and no one really caught on."

He looked at me with sorrow in his eyes. I put my hand on his arm.

"It was an ugly way to make a living, but it was how I got started. It was how I managed to make enough money to get a decent office. Then, I made enough contacts through Carol and Benji that I was able to build up my own reputation and my own business and I worked my way up to this." He spread his hands out wide to emphasize the grandeur of what he had achieved.

"When I married Carol, well, Benji came with her. Once the VCR scam played out, Benji always had another scam right behind it and I was always sucked into it. Benji never needed the money from these scams. He just always wanted to see if and for how long he could get away with each of them. Carol was aware of all of it and while she didn't approve, she didn't really care what he did as long as he stayed away from her political friends or her pet projects."

He paused for a minute and sighed. "What I didn't know at the time was that Benji recorded every conversation he had with everyone. Well, everyone but Carol. You will never find Carol on one of his tapes. Trust me. I tried to find one."

He continued. "After Drew was born, the firm had grown and I didn't need Benji anymore. I wanted a legitimate legacy to leave my son. I told Benji I was done and that his fun and games had to stop. He got pissed and told me about the tapes and how he could ruin my career and get me disbarred from the practice of law. Everything I worked so hard for to build for Drew would be gone. So, all of these years, I've been trapped like a bear in a trap trying to find a way to gnaw my leg off so I could be set free."

"And then you found the tapes and decided to turn the tables?" I asked. I understood that feeling.

He nodded. "I was at Benji's house up in the Hamptons one week by myself and I found a wall safe. I cancelled my golf plans and spent three days working on figuring out the combination to get that damned thing open hoping there would be something useful inside. Some way to pry myself out of the trap. When I finally cracked it and heard what was on some of the tapes, including Carol's dearest friend Birdie, I came up with this plan. I took pictures of all of the tapes and left them there. I had Elise help me with the paperwork creating the companies. We bought identical tapes and we painstakingly copied the handwriting that had been written on each one."

"Damn. That's a lot of work."

He laughed. "You're damn right it was. I went back to the house a few months ago and switched the tapes out and took the real ones. Elise was helping me catalog them so I would have more leverage to make sure Benji would pay to get them back. I was certain once Carol knew that Birdie was in danger she would force Benji to make the deal. Elise and I fought a few times because she wanted to turn them over to the police." His voice choked up again at the mention of her name.

"She was always careful to put them back in the safe up here in my office every night when she was finished working on them. But the night she . . ."

His voice cracked and I could see tears well up in his eyes. "The night she left here for the last time . . . the tapes weren't back in the safe. I couldn't find them. I figured Carol and Benji must have gotten them when they took her. Then Benji kept asking for reassurances that he would be getting the originals back at the time the money was transferred at the merger signing. Carol kept demanding that I give them back and drop the entire merger scheme. So, I knew they didn't have them, but since I didn't have them either, everything was falling apart."

"So, Carol lost her patience and just wants me to eliminate you altogether. Wow! She is a serious thundertwat."

"I'm assuming you have an altogether different plan now that you have the tapes."

I nodded. "I do."

"And may I ask what it is that you plan to do?"

Now that the confessions were exposed, it was time to get down to the brass tacks. "I want you to sign over ownership of the condominium to Drew."

He nodded. "I would have done that by now if it hadn't been for Carol. She loves him, but she wanted some control after he dared to assert his independence and went to France and then to Haiti. Her name is not on the paperwork though, so I can easily draw that up."

"Mal is handling that as we speak. And I'm not done."

"Mal? You mean Tristan-Malcolm?" His laugh filled the room. "Well, I had hoped by putting you two together you would be so busy fighting that neither of you would notice what was really going on, but I can see I was entirely wrong on that front. What else do you want?"

"You are going to sign over the ownership of Rusk Communication to Drew and have the money from the merger wired into an account set up in his name. Mal is also drafting that paperwork up and setting up that account."

"And what does Mal get out of all of this?" He stood, walked over to the window and stared out over the view.

"You are going to retire early and leave him as the managing partner of the firm."

"And what am I supposed to do?"

"Well, I'm assuming you have some of your own money saved up somewhere. A failsafe in case your plan went south. I would suggest maybe you go visit Paris."

He turned to look at me. "Why on Earth would I go to Paris?"

I got up and walked over toward him. I handed him the purple folder. He opened it. His eyes softened and a smile crossed his face.

I gestured toward the window. "You might not have this view, but you might have a second chance to get things right over some croissants and whiskey."

He put his arm around my shoulder and continued staring at the picture. "I underestimated you. My son is a very lucky man to have you in his life."

It was my turn to get choked up. "Well, I don't think I will be in his life much longer, if I even still am at this point."

He pulled me into a side hug. "Why would you think that? You are doing all of this for him, right? I mean you haven't even asked for a thing for yourself. Why aren't you having me transfer the money to you?"

I looked down at my shoes unable to look him in the face. "Because I don't deserve it. I'm not a good person. I'm blackmailing his father and I'm planning on taking down his mother and his uncle. I am pretty sure no relationship can survive any of those things."

"Well, you aren't killing me, so that has to count for something."

He turned and pulled me into a full bear hug. If I closed my eyes, I could imagine it was Drew's arms comforting me. I shook off that thought, gathered my senses, and stepped back to look at Richard.

"Maybe." I didn't believe that for a second.

"Now, we need to talk about how to get through this evening and keep you alive so you can go to Paris after we take down your bitch ass wife."

"Just tell me what you need me to do."

CHAPTER 40

AFTER LEAVING RICHARD TO CONTEMPLATE his part of the plan, I went to my desk and dropped off the bug and went to see Mal. I walked in without knocking, headed straight to the pizza box, which was still perched on his desk, and grabbed a piece.

He looked up from his papers and half-scowled at me, but I could tell he didn't really mean it. "What the hell? Did you leave your manners at the door? I'm not running a cafeteria here."

"Dude, you do not know what I just went through. I need to stress eat. Plus, I just know that bitch is going to have rabbit food on the dinner menu tonight. I may die if I don't eat."

"First, don't ever call me dude again. Second, oh my God, you whine like a child when you are hungry. I don't know how Drew puts up with it. Third, how did Richard take the news?"

"Drew knows to feed me before I whine. Or at least he did. I don't know what he's going to do now." I couldn't bear to think of Drew never cooking for me again. "Richard took it pretty well once he realized that death was an option." I continued shoveling the pizza in my face.

"And you are sure he is on board with the whole plan? This is Richard we are talking about and it is a lot of money for him to be walking away from voluntarily."

"He's fine. The money is staying in the family since it is going to Drew. You should have seen his face when he saw that picture of Shey Redling. He's probably booking his flight to Paris right now." I grabbed a second piece of pizza out of the box. "My instincts are pretty on the money. So, I promise you. He's good to go and on board."

Mal let out an unexpected bellow of a laugh. The laugh grew louder and he actually doubled over in his chair having what could best be described as a giggle fit.

"Your instincts are on the money?"

The laughter started back up in another long fit. "That is adorable that you still think that after all you have been through the past few weeks. Oh hell, after being up all night, I needed a good laugh. So, thank you for that."

I opened my mouth to protest but found myself joining him in laughing at the absurdity of my comment. "Well, you can't say I'm not due to be right for once. Statistics have to be on my side. Of course, my grandmother always used to say, *some people are just born to be statistics.*

So, it is possible everything could go wrong tonight and I will end up as a sad, cautionary tale of a statistic."

"Your grandmother had quite the sunny outlook."

"You can't say she's wrong though. I even cross-stitched it on a pillow. Drew loved it. Again, the thought of no longer having a future with Drew abruptly stopped my trip down memory lane and my smile faded.

Mal sensed the direction of my thoughts. "Ally, you don't know that it is over. You can't go into tonight worried about that. You have to stay focused."

"I will." I walked over to the box to grab a third piece of pizza because the stress was causing my body to demand more carbohydrates and empty calories.

Mal's phone dinged and he picked it up. "It's Max. He says, and I quote, *Drew heard. He's in a tailspin but I've got this. He will be there.*"

"That's hardly comforting. What if this whole thing falls apart?" I slumped down in the chair across from Mal. Then I perked back up. "Hey, since when do you and Max have each other's phone numbers? Is there something I should know about?" I pulled out my sing-song voice to both annoy Mal and to distract myself from the potential shit show I was about to walk into in a few hours.

Mal furrowed his brow at me and gave me a warning look that almost made me pee myself. "We have made arrangements to meet and listen to the events in the town car outside the house in case something goes wrong. Don't make this into something that it is not and that most certainly wouldn't be of any concern to you."

"Got it. I will add match-making to the list of things you do not like. I will add it right under being amused." I smiled at him and even dared to stick my tongue out at him.

He shook his head and sighed. "Just go get ready for tonight. I still have work to do."

I got up and walked towards the door.

He called out to me. "And one more thing."

I turned around and saw his steel blue eyes looking at me, a sense of déjà vu washed over me leaving after our first meeting.

"If you even think for a moment that you are in danger, you call out my name, and I will be there for you."

I smiled as I fought back the tears that were threatening to flood my eyes. "I know you will."

CHAPTER 41

I SMOOTHED THE WRINKLES OUT of the marmalade A-line dress Carol had practically ordered me to wear. I remembered back to when we bought it and the condescending tone she had used to correct me on the color being marmalade after I commented that I really didn't like to wear orange. I couldn't wait to burn it in a heap along with the rest of the clothes she had bought for me. I checked the pocket of the matching cardigan to confirm the bugs were still present. I had checked for them at least five times on the cab ride over. I chanted "I've got this" along with the intro to Eminem's "Lose Yourself" in my head several times before finding the courage to ring the doorbell and get the night over and done with.

Carol opened the door. She must have given the staff the night off again so there would be no extra witnesses to her nefarious spin on family dinner night. My plan had counted on that, so I was glad that she was predictable.

"Allison, it is so good to see you. I was afraid you weren't going to make it." She grabbed me into a tight hug and whispered in my ear. "Don't even think of trying to screw me over tonight." She released me from her grip and took my purse and put it in the closet. Richard was right, she was always careful to not be recorded. Unfortunately for her, she didn't know there were four other bugs in my pocket.

"Come in. Drew is already here. We are just waiting for Richard to come out of the study. He's finishing something he claims is urgent for the merger tomorrow."

We walked down the long hallway and took a right into the sitting room. The study where Carol's grand finale was supposed to be staged was just across the hall. Ms. Brown in the study with the insulin.

Drew was standing at the small bar in the corner pouring a drink. I wanted to run to him and apologize and kiss him. I wanted him to tell me that everything was going to be OK. I knew that it wasn't going to be, but I just wanted one more of those moments. I needed one more of those moments. He turned and our eyes met briefly and then he looked away.

"Mother, would you like a drink?" He seemed firmly entrenched as the sole member of Team Carol.

"I would love one, honey. Allison, how about you?"

I willed a fake smile onto my face to keep the tears from flowing. "Sure, I will have whatever is easiest."

"Drew, you might as well make a drink for your father as well. Hopefully, he won't keep us waiting too long so we can get started on our meal."

Drew poured out four bourbons and water and handed me one without saying a word. He left the drink for his father on the bar and walked to the other side of the room ostensibly to get as far away from me as he could. Thank God I had on the cardigan because the chill in the room was beginning to get downright frosty. Carol nodded over to the drink at me and walked over to talk to Drew.

I took out the vial she had given me and dumped the contents into Richard's drink, all the while knowing Carol was watching me out of the corner of her eye. She smiled approvingly at me and ever so slightly raised her glass as if to toast me for following her commands. I nodded back. Fuck you bitch. That's nothing but crushed up baby aspirin.

Richard entered the room with his trademark smile and cheery demeanor. "Sorry to keep everyone waiting. A last minute emergency came up but it is all taken care of and everything is all set for tomorrow. So, tonight we celebrate!"

I carried his drink over and handed it to him. He greeted me with a kiss on both cheeks. "Ally, you look lovely as always. Drew, you are a lucky son of a bitch to have this woman at your side."

Drew mumbled something under his breath that I didn't hear. I was quite certain it wasn't in agreement with his father. This evening was going to be more painful than I ever thought possible. No amount of role playing with Sarah would have prepared me for his blatant rejection of me. It was even worse that it was taking place in front of Carol, who seemed to be enjoying every moment of it.

Richard gulped his drink down instead of sipping it and made another. "Drew, need a refill?"

Carol interceded, "He's actually had a few since he got here so we should probably sit down and eat soon."

Drew ignored her and walked over with his now empty glass and let his dad refill it. It appeared that the men in the room were intent on getting hammered, which put me on edge about the success of the evening. There was a good chance I would wake up in the morning in Canada, eh? I slowly sipped my drink so at least I had all my wits about me. I noticed Carol's drink similarly remained barely touched. Carol oozed her way over to my side.

"We need to get them to the dinner table so we can get on with this plan." She had obviously perfected smiling and talking in hushed tones.

I whispered through my own fake smile. "Eager to be a widow, are we?"

She scowled at me, which only made me smile more obnoxiously at her before I loudly blurted out, "I'm so damn hungry I could eat a fucking horse. Can we please eat soon?"

Richard's laugh filled the room. "I love that you always say what you are thinking, Ally. No secrets with you." He clapped his hands together enthusiastically. "Yes, let's eat."

Carol kept smiling and hissed. "That wasn't exactly how I would have handled it."

I hissed back. "Too fucking bad."

Richard stumbled on his way to the dining room, which was further down the hall from the study. He grabbed onto Drew. "Whoa! I guess I shouldn't have skipped lunch and then chugged those drinks. Your old man is turning into a light-weight."

I sat down across from Drew. We still hadn't spoken a word to each other. He would barely look me in the face. I hoped Max had made some headway with him. His last text an hour ago simply said, *He will be there. I can't make any promises, but I think he will be fine. I'm trying.*

I was going to have a serious talk with Max about his definition of "fine."

I looked down at my plate and saw the same goddamn autumn salad from the other night. Again! This bitch apparently loved salad or she knew how much I hated it. Thank God for the pizza I scarfed down in Mal's office. I could not get through this evening hungry. I picked at my salad and kept my head down. I didn't want to see Drew blatantly ignoring me.

"So, Drew . . . shit what was I going to ask . . . damn it . . . I can't remember what I was going to ask." Richard's speech was slow and he kept shaking his head as if to clear it and find the right words. I privately admired his acting abilities.

"Dad, are you OK?" Drew reached out and touched his dad's hand.

"I'm fine. Just a little light-headed all of a sudden and woozy. Carol, can you bring out the main course? I need something a little heavier than this salad."

"Sure honey. Allison, would you be a dear and help me with the plates?"

"Absolutely. Because, frankly, this salad fucking sucks." For a moment I thought I saw the barest flicker of a smile just on the edge of Drew's mouth, but then it was gone and replaced by his steadfast refusal to acknowledge me. I had probably just imagined the smile.

Richard barked with laughter again. "God, I love you, Ally."

I followed Carol to the kitchen to retrieve the four dinner plates. I was relieved to see that there was at least some chicken on the menu, even though it was baked, which is the absolute worst kind of chicken. Maybe if this bitch ate some fried chicken, mashed potatoes, and biscuits she wouldn't be so goddamn evil.

"Is everything good with you and Drew? Things seem a bit tense out there." I could practically hear the giddiness in her voice over the development of discord in our relationship.

"We are fine. He's just pouty because I wasn't in the mood to let him fuck me this morning."

"Must you always be so vulgar? It is unbecoming. If you are trying to startle me and lash out because of what you have to do this evening, remember you only have yourself to blame. It is your own actions that put you in this position." She wagged her finger in my face. I wanted to reach up and break it.

"Fuck you." I picked up two plates and headed back to the dining room. Carol followed behind me.

I put a plate down in front of Drew and he didn't even bother to say, "Thank you." I noticed that his bourbon glass had been refilled again while we were gone. This night was going to get much messier than I thought. I was going to kick Max's ass for not doing a better job of wrangling him. After I leaned over in front of Drew to place his plate in front of him, I finally had the opportunity to discreetly slip a bug into his shirt pocket. I had already placed one in Richard's pants' pocket during our embrace earlier in the evening. Carol's outfit had no pockets, so I was shit out of luck in that department. It was probably for the best. That skinny ass bitch probably had some Princess and the Pea-type senses that would have alerted her something was askew.

Richard's eyes were droopy and half-closed. His head dropped forward and then dramatically popped back up. His eyes popped open and he shook his head. Dude was committed to his part like he was trying to win an Oscar. I suppose trying to stay alive does provide some extra motivation.

Carol admonished him. "Richard, why don't you go lay down on the couch in your study? You are about to end up face first in your plate."

"I'm fine." He picked up his fork and chased a piece of asparagus around the plate trying to stab it. I fought the urge to giggle.

Carol's face tightened and her voice grew loud and stern. "Obviously you are not fine. Go lay down. I'm going to be irate if you are coming down with the flu and I get sick before next week's charity ball"

"Well, we can't have that can we." He slammed his fork down, got up and staggered out of the room down the hall and toward the study.

Carol let out what I knew to be a disingenuous disapproving sigh and shook her head. The three of us ate in silence for a few minutes. I pushed my food around the plate and wished this was the kind of house where you could just get up and go to the fridge and grab a bottle of BBQ sauce. The chicken was bland as hell despite Carol's description of it being basted in a light lemongrass sauce. I added lemongrass sauce to the long list of things I despised about Carol.

Carol decided to retaliate for my earlier "vulgar" outbursts by asking,

"Ally, how was your show last night, did it go well?"

My hate for her continued to grow and I reminded myself that I had to stay focused. "Well, . . . last night I actually just stayed home." I didn't look up from my serious task of food rearrangement.

Drew dropped his knife and fork on his plate. "Ally, just drop the damn act. Mom, she hasn't done a set in months. She's a goddamn liar."

And there it was. He finally speaks to me and the words hit me like a direct blow to my face. In fact, I would have preferred to have been smacked or punched. I couldn't bear to hear another word or see the look of disgust that was probably on his face.

"Excuse me. I have to go to the restroom." I pushed back my chair and left the room without looking up. I could instinctively feel Carol's Cheshire Cat smile behind me.

Instead of going to the bathroom, I made my way down the hall to the study. I had only taken a few steps into the room when the shot rang out. Richard shot me.

Mr. Stephens in the study with a gun.

CHAPTER 42

FUCK THAT HURT! I HIT my head on the corner of the desk as I fell to the ground. I clutched my stomach. It stung. Blood began oozing out and staining the marmalade dress. Where had I seen blood ooze like that before? Oh yeah, in the park. On the rock.

The sound of the shot ringing out elicited a "What the hell?" shout from Carol. As I laid on the ground, I heard the footsteps of both her and Drew running to the room. They stopped short when they saw Richard pointing the gun at them both.

"Ally!" Drew screamed and ran towards me and dropped to the ground beside me. "Someone call 911! Honey, you are going to be OK. Everything is going to be OK. I love you, babe." He kissed my head. Finally, the words that I needed so desperately to hear. It had only taken me getting shot to hear them. Who knew?

Drew's scream was filled with panic. "Why isn't anyone calling for an ambulance? She's going to bleed out."

Drew was pressing down on my stomach. The sight of the sticky red ooze bleeding onto his hands and his shirt made my stomach lurch. Would I ever escape the sickening image of the red ooze on the rock? If the man wasn't dead, why couldn't I let that image go? Why was I thinking about that damn sexting jogger when I had more important problems at hand? It must have been the blow to my head. My head hurt like a son of a bitch. Was this how he felt before he died? No. Mal said he wasn't dead. Mal was just down the street. Everything was fine. Maybe Max's loose definition of fine. But it was fine. I had to stay focused.

"Get up son." Richard pointed the gun at Drew. My vision was blurry and it looked like there were two Richards and two guns. I had to squint one eye shut to just see one Richard and one gun. Oh God, please don't let me see two Carols. One is enough.

Richard calmly stated, "No one is calling for help and no one is going anywhere. I disconnected the phones and the security cameras earlier this evening."

Why the hell did he do that? Did I tell him to do that? I didn't remember telling him to do that? What was it that I told him to do? The pain in my head was throbbing so bad that I was having trouble focusing. I closed my eyes and tried to remember what the plan had been, but all I could see was the image of that man laying lifeless and the blood oozing out on the rock. I had done that.

I opened my eyes and saw Richard and the gun pointed in Carol's direction. "Did you really think that I wouldn't find out about your plan Carol?"

Drew looked back and forth from where his dad was standing to where Carol was standing. The pain in my head hurt too much for me to turn and see her face. I would be perfectly happy if I never saw her again.

Drew finally asked, "Mom, what is he talking about? Someone tell me what is going now. We need to call for help."

Richard sneered. "Your mom here was going to have your pretty little girlfriend kill me, isn't that right darling?"

Drew looked at his mom and then down at me. I managed to mouth, "I'm so sorry." At least, I think I did. My brain told my mouth to do it but through all the pain in my head, I wasn't sure my mouth actually complied.

"So, I killed her first. Sorry to ruin your plans, Carol." He pointed the gun at her head.

Drew stepped in between his parents. "That's not true. Mom, tell him that's not true. We need to get her help."

Carol remained speechless. I like speechless Carol a lot more than the talking bitch. Now I kind of wished I could see her face.

Richard turned to face Drew but kept the gun aimed at Carol's head. "Your mom killed Elise. Then she was going to kill me."

He turned back to Carol. "How high of a body count were you willing to go to protect your brother, or were you really just protecting your dear old friend, Birdie? I suspect you'd throw your brother under the bus before her. You two must have bonded quite a bit in college and when you went on all your girls only trips. Is that why you were always such a frost queen to me in the bedroom?"

Holy shit! Did I just hear that or am I now hallucinating? That was definitely not part of the plan. No head injury would cause me to forget that explosive of a firebomb would be hurled at Carol.

"You shut your damn mouth!" Carol screamed.

Seems like someone hit a nerve. If my head wasn't hurting so bad I would be laughing.

Carol continued to yell at Richard. "You got Elise killed the moment you involved her in your blackmail scheme cloaked as a merger deal. Her death is on you. Just like Ally's will be."

Whoa! Stop the train for a second. Who said anything about me dying? I'm not dying. I just hit my head. People don't die from hitting their head. Or, do they? The man in the park might have lived. The image of the red ooze on the rock flooded my brain again. Mal's words came back to me "no open homicide cases." He never said the man wasn't dead. In fact, he had refused to give me any details other than to assure me that there was no investigation so I wouldn't have to worry about being charged. I had to accept the cold hard truth. The man was dead and I killed him. I might never have to pay the legal consequences for my actions but I would have to carry that knowledge and those images with me for the rest of my life. I fought back tears and tried to focus on Drew.

Drew was pacing the floor furiously and pulling his hair. "What the hell is wrong with the two of you? What kind of monsters are you? The woman I love is dying on the floor and neither of you give a shit."

Aww. He still loves me. That's nice to hear. "Owww!" Did I say that out loud or in my head? I put my hand in the ooze and pressed down. Drew continued pacing the room, getting more frantic by the minute.

Richard ignored Drew's pleas for help. "Carol, I'm sorry to disappoint you, but the merger will be going through tomorrow as planned. You will be pleased to know, after I get my money, I will be leaving you. Feel free to snuggle up to Birdie all you want . . ."

Hold up there, dude. You aren't getting the money. Drew gets the money. I know for sure I told you that earlier.

Drew's pacing finally led him over to where Richard was standing and in one swift move he had him disarmed and had the gun pointed at Richard. All those nights of me teaching him Bob's techniques finally paid off. Bob would have been proud.

Carol started to approach Drew. "Thank God, Drew. Now go get your cell phone and call the police."

She smirked at Richard. "It will be hard for that merger deal to go through when you are in jail for shooting Ally, although, I do thank you for that, because it saves me the trouble of getting rid of her later . . ."

A shot rang out and I saw a blur that looked like Richard drop to the ground.

CHAPTER 43

"DREW! WHAT DID YOU DO? Why would you do that?" Carol ran over to him. I could hear the panic in her voice.

"He shot Ally!" He screamed and pointed the gun at his mother. "You just said you were going to kill her. Give me one good reason that I shouldn't just shoot you, too!"

Carol spoke in a soft voice that she probably thought sounded loving and motherly, but it sounded insincere and condescending. "Drew, honey. You need to calm down. You've had a lot to drink. You aren't thinking straight. I can fix this. There was a struggle. That will be the story. I can fix this."

Drew's voice boomed loud and angry. "Just like you fixed Elise? When you had me participate in covering up her murder without me knowing about it? Is that the kind of fix you are talking about?"

He was flailing the gun around wildly as he walked over towards me. He bent down and kissed my forehead.

"Honey, everything is going to be fine. I promise. I'm going to get you help."

There was a softness back in his voice. Maybe we would get a happily ever after and I wouldn't have to move to Canada and buy my milk in bags.

The panic in Carol's voice was palpable. "Drew, I'm sorry about that, but you were the only one who could get in her office and get her things. If you had just found those goddamn tapes in her office, all of this could have been avoided. I told you to get everything out of her office that wasn't paper."

He straightened up and I could see his face was seething with anger. I recognized that anger from the other night.

"Are you kidding me right now? So, this is all my fault? You didn't even tell me I was supposed to be looking for something. I just thought I was cleaning out her office to avoid a scene with dad. But now all of this is my fault? You really are fucking unbelievable."

"I didn't mean it like that, Drew. You know I love you." I could hear the click of her heels as she tried to walk closer to Drew to try to calm him down and get him back on Team Carol.

He raised the gun up to her head and the click of her heels stopped in their tracks. "Then tell me what happened to Elise."

"You don't need to know those details, honey. If you don't know then it gives you plausible deniability."

"Mom, I am all out of fucks to give right now. So help me, I will shoot you too if you don't tell me what happened to Elise."

He stepped closer to her with the gun trained at her head. I briefly hoped that maybe she would pee herself. I would count that as a huge win for Team Ally.

"Fine." Her voice cracked. "If it will calm you down and reassure you I can fix this, I will tell you."

The clicking of her heels started back up as she crossed the floor and settled into a chair. I turned my head and could finally see her face. Thank God, the pain had subsided enough that there was only one of her. She looked defeated. I relished in her pain.

"I had Louis go to the office that night with a flower delivery from Richard knowing that the night security guard would call her down to come get them. When she got down to the lobby, Louis told her Richard had a limo waiting outside and had a special evening planned for the two of them. She got in the limo voluntarily. She didn't have her phone with her because she thought she was just coming down to get flowers. She couldn't call anyone when she finally realized Louis was taking her out of the city. He drove her to the wooded hillside near our property up state. He dragged her out of the car and gave her enough of a dose of insulin to kill her. He buried her in the woods. No one will find her because no one ever goes on that property. No one will think to look for her there."

Tears poured down my face as I thought of how scared Elise must have been. She really was dead. I had tried to hold out hope that maybe Carol just had someone holding her against her will somewhere and that we would find her alive. I had imagined the laughs we would have about all the texts that I had blown up her phone with, pleading for her to help me. She would be gob-smacked that Mal had been there for me and that he had cats. None of that would happen though, because she was dead.

Drew lowered the gun and stared in shock and disgust at his mother. "What is wrong with you? . . . How can you sleep at night? . . . Is she the first person you've done this to or is she just another notch in your belt?"

Carol shrugged. "Honey, politics and power. . . it can be messy sometimes."

"And that's the life you wanted for me? For Ally?" He came back by my side and crouched down beside me.

"You were never supposed to see this side."

"So, I was just going to be the front man who you would use and pull my strings. Just like you have my whole life? Your perfect poster boy. Does a dead girlfriend and dad give me a bump in the polls? Can you spin that?"

Carol snapped back at him. "I told you I can fix it. Look, Ally wasn't the woman you thought she was."

"Don't you fucking say a word about her." He pointed the gun back at her head.

"Drew, she killed a man in the park, she drugged some guys and assaulted them for no reason, and she drugged some pop star to give her friend a boost on Broadway. I think a jury will believe that she is deranged, came in here and killed your father, and in a heroic effort, your father managed to shoot her before he died in order to save our lives."

"That's a great story Carol, except for the fact that I'm not dying and neither is Richard."

I managed to stand up, still woozy from the unexpected and self-inflicted head injury, just in time to see the horror wash over her face as she realized Drew was holding a prop gun and Richard and I were merely covered in squibs of fake blood.

CHAPTER 44

RICHARD STOOD UP FROM THE floor clapping. "That was very big of you to make me a hero in your version of events. I will remember that while you are rotting in prison. If you are lucky, maybe Birdie can be your cellmate."

Carol walked across the room and smacked Richard across the face so hard that his head snapped to the side. She sneered at all of us.

"You think you are cute. You think this will hold up in court and that I won't take every single one of you down for making up this story and lying." She glowered at Drew. "I would expect this from these lowlife pieces of shit who have leached off my tit for all these years . . . but not you. You betrayed me for this . . . this cheap piece of ass? Maybe she might be good down on her knees, but she will never be good enough to deserve my son."

I stepped closer to her not looking at Drew. I didn't want to see his face after what she had revealed that I had done. I didn't want to see the disappointment that I knew would be there. I would try to explain later but not now, not while this conversation was being recorded.

"You know what Carol, that might be true. I might not be good enough for your son but I love him, which is more than you can say. Your son can either chose to forgive me and continue loving me or not. I would rather him leave me than let you drag him down into your cesspool excuse of a lifestyle."

Carol composed herself and her usual air of haughtiness and superiority returned. "You can explain it however you want to, honey, but no one will ever believe a word you say. I have your confession on tape."

"Oh, are you admitting that you bugged me? You must be referring to that recording you have of me rehearsing a monologue that Rena is working on for her one-act play? I was merely helping out a friend. We even rehearsed it today at lunch. Feel free to ask her."

Carol flicked a piece of imaginary dust off her shoulder to illustrate what she thought of my explanation. "So, my son was wasted drunk. My husband was blackmailing my brother. Their testimony doesn't hold a lot of water either. I'm afraid you are in over your head. Better luck next time."

I stepped even closer to her. "Yeah, but here's the thing. Everything you said tonight has been recorded. And that part in the middle where you told us exactly what you had done to Elise, that part is going to be very helpful to the police. I imagine after they find the body exactly where you described it and after Louis turns on you, that will pretty much be all the police need."

She made the mistake of stepping closer to me with her hand raised up to slap me. I grabbed her arm, flipped her, and pinned her to the ground. I twisted her arm until I heard her wince in pain. "What was it you said earlier? Oh yeah, I think it was something like *You only have yourself to blame. It is your own actions that put you in this position.*" I twisted her arm again.

"Let me give you a little advice. Don't ever fuck with a West Virginia girl. Look at a map, we are a state that has been flipping off all the other states for years. We have no fucks to give because Mountaineers are always free."

I released her from my grip and stood up. I saw Richard and Drew were staring at me with their mouths wide open. I walked out of the room and grabbed my purse from the closet. I left unsure if I would ever see either of them again.

I stepped onto the sidewalk and into Mal's waiting town car.

EPILOGUE

I SAT ON THE DOCK with my toes in the water while watching the sunset over the island across the bay from the cottage. I shivered as the late summer air gave way to a windy chill.

"Of course you would run off to Canada and not even think to pack appropriately." Mal handed me a flannel shirt.

"Thanks. I knew I could count on you to cover my ass . . . or my shoulders." I slipped on the shirt.

Mal sat down beside me and handed me a glass of wine.

"Yeah, well don't make a habit of it. I can only cover your ass for so many hours a day."

"Ten months ago, would you ever have guessed we would be sitting here having wine and being best friends?" I smiled and leaned my head over onto his shoulder.

He gently pushed my head off his shoulder. "Don't get carried away. You know I'm just here because of Max."

We both turned and looked up at the house where Drew and Max were cooking at the grill and slam dancing and jumping to Kriss Kross.

"That's our men." I laughed.

"More like boys. I had to come down here to escape all of the bro-ing out. Max actually thought I would jump."

I laughed at the mental image of Mal jumping. "You should try it some time. It is very freeing."

"I let you use Post-it-notes at the office now, so let's take it one step at a time."

"OK, bestie." I leaned my head back onto his shoulder. He let out one of his exaggerated sighs, but this time he let my head stay on his shoulder.

It had been ten months since the scene with Drew's parents. Drew didn't come home that night and I thought for sure it was over between us. He showed up the next morning and we had several days of hard truth telling talks. I told him the truth about the man in the park. I would lie to his mother and to everyone else but not to him. I knew that was a secret that I couldn't keep from him. It would be unfair for Mal and Sarah to know the truth and not him.

After he got over the shock, he was understanding and supportive but also angry that I had put myself in danger and hadn't told him about it. He was angry and hurt that he had to learn about what his father and mother had done and my plan to take her down by having Max play him the audio of the bugged conversation between me and his dad.

I explained I didn't know if he would have believed it any other way because it was so overwhelming. I had barely believed it and I had witnessed it all firsthand.

He confessed he had been working at Max's and had stopped going to his law school classes and that he never wanted to be an attorney. He had been worried about being disowned by his parents and letting me down by not being able to support the two of us. We both agreed to not keep any more secrets from each other and I agreed to work on my anger triggers.

There was a lot of make-up sex. I mean a lot. Whatever amount you are thinking of is way off and you need to multiply it by ten.

Richard is in Paris attempting to woo back Shey and getting fat on croissants. He is happier than he ever was at the firm and thanks me regularly for throwing a wrench in his blackmail plans. I made sure any tapes that had Richard recorded on them mysteriously disappeared.

Elise's body was finally found and she received a proper burial. Louis took the wrap for Elise's murder, claiming Carol knew nothing about his plans beforehand. I'm sure his family received a large cash amount in appreciation for his sacrifice. Drew's mom, Birdie and Uncle Benji all made plea deals on the corporate corruption charges and got what amounted to a slap on the wrist and the briefest amount of time in white collar prison. To quote Sarah, "Fucking white, rich people privilege."

Sarah and Rena are currently starring together on Broadway in a remake of "The Odd Couple" which has gotten rave reviews. Rena is no longer a train wreck waiting to happen, but she did manage to tear a giant hole in Mars News and Media's coffers with her lawsuit, along with the other illegally tapped celebrities.

While Mal may still roll his eyes and will deny that we are best friends, it is a hollow argument betrayed by the fact that Drew and I have dinner with him and Max at least once a week and they come visit us when we are at the cottage in Canada. Honestly, Mal and Max make a pretty adorable couple, so Drew and I need to start stepping up our game.

Drew and I bought a small cottage in Parry Sound. It is the only thing we have splurged on since Drew got the money from the merger, which went off without a hitch thanks to Mal's late-night efforts. Neither of us want to be beholden to the money, but we did both enjoy taking it from Uncle Benji and donating a lot to charity. Don't get me wrong. We aren't living like paupers. We also decided we weren't the type to just sit around all day without something to do. I know, I was as surprised as anyone to learn that about myself. Who knew I had a work ethic? Drew works at Max's restaurant a couple of nights a week and I still go into the office where I'm actually useful. Mal seems to think my particular skill set, which I guess is best described as concocting crazy plans, can be harnessed for good and used in developing legal strategies. I have a plush office up on the penthouse level just down the hall from Richard's old office, which is now occupied by Mal. Susan has also been moved upstairs as part of our elite team of bad-assery.

Every now and then I go to a comedy club and tell a slightly revised and censored version of this story. Everyone laughs because no one thinks that it could possibly be true. I mean who would believe this crazy fucking shit? Would you?